LOCKED AND
LOADED

Books by Mandy Baxter

LOCKED AND LOADED

Mandy Baxter

ZEBRA BOOKS
KENSINGTON PUBLISHING CORP.

http://www.kensingtonbooks.com

ZEBRA BOOKS are published by

Kensington Publishing Corp.
119 West 40th Street
New York, NY 10018

All Kensington titles, imprints and distributed lines are available at special quantity discounts for bulk purchases for sales promotion, premiums, fund-raising, educational or institutional use.

Special book excerpts or customized printings can also be created to fit specific needs. For details, write or phone the office of the Kensington Sales Manager. Attn.: Sales Department. Kensington Publishing Corp., 119 West 40th Street, New York, NY 10018. Phone: 1-800-221-2647.

Zebra and the Z logo Reg. U.S. Pat. & TM Off.

First Printing: October 2016
ISBN-13: 978-1-4201-4107-8
ISBN-10: 1-4201-4107-4

eISBN-13: 978-1-4201-4108-5
eISBN-10: 1-4201-4108-2

10 9 8 7 6 5 4 3 2 1

Printed in the United States of America

ACKNOWLEDGMENTS

Many thanks to everyone at Kensington, including my editor, Esi Sogah, and the awesome cover designers, copy editors, and proofreaders who helped to make this story shine. Also, a huge thanks to my agent, Natanya Wheeler and everyone over at NYLA who continue to support me. As always, I totally own any and all mistakes. I do my best to cross every "t" and dot every "i," but every once in a while, one of those little suckers gets past me.

Chapter One

"Thanks for meeting with me, Mason. Have a seat."

Mason Decker looked at the empty chair opposite Chief Deputy Carlos Carrera and considered asking if he could stand. If he was going to be told yet again that his application to the U.S. Marshals Service had been denied, he'd rather be on his feet when he got the news. After two previous attempts to enter the program, he wondered why the third warranted a face-to-face with the California southern district's chief deputy marshal, rather than the usual consolation letter. Maybe it was a three-strikes-and-you're-out sort of situation.

Mason cleared his throat and settled in the chair. After a year with San Francisco PD and then a five-year stint as an undercover agent for U.S. Customs and Border Protection, he'd been ready for a change of scenery. Apparently, the USMS felt that Mason's history—and family—disqualified him as a viable candidate for their program, despite his glowing service record with CBP. Though in his last interview, they'd noted he'd be well suited for undercover work and suggested he stay on with Customs, that's not what Mason wanted. Which was why he'd left CBP two weeks ago.

His end goal had always been to join the Marshals Service. He'd keep applying to the program until they accepted him. He was more than the family he'd been born into and he wouldn't quit until they let him prove it. Mason just hoped he hadn't been asked here today to be shut down permanently. They couldn't do that? Could they?

Fan-fucking-tastic.

"I'm sure you're wondering why I asked you to come in today." Carrera leaned forward in his seat and rested his elbows on the desk. His dark eyes zeroed in on Mason and he settled back. He wished the chief deputy wouldn't beat around the bush. If he was out, why not just say it?

"Yeah, well . . ." Mason propped his elbows on the armrests of his chair. "Usually you guys send me a letter to tell me my application was shit-canned. Again."

Carrera smirked. "You've applied to the program twice in the past five years. But after reviewing your application and background checks, it was determined that because of your familial relationships, we might not be the right fit for you. The powers that be felt the stress of what might be required of you would be too much."

Was this a joke? "I've been working undercover for Customs for five years," Mason replied. "And I think you know how close those cases related to my *familial relationships.* Last time I checked, no one at CBP had anything to complain about as far as my job performance went."

"True. But you mentioned in your interview that you were looking for a change of pace. You do realize that becoming a deputy U.S. marshal would mean that things wouldn't slow down. In fact, the pace might be a little faster than you're prepared for."

Mason knew what the Marshals Service dealt with. They were the country's most elite law enforcement agency. They went places other agencies wouldn't go and chased criminals that other cops refused to go after. They arrested and transported the worst of the worst. Some of the most dangerous assholes in the world. They risked their lives on a regular basis and rumor had it that most marshals discharged their firearms at least once a day. It was exactly the change of pace he was looking for. Mason was tired of busting smugglers and being used for his particular expertise. He wanted more out of his life and his career.

"I'd like to get out of undercover work, that's all." Not that Mason owed Carrera an explanation.

"We do undercover work."

A slow sigh escaped from between Mason's lips. Why couldn't Carrera just tell him they weren't going to take him and leave it at that? "I'm aware of that. But most of your undercover ops are short-term."

"True." For a long moment Carrera studied him. The other man's scrutinizing stare made Mason seven different kinds of twitchy, as though he were trying to crawl right into his head and take a look at what Mason had going on up there. "You're one of their top undercover guys. And good at your job from what I hear. Why do you want to leave it?"

His entire life he'd been followed by the stigma of his dad's reputation. Mason didn't want to talk about it. In his job, he didn't want his worth to be equated to his upbringing. "Because I want to be a deputy U.S. marshal." He fixed Carrera with a stern stare. "It's been my goal since I joined the police academy."

Carrera pursed his lips. "And you're not interested in undercover work anymore?"

"I'm tired of being used specifically for busting smuggling rings and nothing else." Mason wasn't a one-trick pony. His skills and knowledge went way past knowing how a con artist and smuggler operated.

"That's too bad."

"Yeah?" Mason couldn't keep the disdain from his tone. "Why's that?"

"Because I have a proposition for you."

Mason didn't like the sound of that. He couldn't muster up any enthusiasm in his response. "What?"

Carrera regarded him for a quiet moment. "Kieran Eagan is back in the city."

Mason let out a disbelieving chuff of laughter and shifted in his seat. If he'd known this was why he'd been asked to meet with Carrera, he never would have come. "You're kidding, right?"

Kieran Eagan was one of the world's most infamous diamond smugglers. He'd managed to elude law enforcement agencies—including U.S. Customs—for the past few years. He was damn good at what he did, had learned his skills from the best in the world. Irreverent. Daring. Smart. Kieran was the total criminal package. The white whale that every cop would love to bring in.

"The Justice Department has formed a joint task force to bring down an up-and-coming criminal syndicate known as Faction Five. Eagan is believed to be a potential player. Customs, FBI, the Office of the U.S. Attorneys, and the Marshals Service are all involved."

This wasn't about his application at all, was it? They wanted him because they wanted Kieran. "No." Mason gave an emphatic shake of his head. "No way in hell."

Carrera held up his hands as though that was enough

to calm Mason's building annoyance. "Hear me out. You already have the connection. You know how Eagan thinks, what his next move will be. Right now, arresting him is less of a priority than finding out what he knows about Faction Five. If you help us out on this, I can help you out, Mason. I can fast-track your application and get you into Glynco."

Apparently the USMS wasn't above extortion to get what they wanted. Or in this case, coercion. Dangling something Mason wanted just out of his reach. All he had to do was play ball. "We want to use Kieran as an asset. We're after bigger fish than a diamond smuggler. You can bring him to us." Carrera was quick to assure Mason that he'd be doing nothing more than using Kieran for intel. As though that would somehow entice him to sign on.

Mason swore under his breath and released the air from his lungs in a forceful gust. "CBP knows you're talking to me?"

"We're working closely with Customs on this," Carrera replied. "Gene Fry was the one who suggested we approach you."

Of course. His own former supervisor had thrown him under the bus. "How long has the task force been working on this?" At this point Mason wouldn't put it past them to have orchestrated his rejected applications in order to gain his cooperation for this operation.

"A few weeks." Carrera swiveled his chair back and forth. "I know what you're thinking, Mason, but this isn't some big conspiracy. You can get close to Eagan. We need to know what he knows. Take my offer as the compliment that it is. Accept the job and help us identify the key players so we can bring this syndicate down."

Mason hated duplicity, which, considering his upbringing, sort of made him a hypocrite. "If you talked to Fry, then you know we had a deal about me working any Customs cases that might involve Kieran." That Carrera even had the nerve to ask him to do this made his gut bottom out.

"I do," Carrera replied. "And I also know that as far as integrity goes, no one with CBP ever questioned yours."

Did he think that assurance would somehow make Mason feel better about what they wanted him to do? "Kieran has been smuggling diamonds out of conflict areas for a long damned time. He's the best. There's a reason why no one's been able to make an arrest stick."

"Like I said"—Carrera leveled his gaze—"we're not interested in taking him down. Right now, our priority is Faction Five. Justice wants this syndicate squashed before they have a chance to gain any traction. And we want you to help us do it."

"What is Faction Five?" Whoever they were, if Kieran was working with them it was because it would directly benefit him somehow. He didn't play well with others and he sure as hell didn't share his money or his business connections.

"We're not entirely sure." At least Carrera had the balls to admit it. "But we have some ideas. We're hoping that by getting close to Eagan, you can help us figure it all out."

It was obvious Kieran was one rung on a ladder that went a hell of a lot higher than Mason's pay grade allowed him access to.

"Who's heading up the task force?"

Carrera leaned back in his chair. "Charlie Cahill with the U.S. Attorneys office."

A lawyer. Great. In Mason's experience, all lawyers managed to do was fuck everything up. He preferred to deal with them after the investigation was complete. And even then it was never a pleasant experience. "And if I agreed to join the task force, who would I answer to?"

"Well, since you're not officially affiliated with any agency right now, you'd answer to me."

Mason felt the noose of Carrera's offer tighten around his neck. "Temporary deputy marshal status?"

"Something like that."

The chief deputy was certainly making Mason an offer he couldn't refuse. At this point, his options were few. He was officially unemployed and his job prospects weren't looking great. He wasn't interested in returning to the San Francisco PD, and even though CBP wanted him back, he was done with the way they'd pigeonholed him. His options were either take this gig or work as a rent-a-cop somewhere. And as far as Mason was concerned, that *wasn't* an option. Was he ready to make the ultimate sacrifice to get what he wanted?

"I'm in," he said after a long moment.

"Good." Carrera scribbled something on a notepad before tearing the sheet off and sliding it across the desk toward Mason. He scooped it up in his hand and glanced at the address. "We'll brief you tomorrow morning at nine. Don't be late."

Mason pushed himself up from the chair. "Yeah. I'll be there."

He left the chief deputy's office without a word in parting. Despite the fact he was getting what he wanted in the long run, Mason couldn't shake the feeling that he might have just made the worst decision of his life.

* * *

"Can I get another Bloody Mary, Lacey?"

"Sure. Rough day?"

Weren't they all?

Charlotte Cahill pushed her empty glass toward her friend and eased one foot out of its stiletto, letting the shoe dangle from her toes. It wasn't quite barefoot, but good enough. The only thing that had got her through the day was knowing that the bar—and her friend— were just around the corner from her office. "Remind me again why I declined my dad's offer to join his practice?"

Lacey smiled. She grabbed a bottle of vodka from the bar and poured a generous shot into a clean glass. "Because you hate stuffy corporate types, you're not in it for the money, and you get a rush from taking down the bad guy, which you'd never get reviewing contracts and mergers all day."

"Oh yeah." She snapped her fingers. "I forgot."

"You're good at the whole adulting thing, Charlie," Lacey said. "Don't let the man get you down."

Charlie suppressed a chuckle. Lacey had been her toughest competition in law school and had been on track to graduate cum laude before she'd decided to drop out. There were days—like today—when Charlie wished she'd followed in her friend's footsteps. But whereas Lacey had decided she couldn't handle the stress that came with being an attorney, Charlie had thrived on it. Hell, she'd been raised by one of the top corporate attorneys in the state. The law was in her blood.

Lacey slid another Bloody Mary in front of Charlie, who dunked the skewer into the glass and took an olive from the tip with her teeth. Lacey asked, "What happened at the salt mines to make it a four cocktail sort of day?"

"Oh, nothing much," Charlie replied. "A couple of weeks ago I agreed to head up a multiagency task force to take down an esoteric crime syndicate that's currently soliciting new members and may or may not be headed up by cops and maybe a senator or two. I'm going on day fourteen of almost no sleep and I'm pretty sure I'm on my way to an ulcer."

Lacey paused and her blue eyes went wide. "I stand corrected. This isn't a four cocktail sort of day. This is a fifth of bourbon and eat a whole cheesecake by yourself sort of *month*."

Charlie laughed. "More or less."

"Good for the résumé, though."

True. Though if all Charlie was after was a shiny résumé, she would've joined her dad's firm like he'd wanted. She wasn't after those sorts of accolades. She didn't want to be respected. Charlie wanted to be feared.

She wanted those big-time criminals to quake in their boots at the mention of her name. She wanted them to know that when she decided to come after them, they could kiss their freedom good-bye. This task force was her chance to prove herself as a certifiable badass. It would make or break her career.

Lacey flashed a confident smile. "If anybody can rock this, it's you, Charlie."

She sure as hell hoped so.

"Hey, I get off in twenty minutes. Wanna go grab a bite?"

Dinner with Lacey was definitely a better alternative to her plans for tonight. "Can't." Charlie leaned over her straw and took a nice, long pull, draining a couple of inches from her Bloody Mary. "I'm meeting my dad. He should be here anytime."

"Uuuuugggghhhh!" Lacey made a show of collapsing over the bar. "You're a glutton for punishment. You know that, right?"

True, Charlie and her dad's relationship could be described as amicably antagonistic. And an evening spent listening to him chide her about her career—and life—choices usually ended with a couple of Excedrin and a glass of wine. "It's our monthly dinner date," she replied before downing another couple inches of her drink. "If I blow him off, I have to deal with my mom. And believe it or not, that's a hundred times worse."

"We could meet up afterward?" Lacey suggested. "We could catch a movie or I could just come over to your place and hang out."

There was no doubt she'd need to decompress after dinner. "I'll text you when I'm on my way home. If you bring the cheesecake, I'll grab a bottle of wine."

"Deal." Lacey glanced over Charlie's shoulder before leaning in toward her ear. "Dear old dad's here. Good luck. Hey, Mr. Cahill!" Lacey straightened as she called out. She could go from zero to charming in a second flat. "What are you drinking tonight?"

"Macallan 25, neat," he replied in his crisp, clear voice. He leaned in and kissed Charlie's cheek before sitting down beside her. "When are you going to give up on being a bum and finally take the bar exam, Lacey?"

"When hell freezes over," she replied with a smile. She poured the ridiculously expensive scotch into a glass and placed it on a cocktail napkin. "I'll leave the lawyering to Charlie."

"Hmmm." Robert Cahill gave Lacey an appraising look before he sipped from the glass.

Lacey gave Charlie one last wide-eyed glance before she hightailed it for the opposite end of the bar. Charlie mouthed *coward* and Lacey nodded in agreement, giving a quick shrug of her shoulders before she focused her attention on a couple who'd just bellied up to the bar.

"So, kiddo. How's the life of civil servitude treating you?"

"Fulfilling as ever," Charlie said. "How's the corporate shark tank?"

"Pays the bills."

Understatement of the century. No one could ever say Robert Cahill wasn't good at what he did. His firm handled clients from some of the richest corporations in the world. Charlie made pennies compared to her dad's two-grand-per-billable-hour rate, hence his disdain of her "civil servitude." He'd expected her to join the firm when she graduated law school, and almost five years later he was still pretty butt-hurt that she'd chosen the Office of the U.S. Attorneys over the private sector.

Charlie watched her dad from the corner of her eye. Decked out in a perfectly tailored suit, not a graying hair out of place, distinguished and refined, he screamed one-percenter. He sipped from his glass and set it gently back down on the cocktail napkin.

"What are you working on right now?"

They had this conversation once a month. She couldn't figure out if her dad was truly interested in what she was doing or if he was looking for something to use against her. To convince her to ditch criminal law once and for all. She hated to admit that part of the reason she pushed herself so hard was because she wanted to prove a point to him. To show him that she didn't have to make two grand an hour or negotiate billion-dollar deals to have worth. What she did *mattered*. She just wished her dad could see it.

"I'm actually working on something pretty big." Excitement leaked into Charlie's voice as she turned to face her dad. "I'm heading up a multiagency task force."

Her dad glanced at her from the side of his eye and his brows arched. "Oh yeah? What sort of task force?"

Technically, she wasn't supposed to be talking about it. She'd told Lacey because that woman was a vault, and Charlie knew that whatever they discussed would never see the light of day again. She doubted her dad would mention it to anyone at his firm or anywhere else, for that matter. He might have been disappointed in her decision to practice criminal law, but he'd never betray her confidence.

"FBI, U.S. Customs, the Marshals Service. It's a pretty big deal."

"Sounds like it." Her dad tipped his glass and studied the amber liquid inside. "Who are you after?"

Charlie trusted her dad, but she still wasn't going to name any names. "Some pretty big fish with even bigger plans," she said. "If I get the job done, I'll be exposing corruption at several pretty high levels and taking down a few bad guys in the process."

Charlie turned to face her dad. His expression was drawn, lips pursed. Concern etched his features and lit his light blue eyes. "They're all bad guys in your line of work, aren't they, kiddo?"

Worry leaked into his tone and it tugged at Charlie's heart. Maybe her dad's opinion of her job wasn't merely based on his disappointment that she hadn't followed in his footsteps. "I'll be okay, Dad. I'm surrounded by elite-level law enforcement. No one's going to let anything happen to me. Besides, I'm behind the scenes. Not hands-on."

"I know, Charlie," he said. "But I'm still your dad and I can still worry about you."

She gave him a soft smile. "Are you ready to eat? I skipped lunch and I'm starving."

He scooped up his glass and stood from the bar stool. "Me too. Let's go get a table."

Charlie grabbed what was left of her drink and followed her dad into the dining area. She didn't want to admit to herself, let alone him, that this assignment had her a little spooked. But Chief Deputy Carrera had promised her only the best of the best would be appointed to the task force.

She sure as hell hoped so. Because she was after the sort of people who couldn't risk exposure and would go to any lengths to protect their identities and their secrets. When power and money were involved, the rules didn't apply. Anything goes. And not only was Charlie prepared to expose Faction Five's leaders, she was going to use one of the world's foremost diamond smugglers to get to them.

Danger or not, she wouldn't stop until she took them all down.

Chapter Two

Mason pulled into the parking garage of the Phillip Burton Federal Building in San Francisco and killed the engine. He'd slept all of about two hours the previous night and he was still wondering if his decision to become a part of Carrera's task force was a huge mistake. Especially now that he knew the chief deputy had been fully aware of Mason's history. And not just the part that made him look like a chump for leaving CBP because he was tired of being used solely for undercover jobs. It all seemed too good to be true. A red flag if Mason ever saw one. Then again, he was being asked to do something he swore he'd never do in order to get a chance at joining the U.S. Marshals Service. So this wouldn't exactly be a cakewalk. Still, Mason couldn't fully let his guard down. *Always suspicious.* He let out a snort. Maybe he was more like his dad than he wanted to admit.

His hands clutched the steering wheel and he stared straight ahead. He could back out now. Tell the Marshals Service to fuck off, swallow his considerable pride, and work private security somewhere. He didn't have to be a rent-a-cop. There were plenty of corporations and wealthy people out there looking for protection. Shit, he'd probably make a hell of a lot more money in the private sector. Once he was away from government scrutiny he might even be able to finally escape his past.

"Shit."

Mason let out a gust of breath as he reached for the handle and pushed open the door. Against his better judgment he hopped out of his Camaro and headed inside. It was because of his past that he was going through with this. Not only to prove a point to Carrera and anyone else who might have doubts about him, but to prove to himself that his past didn't have any hold on him. Mason wasn't like his family and he never would be. He was better than his upbringing. Better than the opinions of guys like Carrera who measured him by his relations.

He checked in at the front desk and pinned the visitor badge to his shirt. He supposed he'd be given a temporary ID badge or something once he was briefed. Until then, he was nothing more than the chief deputy's invited guest. His footsteps were heavy as he headed for the bank of elevators. He waited for an empty car and stepped inside.

"Hold the elevator!"

The last thing Mason wanted was to exchange small talk with a stranger in a cramped metal box. Already he felt the walls closing in on him, and the door hadn't even slid shut. Rather than hold the door, he pushed the button to close it. He didn't feel all that personable and he made no apologies for it. Whoever wanted a ride up could wait for the next car.

A slender hand shot into the crack just before the door closed completely. It bounced for a brief moment and slid open, to Mason's disappointment. A huff of breath preceded a tall, curvy woman who stepped into the car. She swept the curtain of her wavy strawberry-blond hair away from her face and her dark blue eyes narrowed as she shot an accusing glare Mason's way.

Pretty. But the way her gaze raked Mason from head to toe made him feel as though he was being measured up. Whoever she was, she had a chip on her shoulder and obviously was just as thrilled about sharing the elevator as he was. Well, too damned bad. She's the one who'd insisted on taking this car. She'd just have to suck it up and share the air that felt like it was diminishing by the second.

"Sixth floor, please."

Her voice had a husky timbre to it. Warm and sweet as fresh honey. It made the fine hairs stand up on the back of Mason's neck and he reached back to rub the sensation away. He didn't move to punch the button—he was already heading to the sixth floor—and she turned to cut him an exasperated look. Jesus. How dare he not jab his finger on the six, the second the words came out of her haughty mouth.

Mason indicated the lit button panel. "Already done, princess."

Her eyes widened a fraction of an inch and her lips parted. Color rose to her cheeks and she drew in an indignant breath as though ready to let him have it. Mason cocked a brow and met her steady blue gaze, all but daring her to say something. He wasn't in the mood to deal with bullshit of any kind, and she'd be just as good as anyone to take the brunt of his frustration.

She didn't break eye contact. For a long, tense moment she simply stared. Mason could be damned intimidating when he wanted to be. He had a good six inches and fifty or so pounds on her. She didn't cower, though. Didn't even flinch. The hard line of her mouth softened and curved into a tantalizing smile that nearly blinded him.

"Thank you." The words slipped from between her lips in an almost silky caress. She gave him one last look that speared straight through him before she turned around and dismissed him completely.

Damn.

If not for her expression, which very clearly conveyed to Mason he was no better than a piece of gum stuck to the bottom of her expensive stilettos, he might have reconsidered his shitty attitude and tried to warm her up to him a bit. The light locks of her hair brushed her shoulders in a blunt cut with soft, haphazard waves. Her crisp suit jacket and matching skirt hugged every round, supple curve of her body. Her crisp attitude wasn't his cup of tea, but her body checked every box on his *hell yeah* list.

A sweet, floral scent hit Mason's nostrils and he breathed in deeply. His brow furrowed as he realized they'd almost reached the sixth floor and he hadn't broken out into a cold sweat or experienced an ounce of panic. Usually, tight spaces made him twitchy as fuck, but his companion in the cramped car had distracted him from his own ridiculous anxiety.

Huh.

The elevator chimed and the doors slid open. His companion rushed from the elevator as though her heels were on fire, leaving Mason to stare after her. She hung a quick right and disappeared down a hallway. Her speedy exit wasn't exactly the boost to Mason's ego that he needed to get him through the rest of the morning. The fact that she couldn't seem to get out of the elevator fast enough was more like a kick to the nuts.

Awesome.

The elevator doors threatened to close him back in and Mason took a wide step out into the hallway. He rolled his shoulders and stretched his neck from side to side in an effort to release some of the tension that already pulled his muscles taut. So far, his day wasn't turning out so hot. If he didn't experience an uptick soon, he doubted he'd make it through the briefing without stroking out.

"Can I help you with something?"

Mason looked up to find a cheerful older woman smiling up at him. Her sympathetic expression, coupled with elevator-woman's obvious disgust, told him he was doing a pretty damned good job of broadcasting his emotions this morning. Something that he'd have to shut down in a hurry if he was going to work this operation with Carrera.

"Yeah." Mason brushed a hand through his hair. "I'm looking for conference room B."

Her eyes narrowed and her lips curved wryly as she studied him with much more interest. "You're with the Faction Five task force?"

Mason fixed a pleasant but not open smile on his face. He knew better than to admit or deny anything when involved with these sorts of clandestine operations.

The woman's smile broadened as though Mason had passed some sort of test. "I'm Meredith. Charlie's assistant. They're getting ready to start in a few minutes. I was headed to the conference room if you'd like to walk with me."

"Thanks." Mason fell into step beside Meredith. "I'm Mason Decker, by the way."

"Oh, the wild card," Meredith said with a chuckle.

Mason's gut twisted into a knot. What was better

than walking into a room full of high-ranking officials knowing that most of them didn't think you were capable of getting the job done? He'd rather someone dropped him into the gorilla enclosure at the zoo.

"That bad, huh?"

"I have a feeling it's a little overblown." Meredith turned and winked at him. "Want a little advice before we go in?"

Couldn't hurt. "Sure."

"Don't let Charlie intimidate you."

Great. He didn't know anything about the assistant U.S. attorney who was heading up the task force, but from the sound of it, he was a guy who liked to throw his weight around. The last thing Mason wanted was to get into a pissing match with some stick-up-his-ass attorney who thought that because he had a fancy degree, he knew more about undercover ops—or Kieran Eagan—than Mason did. If he was going to be a part of this task force, everyone involved needed to know from the get-go that if it was his future on the line, *he* was in charge. Period.

"I'm used to working with those sorts of guys," Mason said. "But thanks. I'll try to keep my chin up."

Meredith chuckled in a way that made Mason think he was on the outside of an inside joke. "You do that, kiddo."

The conference room was already full when they walked in. Mason let out a gust of breath as he tried to gain his bearings. He liked to be the guy seated and eyeballing the people walking through the door, not the other way around. Already, he felt at a disadvantage, which wasn't going to do much for his confidence. If he was going to be face-to-face with Kieran Eagan, he needed to be at the top of his game.

Mason paused just inside the doorway as he caught

a glimpse of shining strawberry-blond hair. His mystery elevator-woman stood at the head of the long table, one arm braced on the polished surface as she studied the contents of the open file folder in front of her.

"Charlie," Meredith said, drawing the attention of the room. "This is Mason Decker."

Mason's gaze wandered to the men in the room, but instead, cranky-elevator-lady's head snapped up from whatever held her concentration. Her deep blue eyes narrowed as her mouth puckered. She let out a slow sigh and Mason swallowed down a groan as he realized why Meredith had been so amused. Was it too late to back the fuck out now?

"Have a seat." Her warm, honeyed voice rang with authority. He could see why Meredith had thought it best to warn him. *Damn.* Working with the petulant assistant U.S. attorney was going to be an uphill battle, that was for sure. "Okay, everyone, let's get down to business."

Charlie's composure threatened to slip the moment Meredith introduced her to Mason Decker. It was just her luck that the rude jerk from the elevator would be the guy Carrera suggested as their inside man. Charlie had dealt with guys like him before. Confident, tough, with panty-melting good looks and a dismissive attitude that had women dying to get their attention. Well, too bad for him she wasn't the least bit interested in attracting his interest. Instead of giving in to her annoyance, Charlie gave herself a kick in the ass and swallowed down the flustered indignation that would have otherwise made her appear as though she wasn't in charge. The last thing she needed was for this operation to go off the rails before it even had a chance to leave the station.

The former Customs agent took a seat directly across from her at the other end of the table. He leaned back in the chair, arms folded across his wide chest, his intense light green eyes focused on her as though daring her to do something he would find even marginally impressive. *Cocky SOB*. No doubt Mason Decker's ego was as big as his large, muscular frame. Charlie couldn't help but worry he'd prove to be an enormous pain in the ass. She needed this operation to run by the book and as smoothly as possible. The future of her career depended on it.

She tried to ignore the unnerving intensity of his gaze and the way his nearly black hair brushed his brow in a haphazard and outwardly defiant way. The bulk of his frame, packed with solid muscle, and the square cut of his jaw, rough with a few days' worth of stubble, didn't faze her nor did his full lips that curved into a sardonic smirk. Carrera was right about one thing: Decker was perfect for the job. He'd be right at home with guys like Eagan. Rough around the edges. Arrogant. Unapologetic. Ruthless. He was by far the most intimidating man in the room. Hell, probably the entire building.

Charlie stood at the head of the table. All eyes turned to her and she swallowed down her nerves. She was a badass, damn it. Her dad always said that self-doubt had no place in the courtroom or the boardroom. It was time to prove herself.

"For those of you who don't know, I'm Assistant U.S. Attorney Charlotte Cahill and I'm heading up the Faction Five task force that you've all been asked to be a part of. Several months ago, the Marshals Service received a tip about the formation of a large-scale crime syndicate known as Faction Five. According to the informant, the heads of Faction Five are law enforcement and holders of public office. Right now, we're looking at everyone from local PD to FBI, federal judges, and even members of Congress. A new player entered the mix a couple of months ago. We've been tracking the activity of Kieran Eagan, who most of you know since you've all tried to arrest him for something at one point or another."

The comment generated a few chuckles and managed to break the ice. The tension in Charlie's shoulders relaxed by a small degree and she chanced a look Mason's way to find the same inscrutable expression on his face. Well, she guessed it was impossible to please all of the people all of the time.

"Eagan's got a pretty good thing going. He's managed to elude arrest and indictment for several years while he's been busy smuggling diamonds out of the DRC and into India, where they're being cut, polished, and laundered. Eagan's managed to cut out the middleman by doing most of the legwork himself, including forging the Kimberley certificates for the diamonds. The FBI and CIA have kept a close eye on him and it's become apparent that Eagan is trying to amass a small fortune from the proceeds of the diamond sales. We're assuming he's generating seed money to help fund Faction Five."

A low murmur spread throughout the group. Once again, Charlie's gaze found Mason's. The indifference melted from his expression and a deep furrow cut into his brow. He leaned forward in the chair and let his elbows rest on the table. For some damned reason, she found his undivided attention far more disarming than his cool indifference.

Charlie tore her gaze away from Mason's and cleared her throat. "We're not sure what Faction Five's motives are at this point. We have to assume that if its leaders hold positions of authority, they're offering their members a certain level of autonomy. If that's the case, Faction Five could potentially become one of the most dangerous—not to mention lucrative—crime syndicates in the nation, if not the world."

"Does anyone know how Eagan got involved with them?" Charlie glanced over at Gene Fry from Customs and Border Protection. From what she'd been told, Fry had been Mason Decker's supervisor before he left CBP a few months ago. "As far as any of us knows, Eagan is a lone wolf and doesn't do business with syndicates. Otherwise he'd have to share the glory," Fry said.

Another round of chuckles followed Gene's comment. The only person in the room who didn't seem amused was Mason. Interesting. "We think we know how," Charlie replied. "But we're more interested in the possible intel he might be able to provide us with. The FBI, DHS, and CIA have all been investigating Faction Five. Eagan is a relatively new player. He's only recently become involved with them and is quickly raising capital with the sale of blood diamonds. Our goal is to use Eagan to infiltrate Faction Five, or at the very least learn more about the founding and controlling members of the group. If we can get close enough to Eagan, we're confident we can take Faction Five down in the process."

Across the room, Mason let out a soft snort. The indignation Charlie had tried to squash made an unwelcome reappearance. She turned her attention to him. "Is there something you'd like to add, Mr. Decker?"

"If your informant about Faction Five is right, then Kieran already knows you're watching him." Mason's deep voice commanded the room. Embarrassment heated Charlie's cheeks and a lump of annoyance rose in her throat. "His guard is already up. No way is he going to serve up Faction Five to you on a silver platter."

Charlie pinned him with an intimidating stare of her own. "No one but the people in this room knows about this task force." Well, aside from her dad and Lacey, but Charlie knew they'd take her secrets to the grave. She'd made sure to keep the investigation into Faction Five's existence as quiet as possible. "What makes you think he knows we're watching him?"

Mason hiked a shoulder. "Because he's not stupid."

Charlie gaped. This was the guy who was going to gain Eagan's trust? Mason Decker was a piece of work. "And you think that the combined agencies in this room are?"

His jaw squared. "I'm not saying that."

Really? It sure as hell sounded that way. "All right. Then why don't you tell us what you know about Eagan that the rest of the people in this room—people who've spent *months* investigating him—don't know."

She waited for a smart-assed response that never came. Instead, Mason clamped his jaw down and once again leaned back in his chair, arms folded across his wide chest.

"We can all agree that with so many agencies working together, tensions among the group are going to be high until we manage to take Faction Five down," Chief Deputy Carrera interjected. "I think I can speak for Mason and CBP when I say that no one knows more about Kieran Eagan than Mason does. Despite what anyone might think to the contrary, he's going to be an asset to this team. We're all working toward the same goals here."

From the corner of her eye, Charlie noticed Mason hold Carrera's gaze. He cocked a challenging brow, and Charlie wondered what the silent exchange might have meant. At any rate, the briefing had gone off the rails pretty damned fast. Exactly what she'd been trying to avoid. She needed to get them all back on track. She had to put Decker's cocky attitude to the back of her mind and think about the big picture. Charlie needed a win.

"You're right, Carlos. We're all on the same team here." Charlie refused to let Decker's pessimism rain on her parade. "What's important moving forward is that we're able to use Eagan as an asset to build a solid case against Faction Five. We can thank the U.S. Marshals Service and Mr. Decker for that."

No one acknowledged her, but Charlie didn't expect it. It was tough enough to get so many agencies to play nice and cooperate. It was her job to make sure that everyone got along and stayed on task. The rest of the briefing went smoothly, with Charlie pretty much glossing over everything that most of the people in the room already knew. By the time she'd concluded, her confidence was back in full force. That is, until the room began to empty and the only two people remaining were Mason Decker and Carrera. This was the part of the briefing she'd been dreading. One-on-one time with the arrogant, know-it-all former Customs agent was bound to siphon all of that newfound confidence right out of her.

"All right, guys," Charlie said when the last body filed out of the conference room. "Let's get down to brass tacks."

Chapter Three

Assistant U.S. Attorney Charlotte Cahill had one hell of a chip on her shoulder. Her deep blue eyes narrowed as her gaze locked on Mason. He had a feeling that she was the sort of person who hated to have her authority challenged. And he'd called her out in front of the heads of almost every federal law enforcement agency in the region.

So far, this gig was off to a stellar start.

She settled down onto her chair and studied Mason for a quiet—and not a little unnerving—moment. Her full lips pursed as she watched him and Mason was willing to bet that hardened criminals withered under that scrutinizing stare. She was trying to get under his skin. Assert her dominance and let him know exactly who was in charge. It didn't faze Mason one bit. She could think she was in charge, but the fact of the matter was, the second he made contact with Kieran, Mason would be running the show.

Of course, his own domineering attitude—not to mention his own deep-seated disregard for authority—had probably only added to the reasons the USMS continued to reject his applications to join their ranks.

Now, his only option was to buy his way in by doing something he'd vowed he'd never do. And he'd be answering to the woman who stared at him as though she could see right into his soul and found it somehow tainted. *Join the club, lady.*

"I don't usually have these sorts of meetings without everyone on the team present," she said in a crisp, matter-of-fact way. Mason pegged her as a control freak. No doubt going off script was sending her OCD into a tailspin. "So what did you want to discuss, Carlos?"

"I thought it would be a good idea for you to get a little background on Mason beforehand, Charlie." Carrera rested his hip on the edge of the conference table as he turned toward Charlie. Mason loved being talked about like he wasn't there. This was bound to be the cherry on top of a perfect day. "We won't gain Eagan's trust without him."

Charlie focused her attention on Carrera. "Why do I feel like I'm about to be managed?"

"Because you are," Mason interjected.

Carrera cut him a look and let out a long-suffering sigh. The chief deputy might have wanted to sugarcoat it for Charlie, but Mason didn't like to play games. Might as well get all of his shit out in the open now.

Charlie's eyes narrowed. "What's this about?"

"There are a few things about Mason that you need to know before we launch this operation." Carrera gave Mason a sidelong glance. "First off, he's no longer with CBP and he's not technically employed by the USMS, either."

"So . . ." Charlie turned toward Mason, her brow raised in question. "What agency, *technically*, do you currently work for?"

"None," Mason said flatly. "Before Carrera called, I was *technically* unemployed."

Her eyes went wide and Charlie leaned forward in her chair as she fixed that withering stare on Carrera once again. "You're kidding, right?"

"I gave my notice to CBP a month ago. My last day was about two weeks ago." Mason settled back into his chair. "And every single one of my applications to the Marshals Service has been rejected." He probably didn't need to fill her in on that last part, but for some reason, it gave Mason a perverse sense of satisfaction to see her feathers ruffled.

"You want to explain this, Carlos?" Charlie's head looked like it was about to explode off her shoulders. "You know how important this operation is. We can't move forward if any of the members of this team are anything less than fully vetted and capable."

"Mason's capable," Carrera assured her. "He's the most capable man for the job."

"And I'm supposed to believe that because . . . ?"

"Because my dad taught Kieran Eagan everything he knows," Mason said.

He almost wished he could drop the bomb again, just to see the expression on Charlotte Cahill's high-and-mighty face. Her jaw hung on its hinges for the barest moment before she regained her composure. "What?" Her bemused expression transformed to one of realization. "Your father is Jensen Decker?"

Mason fought the urge to cringe at the mention of his father's name. There wasn't a law enforcement agency in the world that didn't know of the infamous smuggler and forger. It was Mason's misfortune that he'd been born Jensen Decker's son, and it was his father's misfortune that his son had decided to spend his life upholding the laws that Jensen insisted on breaking.

"Where is dear old dad, now?" Mason asked with not a little sarcasm. "Victorville? Lompoc? I sort of lost track after they transferred him to San Diego a few years ago."

"Jesus." The word left Charlie's lips on an emphatic breath. She looked at Carrera, her eyes still a little wide. "Seriously?"

Carrera met her gaze and offered up a shrug. "Why do you think he was so successful with CBP?"

"How?" Charlie's eyes slid to Mason once again. It rankled that she insisted on continuing to talk around him rather than to him. "He worked undercover, didn't he? How could he possibly maintain a cover with such an illustrious father? Every smuggler and forger in the world must know who he is."

Mason folded his arms across his chest as he studied the assistant U.S. attorney. She was heading up a task force whose main directive was to make arrests with the aid of undercover intel and she acted as though she had no idea what *undercover* even meant.

He decided to hit her with a dose of her own medicine and said to Carrera, "Is she for real?"

A smile threatened to surface at her expression, half-flustered, half-enraged. Mason swallowed the urge down and kept his own face passive.

"Charlie's one of the best prosecutors in the state." Carrera's brow puckered and the older man scrubbed a hand over his face. "Why do I suddenly feel like a referee—or worse, a teacher breaking up a fight between a couple of teenagers? We're all professionals here, right?"

"At least two of us are," Charlie groused.

Jesus. Why was he even still sitting here? Carrera was

all but blackmailing him to use Kieran to bring Faction Five down. He wasn't out anything save a job if he got up and walked the fuck out of here. Mason wanted to get back into undercover work about as much as he wanted to take a bullet to the head. Throw Kieran into the mix and Mason really would rather be six feet under. All of this was an utter waste of his time.

Mason pushed out his chair and Carrera held up a staying hand. "Hang on a second, Mason." He leaned toward Charlie, his dark brows drawn over his eyes. "If you want a win, Charlie, we need Mason to get it. No one knows more about Eagan than Mason does."

Charlie pursed her lips. Mason was beginning to think she did it only when in deep contemplation. He bet he could create one hell of a drinking game if he watched her in court. "If Eagan is that close to Jensen Decker, then Mason's cover is already blown. He's useless."

Useless? Mason was tired of being jerked around. He stood and strode to the door, ready to slam the damn thing behind him.

"That's the point, Charlie," Carrera said. "We want Eagan to assume that Mason has flipped."

Mason paused at the door and turned around. Charlie's lips further puckered, as though she'd just sucked on a particularly sour lemon. It made her look too young. Almost cute, in a petulant sort of way. He paused at the door and watched as her expression changed. Softened. She brushed her fingers through the length of her strawberry-blond hair, and Mason counted at least five variations of color that played off of the light. Pretty.

Too bad she was a total control freak.

"Do you think Eagan will buy it?"

Carrera smiled as though sure he'd won her over. "Either way, I don't think he'll be able to resist."

It was certainly nice to see Carrera could be so cavalier with someone else's life. Mason swallowed down a snort. He was right, though. Kieran's curiosity would get the best of him. He'd let Mason into the operation to satisfy that curiosity.

"Are you up for this?"

Mason's gaze met Charlie's. He was surprised she deigned him worthy to address without the aid of a middleman. And even though he considered her a raging pain in the ass, he understood where she was coming from. The buck stopped at her desk. If shit went south, she'd be the one to pay the price. Mason got that. Hell, he'd lived through it.

"Yeah," he said. "I am."

Was he, though? Mason wished he was as sure as he sounded.

Charlie didn't want to admit it, but they might've struck gold with Mason. Never in a million years would she have guessed the former Customs agent was the son of an infamous criminal. Jensen Decker's reputation was far-reaching. Hell, she'd studied two of his trials while in law school. He was the sort of criminal that Hollywood producers made movies about. Counterfeiter, master forger, smuggler—the ultimate con man. Not to mention good-looking and charming to a fault. He'd managed to avoid prosecution and evade capture for years before the Marshals Service had arrested him in 1999. Which would have made Mason about sixteen or seventeen years old at the time. What on earth had prompted him to leave the trail his dad had forged, to strike out on his own? A twinge of jealousy tugged at Charlie's chest. She'd barely veered off her own father's path. More to the point, she'd walked safely beside it.

The unwavering confidence in Mason's tone was the boost that Charlie needed to see this through. It was a dangerous game they were about to play. One that could easily cost Mason his future in law enforcement, if not his life, if Eagan found out what they were up to. Hell, maybe he already knew. A wave of anxiety crested and Charlie forced the worry away.

"You said Eagan probably already knows we're watching him. Aren't you worried that he'll assume you're working for someone from the get-go?"

Mason hiked an unconcerned shoulder. How was it possible for someone to look so nonchalant and so menacing at the same time?

"I'm going to let him assume that I'm working with the government," Mason said. "There's no reason for him to think I've left CBP, and I'll let him think that I can help him get his product through customs without detection."

Charlie rolled her bottom lip between her teeth. "A double agent?" It was risky, but the payout could be huge if Eagan took the bait.

A half smile tugged at one corner of Mason's lips. "Exactly."

This operation was becoming more complicated by the second. "That wasn't the plan the task force had in place for an undercover marshal," Charlie replied.

"*Technically,*" Mason stressed yet again. "I'm only a temporary marshal. And I'm changing the plan."

Heat rose to Charlie's cheeks. It didn't matter that his plan was sound. Mason Decker thought he could change the rules whenever and however he damn well pleased, and it pissed her off. Charlie lived her life by rules. Hell, her entire existence was about order. The anxiety of butting heads with Mason might kill her long before she ever got the chance to see any of Faction Five's members stand before a judge.

"You're not in charge." The hot retort escaped unchecked from Charlie's lips. She wanted to tell Mason Decker that he was a coarse, rude, selfish, arrogant pain in her ass, and if she had it her way, she'd deposit him right back on the street that Carrera scooped him up from. Her pride stemmed the flow, though. Her burning need to win at all costs cut off the words before they escaped.

"No," Mason agreed darkly. His nearly black brows cut severe slashes above his brilliant green eyes. "I'm sure as hell not. But no one knows Kieran better than I do."

Charlie sensed there was more to Eagan's relationship with Mason than simply being Jensen Decker's apprentice. Until she could do a little digging, she decided not to press Mason on the issue. "All right. I'm sure Carrera told you you'd be working with a partner on this one—"

"I work alone," Mason interjected. "Period."

"That's not how this works," Charlie said. "It's for your safety as well as everyone else's that you have a partner."

"It's safer for everyone if I do this alone." Mason's tone brooked no argument. "You can find someone else to bring Faction Five down if you don't like it."

Sweet fiery hell, the man was stubborn! Charlie cast an exasperated glance Carrera's way and Carrera simply shrugged his shoulders. Apparently he was at a loss as to how to handle Mason as well.

"Everyone involved will have to sign off on it," Charlie

said. "You might want to work alone, but this task force is a *team*."

Mason shrugged as though he didn't care either way. Charlie was sorely tempted to lay her fist into his smug jaw, but going by the chiseled-from-marble look of it, her hand would break long before his jaw would.

Charlie rounded the table and walked up to Mason. He towered head and shoulders above her. Broad, imposing, and maybe even a little tempting. But good looks aside, the future of Charlie's career swung on a hinge that Mason Decker controlled. It was an unfortunate truth. "Can you get Faction Five for me?"

He gave a crisp nod of his head. "Yeah."

Charlie turned to face Carrera. "Make sure he's ready to go."

Carrera's smug expression told her they were both going to get what they wanted today. "I'll deal with getting everyone to sign off. No need for you to bother."

"All right." Carrera had a rapport with everyone on the task force. No doubt he'd convince all of them that bringing Mason on—and letting him work alone—was the right thing to do. She turned back to face Mason. "I'm trusting you. Don't make me regret it." Without another word, she walked past him and out of the conference room.

As she made her way down the hallway, Charlie took several cleansing breaths. Most of the time, she was cool as a cucumber under pressure. Completely unflappable. Mason Decker got under her skin like few people could. She didn't know what it was about him, but she found it infuriating as hell.

"Did you see his eyes?" Meredith fell into step beside her and the tension that Charlie had been trying to release made an unwelcome reappearance. "I swear they were the color of seafoam."

Charlie rolled her eyes. Yeah, the guy had pretty eyes. So what? "I hadn't really noticed."

"Are you kidding me?" Meredith clucked her tongue as though she felt sorry for Charlie. "You must be blind, kiddo, because that man was a sight to behold."

Ugh. *So* melodramatic. "You think every man under forty who walks through the door is a sight to behold," she teased. "Remember the SFPD guy we met with last month? I thought you were going to leave that deposition on a stretcher."

Meredith chuckled. "He was a cutie. But that Mason Decker . . ." She mocked a swoon before she leaned in conspiratorially. "Can you imagine what a man like that could do in bed?"

Charlie's step faltered. It was true that Mason looked as though he could rock a woman into next week. His attitude, on the other hand, didn't do a damn thing for Charlie. "Bossy and demanding gets your motor going, huh, Mer?"

Her eyes bulged as she looked at Charlie. "Um, it doesn't for you?"

Charlie's stomach did a pleasant little flip as she thought of the intensity of Mason's expression earlier in the conference room. She pursed her lips. "Not a damned bit."

Meredith chuckled. "Liar." Her phone chimed and she checked the alert. "You're due in court in a half hour, don't forget."

Shit. Charlie had been so wrapped up in what Mason had unexpectedly brought to the table, court had completely skipped her mind. "We'd better get a move on. I want to review my notes beforehand."

Meredith handed over a file folder. "One step ahead of you."

Charlie flashed her assistant a smile. "Thanks."

There probably wasn't a woman alive who didn't perk up when Mason walked into a room. Hell, he'd commanded the conference room today and he'd barely said a word. "Growly voice and alpha-male charisma aside, what did you really think of him?" She knew that when it came down to it, Meredith wouldn't pull any punches and she was one hell of a good judge of character.

"I think if you want to take down Faction Five, you're going to need him," Meredith replied. "You need someone as hard as the guys you're trying to bust, Charlie. And he's the real deal."

Sort of what Charlie was afraid of. "I can't believe his dad is Jensen Decker." She gave a disbelieving shake of her head.

"No kidding?" Meredith let out an appreciative whistle. "His most-wanted poster was worthy of being framed," she said with a laugh. "His son definitely inherited his good looks."

Was that all he'd inherited, though?

"I'm worried about his connection to Eagan," Charlie admitted. "Blood is thicker than water."

"True."

Had she been wrong to put her trust in the former Customs agent? Guess she'd find out soon enough.

Chapter Four

Mason sat at a small square table in the visitors' room at San Quentin State Prison. His gut churned and the acid ate away at the lining. The only thing he might come away from all of this with was an ulcer. He hadn't seen his dad in years. Not since the marshals had ambushed him at the Mexico border and hauled him off to jail. Fifteen years. Jesus. Mason and Kieran had both been kids when Jensen's shit finally caught up to him. Mason had tried to visit his dad once, before he'd revealed his postgraduation plans and been effectively shunned. According to his dad, working law enforcement brought the ultimate shame upon his family name. Mason snorted. Only in his fucked up life would one of his parents be ashamed that he'd decided to pursue law enforcement as a career.

Carrera had orchestrated his father's transfer to San Quentin shortly after Mason's meeting with the task force a couple of weeks ago. Right around the same time Mason had finally been given the green light to reach out to Kieran. He should've felt a twinge of guilt that he was using his dad as an unsuspecting accomplice to connect with Kieran, but he couldn't seem to muster anything but apathy. His dad had made his bed a long damned time ago. It wasn't Mason's fault that now he was being forced to lie in it.

How Mason felt about using Kieran to get information on Faction Five was another matter altogether, though. They'd promised to stay far away from each other's business a long time ago. Sort of their way of creating a neutral zone. Kieran got the life he wanted while Mason had been denied his happiness time and again. It certainly wasn't Kieran's fault—the blame for that rested on Jensen. And still, Mason had made the decision to cross the line he'd drawn almost two decades ago. Didn't he deserve to have the life he wanted too? His shared DNA with one of the country's most infamous criminals, not to mention his history with Kieran, had guaranteed him a spot at Glynco when all of this was done. This was about getting intel on Faction Five and playing by the task force's rules to get it done. Okay, *some* of their rules.

He'd come to the prison early, knowing he'd need a few minutes to get his shit together before he let his past collide head-on with his present. The past couple of weeks had been spent rethinking his decision to involve himself with the Faction Five task force. He reminded himself that he wasn't going after Kieran. This wasn't about bringing him down. His reasoning might be on the weak side, but it gave Mason a loophole. Justification for what he was about to do. It wasn't a betrayal per se. He was simply bending the rules. A means to an end.

It was Mason's turn to get the life he deserved.

A loud buzzer sliced through the quiet as a heavy metal door at the opposite end of the room opened wide. Several inmates filed in and settled at tables interspersed throughout the room. Mason's hands gathered into fists and his heart began to hammer in his rib cage. The last time he'd been face-to-face with his dad, Mason was a kid and they'd sat across from each other in a bland, cinder-block reception room just like this one.

He wondered what his dad would say if he found out his son was about to join the ranks of the world's most successful man hunters. The same man hunters who'd stolen his freedom almost two decades ago. The old man would probably have a heart attack on the spot.

Mason knew that prison aged a person, but it didn't lessen the shock as his dad walked across the room toward him. No longer the picture of youth and vitality that Mason remembered, his face bore the proof of a harsh existence and his dark hair ran with streaks of white. A wide, sarcastic smile stretched across Jensen Decker's lips as he pulled out a chair and sat across from his son.

"Funny," his dad remarked. "For some reason, I didn't think I'd be walking into this room to sit across from a grown man."

Mason knew exactly how his dad felt. He supposed that time stood still in prison. Still, the years showed on every line of his dad's face and in the graying of his hair. There was a hollowness in his gaze that Mason couldn't remember being there before his arrest. A tight ball of emotion lodged itself in Mason's throat and he swallowed it down. There was no use hashing out issues he'd long since buried.

"Dad," Mason began. "How've you been?"

"I can't complain." He shrugged. "Food sucks, though."

Mason chuckled. His dad had always had gourmet tastes. Growing up, Mason had rarely eaten a meal that wasn't five-star. As a kid, all he'd wanted was

McDonald's, and he'd hated his dad's fancy fucking tastes. He supposed that he'd inherited something good from his father, an appreciation for well-prepared food.

"I might be able to do something about that," Mason replied.

His dad cocked an appreciative brow. "Smuggle in a half dozen fresh oysters and I'll be impressed."

Mason's chest burned. That's what it would take to get his father's approval. To prove himself a halfway decent smuggler. He tried not to let the bitterness eat him alive. "Done."

Ego was a trait that criminals not only valued, but respected. Whether they were gangbangers or high-end forgers. "I'll hold you to it." His dad flashed a quick smile, reminding Mason of the man he remembered from childhood.

"Have you been painting?" Mason asked. Jensen Decker could put any Renaissance master to shame with his skill. Hell, he'd painted a reproduction of the *Mona Lisa* that would have brought da Vinci to tears.

"A little." His dad's artistic skill was impressive and it was the only good thing Mason had inherited from him. "There's not much else to do in prison. I did one of Van Gogh's irises a few months back that I bet I could have snagged a couple million for."

Always forgeries. Too bad he never painted anything original.

A space of silence passed. Mason couldn't recall a more awkward moment in his entire life. This notion of cozying up to his dad was a horrible idea. One that was sure to blow his cover. Jensen's gaze narrowed as he studied him, his eyes nearly the same color as Mason's. "You're the last person I would've ever pegged to jump ship on his convictions. What happened?"

Mason might've decided to walk the straight and narrow, but he'd inherited at least one more of his dad's traits. He could bullshit like a master. His ability to sell his cover story was what made him a great undercover agent.

"I got jerked around one too many times." Mason offered up a shrug. "Shit pay. Shit benefits. No advancement. CBP put me on probation and there was an investigation after a few South American emeralds went missing from the evidence room."

His dad's eyes lit with excitement. "What happened to the stones?"

Mason slid one balled fist across the table and splayed his fingers out. When he pulled his hand away, three grade-AAA emeralds sat on the table in front of his dad. It was a gamble to offer up a prize like this right off the bat. It could come off as contrived. But Mason was willing to bet that the shining green gems would dazzle his dad. Remind him of the life he'd been forced to leave behind.

"Damn," Jensen said on a breath. "Very nice."

He reached up, wrists cuffed together, and scooped up the emeralds before settling his hands in his lap. Thanks to Carrera, the guards would be a little lax with his dad for a while, allowing him to settle into a false sense of security. Mason doubted his dad would barter away the emeralds. More likely, he'd covet them as a symbol of his son finally turning his back on the law.

"Kieran didn't believe me when I told him you finally wanted to work with him." His dad's expression grew serious and Mason's muscles tensed. "He said you were working an angle."

Of all the things Kieran Eagan was, stupid wasn't

one of them. That's why the double-agent cover story was the best. There was just enough truth in the lie to properly sell it.

"Which is why I asked you to change the date of our visit to today instead of Friday." Eagan wasn't stupid, but neither was Mason. He'd gone off script and changed the date of their rendezvous, knowing full well that Eagan would be watching local law enforcement in anticipation of an ambush. No one knew about the change but Mason. Something that was bound to ruffle the feathers of a certain assistant U.S. attorney. "Ever since my probation, CBP has been keeping close tabs on me."

His dad let out a derisive snort. "Dogs with a bone," he muttered. "Every last one of them."

Mason knew his dad thought of his crimes as victimless. He'd smuggled, stolen, and conned from those he'd felt could afford it. *They've got insurance,* he'd say. *Which, if you ask me, is the biggest racket there is. No one's out anything but the insurance company, and they're robbing their customers blind already.*

There still wasn't any guarantee that Kieran would show up today. But like he'd assured Carrera, he had to believe that after so many years of radio silence from Mason, Kieran's curiosity would get the better of him. Even the best criminals had a fatal flaw. Unfortunately, Kieran's was his relationship with Mason. "Yeah, well, I'm here because CBP thought they could jerk me around. They used me for undercover shit, refused to advance me. Exploited my knowledge and connections and didn't offer me a single reward for it. So, fuck them. It's time I worried about myself for a change. Paybacks are a bitch."

"That they are." Jensen chuckled. "Don't think for a second that I'm ready to trust you though." His gaze hardened. "I haven't seen or heard from you in over ten years. Suddenly you come out of the woodwork, flipped, and ready to fuck over the same people you've idolized since you were a kid? Even you've got to admit that it's shady."

Mason never thought it would be an easy sell. This was the part he'd been dreading. Every lie needed a bit of truth to it to be truly effective. And Mason's truth was one he'd tried to bury in the darkest recesses of his mind over the past several months. "I promised Kieran that nothing would come between us. That I'd always put him before the job. A month ago, the Marshals Service came to me. Because of you, they've rejected every single one of my applications. But they wanted to make a deal. They dangled a spot with the next training group at Glynco if I agreed to help them bring Kieran down. That's not going to happen. I made a promise to him and I'm keeping it. The marshals can fuck off. But I'm broke. CBP is never going to advance me. Kieran promised me that he'd always be there for me no matter what. I'm ready to collect on that promise."

"They bent you over a barrel, that's for sure," Jensen replied. "No Kieran, no Glynco."

"Yup. I'm sick of bending over backward for CBP for no reward, and I'm sure as hell not going to work as a rent-a-cop or mall security somewhere. I'm tired of playing games. Tired of being poor. Of swimming upstream. Of doing every goddamned thing by the letter and still getting screwed in the end. I'm done. With all of it."

Mason drew in a deep breath through flared nostrils. That was a hell of a lot of truth to spit out all at once.

His dad's lips thinned as he regarded him. "It's about damned time."

* * *

Charlie slammed the phone down into the cradle with enough force to break the damn thing. Heat rose to her cheeks as her temper flared. "That son of a bitch!"

She grabbed her purse and headed out of her office. The door slammed behind her and Meredith gave her a questioning look.

"Cancel all of my meetings for the rest of the afternoon."

Meredith opened a window on her computer and scrolled through the calendar. "What's up?"

"Mason Decker," Charlie said through clenched teeth.

Meredith's gaze widened a fraction, but she kept her mouth shut. "Want me to call Carrera and get him involved?"

"No." She'd be paying an in-person visit to the chief deputy's office later. "Just call me if anything pressing comes up."

"Can do." Meredith's fingernails clicked on her keyboard as she typed. "But Charlie, try to calm down. You look like you could use a Xanax."

There weren't enough drugs in the world to help her deal with Decker. She let out a chuff of breath. "I'll touch base later."

Thirty minutes later, Charlie pulled into a parking space at San Quentin, her hands still wrapped around the steering wheel with a death grip. When she'd gotten the call from the prison that Jensen Decker was scheduled to receive not one but two visitors today, her head had nearly blown right off of her shoulders. Mason had been given the green light to use his dad to reach out to Eagan, but only under U.S. marshal surveillance. They'd agreed Mason could meet with his dad two days from now. What was he up to? The double-agent angle of his cover left Charlie with a bad feeling in the pit of her stomach. How could they be certain that he wasn't double-crossing them and working with Eagan? Mason was a wild card as far as she was concerned. He couldn't be left to work unchecked. It had been foolish for any of them to put their trust in him.

Charlie got out of the car and took a moment to gather her thoughts. By being here, she wanted Mason to know that he couldn't get anything past her. That she had his number, and damn it, she would *not* be made a fool of. He wasn't in charge. Not even close. Scheduling meetings off the books—unacceptable. Not to mention damned shady. Charlie wanted the win but not at the expense of sacrificing her integrity. Decker obviously wasn't trustworthy. Even if he managed to get anything on Eagan, who would believe him? An unreliable witness was useless. Not following proper procedure would sink her case.

They could find another way to flip Eagan. Mason was out and Charlie was going to put an end to his involvement with the task force right here and now. She'd bring conspiracy charges against him so fast it would make his head spin.

She smoothed a hand over her hair and headed into the prison. She showed her DOJ badge and signed in at the front desk.

A moment later, one of the prison staff met her. "Charlie?" He reached out and shook her hand. "Evan Hill. I'm the chief facility security supervisor. Decker's in the visitation area with his father right now."

Charlie fell into step beside him. "How long has he been here?"

"Not long," Evan replied. "A half hour or so."

"And no one else has shown up yet?"

"Not yet." Charlie quickened her pace to keep up with Evan as they hustled down the hallway. "Besides Mason Decker, there's a Max Clark on Jensen's visitors list for today."

The name didn't ring a bell, but that didn't matter. It could be an alias. Adrenaline pooled in Charlie's muscles. If this Max Clark was in fact Eagan, it would be best to ambush Mason and get him the hell out of there before he showed up.

God, Charlie. What in the hell are you doing?

She was a planner. Flying by the seat of her pants wasn't Charlie's thing. She wouldn't be made a fool of, though. Not by Mason Decker, or anyone. No way was she going to lose control over her task force or the people in it. She was in charge. Period. She didn't need Mason to get the win. Carrera would just have to live with her decision to remove him.

A loud buzzer preceded the opening of a heavy metal door that led to the visiting area. "There are guards inside. If you need help or run into trouble, you'll be covered."

She smiled her appreciation at Evan. "Thanks." The only person who was going to need help was Mason Decker after she raked his ass over the coals.

From across the room she spotted him deep in conversation with his father. For a moment, Charlie was taken aback by the similarities between the two men. They shared the same rugged good looks, the same striking green eyes and sharp features. Through Jensen Decker, Charlie got a glimpse of what Mason would someday look like, and it proved that he'd only get better with age. Good looks or not, Mason had screwed the pooch. No one fucked with Charlie's task force and got away with it. Not when she stood to lose so much.

Her heels clacked on the industrial flooring as she strode toward their table. The sound drew Mason's attention and he caught sight of her from the corner of his eye. A momentary glimmer of shock crossed his face, but he recovered quickly and replaced it instead with recognition. Jensen's brow furrowed and his mouth formed a hard line. He murmured something to Mason and he gave a quick response before pushing out his chair and turning toward Charlie.

"You're late." His growled response sent a tingle up Charlie's spine. "But Kieran isn't here yet so it's no big deal."

What in the hell . . . ? His words threw her for a loop. She opened her mouth to let him have it, but before she could say a single word, Mason cut her off.

"Jensen, this is Charlie Sinclair. She brokers in rare gems and her specialty is diamonds. Charlie, meet the infamous Jensen Decker."

Diamonds? Sinclair? *Huh?* Charlie looked at Mason. The hard glint in his eyes and the stern set of his jaw told her that she'd better roll with the punches or the consequences could be dire. She'd seen defense attorneys look at their clients that way. Especially when they knew their case didn't have a leg to stand on.

Shit! Charlie was beginning to think that waltzing in here to shit-can Mason might not have been the best idea.

"It's an honor to meet the legend in person," Charlie replied as smoothly as she could, despite the shock that hadn't quite worn off. It was true, though. Jensen Decker was a rock star among criminals. She still had no idea in hell what was going on, but she'd play along—for now. "Sorry I'm late."

Jensen turned a caustic eye on his son. "It would have been nice if you'd told me beforehand you were inviting another player to the table. Kieran isn't going to like this."

A corner of Mason's mouth hitched in a sardonic smile. He snagged a chair from a nearby table and pulled it up for Charlie to sit. "Are you kidding? He lives for shit like this. It won't faze him in the least."

Jensen looked as though he wanted to disagree but held his tongue. "So, tell me, Charlie, how long have you been a broker?"

She hated being put on the spot. *Hated it.* Improv wasn't exactly her thing, but it appeared as though she had no choice but to wing it. "About five years. I was a buyer for Tiffany's before that."

"Decided to move out of the private sector, huh?"

"Yeah, well." Charlie laughed. "You've gotta go where the money is, know what I mean?"

Jensen winked. The man was certainly as charming as his reputation suggested. Not even close to as growly and grumpy as his broody son.

"Where are your stones coming from?" Jensen asked.

It was a damn good thing she'd brushed up on the black-market diamond trade prior to convening this task force. She suspected it might be the only thing currently keeping her ass out of a sling. "India mostly. I don't dabble with the raw material. I won't touch a single stone until it's cut and polished and accompanied by a passable Kimberley certificate."

Jensen snorted. "Most brokers don't like to get their hands dirty. You let the smugglers do all the heavy lifting and pull in a hefty commission in the process."

Charlie shrugged. "I have the connections. Without the buyers, there would be no need to smuggle the stones out of Africa in the first place. Guys like you have a job because of people like me."

Jensen broke out into good-natured laughter. "True." He looked at Mason. "I like her."

Mason cut her a look from the corner of his eye and Charlie let out a slow sigh that she hoped no one noticed. She kept her hands in her lap, clenched tight to keep them from shaking. She hadn't been this nervous since the bar exam.

The buzzer signaled that the door to the visiting room was about to open again and Charlie jumped. Beside her, Mason took her forearm and gave a gentle squeeze. She really wished she was better at deciphering nonverbal communication, because she wasn't sure if the contact had meant to be reassuring or a warning.

All eyes turned toward the door, and an anxious knot rose in Charlie's throat. Things had gone from bad to worse as Kieran Eagan crossed the room to where they sat. Of all of the stupid decisions Charlie had ever made in her life, waltzing in here to confront Mason was by far the stupidest.

So far, she was doing a bang-up job of proving who was in charge.

Chapter Five

Mason teetered between feeling the urge to protect and throttle Charlie all at once. Of all the people he could have imagined walking through that door, she was dead last. So far, she hadn't managed to screw him over, but that wasn't saying much. She could have blown his cover right off the bat, and it was a miracle she'd gotten Mason's hint and played along.

Charlie Cahill wasn't stupid—current situation aside—and for that, Mason could be thankful. They'd yet to pass this quickly contrived cover story over on Kieran, though. It was way too soon to get comfortable.

"Hell, Mason, if I'd have known you were bringing a beautiful woman with you I would have made sure to be here on time."

Mason stood and Kieran rounded the table to embrace him. It had been almost a decade since he'd seen his childhood friend, his adopted brother, the surrogate son his dad wished Mason would've grown up to be like. For a long time, Kieran had been Mason's only family. His confidant. Sometimes it was hard to believe they'd chosen such different paths, considering their shared upbringing. They were two sides of the same coin and Mason was shocked to realize how much he'd missed Kieran.

"Charlie." Mason pulled away. "This is Kieran Eagan."

She let out a slow breath and Mason hoped she'd be able to keep it together long enough to get this meeting over with. He still couldn't believe how she'd managed to fuck up what had been a perfectly orchestrated plan. Good God, how had she even known he was here?

She held out her hand and Kieran took it. "Nice to finally meet you, Mr. Eagan."

Kieran flashed a cocky grin. "Call me Kieran."

He continued to hold Charlie's hand and held eye contact for a moment too long. Mason's gut clenched. Kieran was purposely trying to unnerve her. Rattle her into slipping. Revealing something. She let out a nervous laugh and angled her head to glance at Mason over his shoulder.

"You never told me he was so charming."

Some of the tension released from Mason's muscles. He needed her to be the haughty woman from the elevator. The badass bitch with a chip on her shoulder. If she could do that for him, Mason could float the rest. He could get them both out of here today and hopefully still keep the task force on track. She just had to keep it together for fifteen minutes. A half hour at the most and they'd be home free. Sort of.

Charlie turned back to Kieran. His smile remained pleasant as he finally released her hand and took a seat at the table.

"You're the only son of a bitch on the face of the earth who prison agrees with, Jensen," he said with a chuckle. "Seriously, whose palms are you greasing? Because someone is treating you right."

Mason's dad looked at Kieran with all of the affection

reserved for a son. Meanwhile, he treated his *real son*, his own flesh and blood, with suspicion. Like he was the outsider. This job was dredging up all sorts of repressed emotions. Ones Mason had spent most of his life trying *not* to deal with.

"I didn't grease any palms this time." Jensen bucked his chin toward Mason. "Mason organized the transfer here. So far, so good."

A sly smile spread on Kieran's lips and he finally turned his full attention to Mason. He hadn't changed much over the years. A slightly older—and decidedly more sophisticated—version of that same smart-ass homeless kid who'd tried to hustle his dad and then steal his wallet. Jensen had always liked to have a pet project and he'd made Kieran his. Brought him into their home, taught him everything he knew, because Mason had never been interested in having anything to do with the con game.

"Finally using those superpowers of yours for evil, huh? It's been a long time, Mason."

It sure as hell had been. "How've you been, Kieran?"

He flashed a confident grin. "I can't complain." His gaze slid to Charlie. "Looks like you're doing all right too."

"Charlie's a broker," Mason replied.

Kieran's gaze narrowed. "Funny. I'm familiar with everyone in the game. Don't know of any Charlies. Especially one so pretty."

Ugh. The man could talk a saint happily into sin. Charlie seemed unaffected by his charm, and Mason tried not to feel smug. Looked like Kieran couldn't put everyone under his spell.

"I don't think I need a broker." Kieran's tone chilled by a degree.

"You might not need one," Mason said. "But you could use one like Charlie."

Kieran gave her the once-over. She didn't even squirm, which earned her a point or two. Neither did she try to butt in and assert herself, which helped to put Mason at ease. Thank God.

Kieran chuckled. "When you make a change, you make it big, don't you, Mason?" He leaned back in his chair and fixed Mason with his inscrutable, deep brown gaze. "I've never known you to be anything other than a stand-up guy. Hell, you wouldn't even take a free sample without confirming it was free first. What in the hell is going on? Why now?"

Mason gritted his teeth. He'd vowed long ago to never be anything less than 100 percent with Kieran. Playing to his ego and blurring the lines between truth and fiction was the last thing he wanted to do, but he was going to suck it the fuck up and do it anyway. "Because I'm tired of swimming upstream," he said. "I want what you have."

Kieran smirked. Arrogant as ever.

"And what is it that I have, Mason?"

He replied from between clenched teeth, "Everything."

A tense, quiet moment followed. Kieran's discerning expression turned to one of amusement and he broke into raucous laughter. "Mason Decker wants what I have? Did hell freeze over and no one told me?"

Mason cast a nervous glance around the visitors' room. Kieran never did give a shit about attracting attention. No, he lived for it. One of the guys at CBP told him that a group of marshals had been close to apprehending Kieran once. The crazy SOB had jumped off a bridge to evade capture, and gave the marshals the finger all the way down until he hit the water.

"I've got something that could be useful to you, Kieran," Mason replied coolly. "If you don't want it, I'm sure there's someone else out there hustling who'd put me on their payroll."

Kieran gave Mason a shit-eating grin before turning his attention to Charlie. "Tell me more about what *you* bring to the table, Charlie."

Shit. How would she react to being put on the spot? Mason spoke up before she'd be forced to answer. "Charlie is—"

"The woman's got a mouth, Mason," Kieran interrupted. "And not an unattractive one. So . . . what makes you such a special snowflake?"

Fuck.

Mason fought the urge to rake his fingers through his hair. Any outward show of frustration would be a red flag for Kieran. And messing with his hair was one of Mason's tells. There was no way Charlie could convince Kieran she was a black-market diamond broker. None. They were as good as screwed.

Charlie might as well have been thrown on stage at the San Francisco Opera, bare-assed naked, and asked to sing "The Star-Spangled Banner." Her heart hammered in her rib cage as it inched its way up her throat. Her mind swirled with myriad thoughts that were damned near impossible to organize. *Get it together, Charlie. Don't screw this up . . .*

"I have a very limited number of contacts, but I sell to an elite clientele. Most of the people who buy from me want to remain anonymous for obvious reasons.

They're willing to spend millions—tens of millions—on quality stones." She drew on every bit of knowledge she'd gathered in the course of her research on Eagan's operation, hoping she could impress him enough to pique his interest. "They want the certificates. They prefer to appear to be politically correct, but the fact of the matter is that they don't give a shit. My clientele want statement pieces. Gems that flaunt their wealth. They want the big game of diamonds."

"Tens of millions?" Kieran's eyes grew hungry as did his wide grin. Charlie knew from her research that he generated an estimated ten million in income last year. But if she could promise to double or even triple that number, she doubted he'd be able to turn down the opportunity to work with Mason.

"I brokered thirty million in sales in the second half of last year," Charlie replied.

Kieran smirked. "Can you prove it?"

Charlie cocked a brow. "Can you provide me proof of your income for last year?"

He laughed. "Client list?"

Charlie's lips pursed. "Strictly confidential. No one sees it. Not even the famous Kieran Eagan."

"Infamous is more like it, huh, Mason?"

Charlie chanced a glance at Mason from the corner of her eye. He didn't show a single sign of tension. He was so damned relaxed, you'd never guess he'd been estranged for over a decade from the other two men seated at the table. His haunting eyes fixated on Eagan, and one dark brow arched curiously. His full lips spread into a slow smile and he hiked a casual shoulder.

"You said it, not me."

It was apparent there was a history between the two

men. More even than Carrera had let on. What else
had he failed to fill her in on? Had the chief deputy
known Mason had changed the date of his meeting
with his father and Eagan? Charlie's brain cranked into
high gear and she forced herself to stay in the moment.
She couldn't afford to let her concentration slip for
even a second.

"Charlie's connected," Kieran conceded. "Or so she
claims. Which means she can bring in the whales. What
about you, Mason? What do you have to offer me?"

Charlie's stomach curled into an anxious knot. How
far was Mason willing to go to earn Kieran's trust?

"They're watching you." Mason rested his muscular
forearms on the table and leaned in toward Kieran.
"You know they are."

Kieran's dark eyes crinkled at the corners with
amusement. "Who?"

"FBI, CIA, CBP, the Marshals Service. You name it,
they want you."

Kieran shrugged. "What can I say? I'm a popular
guy, but I'm not worried. Federal law enforcement is
populated with self-important, pretentious assholes
and they've got bigger fish to catch than me."

"And I'm one of them," Mason replied, his expression blank.

"Yeah." Kieran flashed a wide grin. "You are."

"Not anymore."

Charlie's eyes met Jensen's. The elder Decker had
been all but silent for most of the meeting. He watched
with interest as Mason and Kieran squared off, his
expression almost pleased. As though his two fighting
children were finally getting along.

Again Charlie wondered, just how close were the two?

"Because you want what I have?" Sarcasm accented Kieran's words.

Mason's jaw squared. "Exactly."

"Calm down, boys." Finally, Jensen chose to break his silence. "No one wants to get into a pissing contest." His gaze flitted to Charlie. "Especially with our current company. No need to hash out fifteen years of bullshit all at once. You'll have plenty of time to do that later. Kieran, you've got product to move and the feds are up your ass. Charlie could help you with that while Mason"—his gaze met his son's—"can help keep the heat off of you with Customs and directed where you want it to be so you can raise a little capital."

Kieran gave Jensen a look as though the older man had already revealed too much. Charlie didn't want him getting spooked. She wanted Faction Five and they needed Eagan to get it done. Taking them down would make her career.

"You think I can trust him?" Kieran asked.

"What could it hurt?" Jensen shrugged.

Kieran let out an amused snort.

Charlie wondered at Mason's continued silent stoicism. He'd made his case, it seemed, and he wasn't about to beg for any favors from either Kieran or his father. Charlie had reached the end of what she could offer as well. She was afraid to open her mouth. To say or do anything that might hurt rather than help them. The silence that settled over the table became thick with tension. Oppressive. Charlie wished she knew more about the history these three men shared, because she had a feeling she was missing a huge piece of the puzzle.

"Why is the CIA watching me?" Kieran flashed a challenging grin.

"I don't work for the CIA," Mason shot back. "How the fuck should I know?"

The arrogant smile once again made an appearance on Kieran's face. "A little uncertainty makes life more interesting, don't you think, Mason?"

Mason tensed, though his expression remained relaxed. She doubted he subscribed to Kieran's philosophies.

"I want money and a reputation I can be proud of," Mason replied. "And I don't want to wind up here after I get it."

A dark cloud passed over Jensen's features. Regret, perhaps? "Make him prove himself, Kieran."

Kieran's gaze sparked. "A test?"

Well, shit. It was probably foolish to have thought that Kieran would just take them at their word and welcome them with open arms.

Jensen looked at Kieran and his lips thinned. "Yeah."

Kieran laughed. Too bad Charlie didn't find their situation quite as funny. "I haven't had this much goddamned fun since we were kids. A game," he said with excitement. "Whaddya say, Mason? You up for a little challenge?"

Mason let out a grumbling sound that conveyed just how excited he was about Kieran's proposal. "Whatever you want. I don't give a shit. Let's just get on with it and quit hemming and hawing, yeah?"

"Abso-fucking-lutely." Kieran pushed his chair out and stood. "You'll hear from me tomorrow." He chuckled again. "This is going to be a hell of a lot of fun."

Charlie's stomach sank. This couldn't possibly be good. Mason glanced up at Kieran, his jaw squared. He didn't say a single word, just locked gazes with the other man.

"Charlie." Kieran reached out and took her hand. "See you soon, I hope."

"Definitely," Charlie replied with a pleasant smile.

"I'll be back to see you soon, old man," Kieran said to Mason's father. "Take it easy."

Jensen responded with an affectionate smile. "Always."

As he turned to leave, Charlie let out a shaky breath. This little family reunion couldn't be over fast enough for her peace of mind.

Chapter Six

Unspent adrenaline pooled in Mason's limbs. He was twitchy as fuck and nothing short of a five-mile run was going to work the excess energy out of his system. Hell, even that might not be enough. Beside him, the *click clack* of Charlie's heels as she walked drilled into his head with the force of a jackhammer. The urge to snatch them off her feet and chuck the damn things was almost too much to resist. An exasperated sigh escaped from between Charlie's lips. The fact that she even had the nerve to act put-out caused Mason's temper to crest. She'd damned near fucked them both over today. Hell, there wasn't even a guarantee that Kieran had bought any of it.

They exited the prison and the *click clack, click clack* increased in tempo as Charlie tried to keep up with him. Mason strode across the parking lot, his breath heaving in his chest as he swallowed down the anger that threatened to surface. He wasn't as mad at her as he was at his own damned self for letting not only Kieran, but his hurtful past, get under his skin.

"Do you want to tell me exactly what in the hell you thought you were doing today, Mason?"

Mason's hands balled into fists at his sides and he clenched his jaw until his molars ground. He turned to face Charlie and met her wild blue gaze.

"What in the hell was *I* doing?" he asked with incredulity. "What in the hell were *you* doing, Charlie?"

"I came to kick your ass off my task force," she spat. "You were supposed to meet your dad and Eagan the day after tomorrow. I told you I was putting my trust in you and you went behind my back—"

Her angry words barely registered. "Do you realize what you've done by following me here today?" Did she have no clue the danger she'd put herself in? "You're in this now, Charlie. You're not just sitting at your desk, micromanaging everyone. You're on Kieran's radar. He's going to expect to see you. I told you that I would only be a part of this operation if I worked alone. And now, thanks to you, I have a *partner*."

"Wait." Charlie stopped dead in her tracks. "What do you mean a *partner*?"

Mason's rueful laughter echoed around them. She really didn't understand the weight of her actions at all. "Part-ner," Mason stressed. "As in, not one but two. Both Kieran and my father assume that we're working together now. What's going to happen if suddenly you're no longer in the picture?"

Charlie's mouth gathered into the pucker that Mason found so distracting. His gaze wandered to her full lips for the barest moment. The last thing he wanted was for Kieran to find Charlie even marginally interesting, and without even trying she'd piqued his interest. Not good. Mason wanted to work alone because he didn't want the responsibility of someone else's safety thrust on him. He'd had enough of that working with CBP. And now he was going to have to watch Charlie like a goddamned hawk. Kieran had always been a competitive son of a bitch. He'd pursue Charlie just to prove that he could get her.

"I didn't think—"

"No." Mason let out a derisive snort. "You sure as hell didn't."

"Fine. I screwed up." Charlie blew out a gust of breath that stirred the wisps of hair that dangled over her right eye. "But you changed the day! What was I supposed to think, Mason?"

"You were supposed to think that I knew what I was doing and stay the hell out of it!"

Charlie's eyes widened. "This is my task force!"'

Mason raked his fingers through his hair before brushing it all forward with a forceful flick of his wrists. He didn't think it was possible to be any more aggravated than he was right now. He rounded on Charlie, stepped right up to her until his chest nearly brushed hers. "How long does it take Kieran to prepare for a job?" Charlie bucked her chin up a notch but didn't respond. "What's his favorite wine? Bourbon? What city does he want to retire to when he's finally had enough of the game? Do you know how he got started? What his favorite cons are? Which ones he still likes to run?" Mason waited a moment and still Charlie didn't utter a word. "Well? Do you?"

"No." The word slipped tightly from between her pursed lips. "But you do?"

"You're damn right I do."

Charlie scoffed. "How is it that you know more about him than all of the agencies on the task force combined?"

"Kieran and I grew up together." Mason reached up to fiddle with his hair. Charlie agitated the hell out of him. "He lived with us for eight years. He visited my dad every month for years after he went to prison. He's my goddamned brother."

Her jaw went slack. Mason had only known Charlie for a few days, but already he enjoyed stunning her into silence. Every bomb dropped cracked away at the giant chip on her shoulder. If she only knew just how far over her head she'd gotten herself today . . .

"I had no idea that Kieran was so enmeshed with your family. You were the wrong choice for this operation."

It was Mason's turn to scoff. "I was the *only* choice." Charlie drew in a deep breath but Mason didn't give her a chance to speak. "Did you drive here?"

Her brow furrowed as a burst of incredulous laughter escaped her full lips. "Of course I drove. Do you think I jogged from downtown?"

"We'll come back and get your car later." He grabbed her by the elbow and led her along none too gently.

"Excuse me?" Her outrage was a little misplaced considering she'd been the one to throw the monkey wrench into his plans. "I'm not leaving my car here."

"Yeah," Mason replied. "You are. You think Kieran just toddled off without a care in the world after this little reunion?" Charlie's heels clicked triple time to keep up with Mason's wide stride through the parking lot. God, that sound drilled right into his damn cranium. "He's probably watching us. Or has someone watching us. Odds are we'll be followed from here on out. Which means you can't go home, either."

Her indignant tone cranked up by a decibel with every word. "What do you mean, I can't go home?"

Mason had to admit he liked her fire. "Do you want him to find out who you really are, Charlie? Because believe me, it won't be hard."

"Oh my God."

She spoke the words under her breath, but Mason caught them just the same. He wasn't helping the situation with his harsh words, rushing her across the parking lot. If Kieran was watching them—and he'd be a fool not to—their behavior would appear antagonistic at best. They were supposed to be partners. Trusting. Comfortable. Confident.

Mason forced his pace to slow and he relaxed by small degrees. The hand that gripped Charlie's elbow slid down her forearm before he released his hold. Her skin was like satin against his. Warm. Mason pushed the momentary distraction from his mind and continued toward his car. They were supposed to be business partners, nothing more.

"My car's over there."

"I can't leave my car here," Charlie insisted again. Her tone had lost a little of its fire. "How in the hell am I supposed to get back here to pick it up?"

"We'll figure that out later." Mason pulled his keys out of his pocket and hit the fob to unlock the shiny yellow Camaro.

Charlie's mouth puckered into an amused half smile and she said, "Well, you've got the right car for the part you're playing."

Fast and sexy, maybe. But hardly up to par for the world he was about to be immersed in. His Camaro was a dilapidated POS compared to the luxury vehicles Kieran and his crew rolled in.

Mason pulled open the door at the same time Charlie opened hers and they climbed into their seats. He couldn't even take the time for a few calming breaths inside the privacy of his own damn car. Kieran had eyes everywhere. He wouldn't be able to truly relax until he was back at his place. Hell, maybe not even then.

"Where are we going?"

Back in time, he wished. To before he agreed to work for Carrera. Mason turned the key in the ignition and pulled out of the parking lot. "My place. I need to decompress and figure out what my next move is going to be."

Charlie glanced his way. "Don't you mean *our* next move?"

"Is there any situation where you don't find yourself compelled to be a total control freak? Like I said, you don't know anything about Kieran. I do. And now I have to figure you into the equation in a way that won't end up getting us both killed."

"I'm not an idiot, Mason." Charlie's melodramatic—not to mention offended—tone should have been annoying, but it was starting to grow on Mason. He'd never met a feistier woman.

"No, but you're not a criminal, either."

She cocked a challenging brow. "And you are?"

He pinned her with his gaze. "Close enough."

Charlie wondered at the sudden sadness in Mason's tone. She'd researched his history with CBP and found Mason to be a stellar Customs agent. One of their best, in fact. She also knew that he'd applied to the U.S. Marshals Service twice in the past two years, and though all of his applications had been rejected, it wasn't because he wasn't cut out for the job. Unfortunately, his apparent attitude toward authority had stood in the way. Charlie had gotten a dose of that attitude today. But whereas Charlie had thought his insubordination was nothing more than arrogance, she realized that Mason simply didn't trust anyone. And given his upbringing, she could hardly fault him for it. Still, she couldn't let that excuse what had happened today.

They drove in silence for twenty minutes or so. Charlie tried to compartmentalize everything that had happened since showing up at the prison and the realization that her entire operation was about to blow up in her face. She had to hope that it could somehow be salvaged. That by some miracle, Eagan bought everything they'd told him and he wouldn't take off yet again. Carrera indicated that he was itching to arrest Eagan, but the rest of the task force knew that Faction Five was the real prize. And it rankled that they needed Eagan to get to the esoteric crime syndicate.

"Why do you think Eagan wants to join them?" she asked. Mason quirked a brow. She'd been more or less thinking out loud, but maybe without the scrutinizing eyes of several heads of agencies on him, Mason would be more forthcoming with information. "Faction Five," she added.

"Honestly," he said, "I'm not entirely sure. It's not like him to get involved in something like this. Kieran prefers to work alone. There's no accountability and no one to screw him over or trip him up. And the political aspect of smuggling never appealed to him. The warlords in the Congo are volatile, and Kieran always hated playing to their egos. I can't imagine being under the thumb of some crazy-ass crime syndicate is going to appeal to him. Kieran is in this business for two reasons: the money and the excitement. The only thing I can figure is that smuggling has lost some of its luster for him and he's looking for a different adrenaline rush."

"Is that why your dad did it?" Charlie asked. "For the rush?"

Mason kept his gaze straight ahead as he negotiated the freeway traffic. "No. For him it was all about easy money."

"Easy?" Charlie laughed. She could never figure out why criminals thought the money they made was *easy*. From her perspective, circumventing the law to make a buck took a hell of a lot more elbow grease than a regular nine-to-five job. "I don't think anything about what your dad did was easy."

"You're probably right," Mason said. "Maybe he just didn't want to have to answer to anyone. Hell, maybe he liked the thrill like Kieran does. I really don't know. He didn't confide in me much. He knew I wasn't going to follow in his footsteps and I guess he didn't see the need to share any deep secrets with me."

The disappointment in his tone sliced through Charlie. Mason wanted his dad to be proud of him, and instead, he found him lacking. Charlie knew first-hand what that felt like. Oh, her dad played nice, but there was something hiding beneath the surface of the constant ribbing for taking a job as a federal prosecutor. He'd wanted more for her. He'd wanted her to join his practice, and her choice to go her own way had let him down.

"What sort of test do you think Kieran is going to lay down for you?" It bothered Charlie, especially since they'd have to pull something together at a moment's notice to make sure that Mason could perform whatever task Kieran set out for him without a single wrinkle.

"*Us,*" Mason corrected. "I told you, you're in this now. We'll be working as a team from here on out."

Anxiety stabbed at Charlie's chest, sending a rush of nervous energy through her bloodstream. If she was busy playing a part, who would run the task force? Carrera was the logical choice. He was already her go-to when she needed something. She had no idea how to play the game she'd thrown herself into. Her presence was bound to only make matters worse. "What will he have us do?"

"Steal something," Mason replied matter-of-factly. "Or fence something. Run a con on someone that will inevitably require me to forge something. And he'll more than likely pay off a cop to catch us in the act and then let us go. So he'll have something to lord over us if we try to fuck him over."

"Eagan has cops on his payroll?"

He gave Charlie a look as though she were painfully naïve. She couldn't even be bothered to care as she took in the beauty of his light eyes. The color really was like seafoam. Unusual. But breathtakingly beautiful.

"Kieran's well connected," he said. "He's got enough money to protect himself."

"Yeah, well, not for long." Charlie settled back into her seat and folded her arms across her chest. She was going to bring that cocky bastard down if it killed her. "When we're through with him, he's going to wish you'd never walked back into his life."

Mason's jaw squared. "Probably."

Another space of silence followed. Mason had seemed unaffected by the role he was playing in all of this, but after gaining more insight into his history with Eagan, she couldn't imagine that he'd be able to remain completely detached. The two had been as close as brothers at one point. Could Mason follow through and use Eagan to bring the members of Faction Five to justice? The possibility for failure seemed so much greater now. But Charlie refused to lose.

Mason glanced at her from the corner of his eye. "Tell me more about Faction Five."

The silence had begun to weigh her down, so Charlie was more than thankful to have something to talk about. "Like I said at the briefing, we don't know very much about them aside from the fact that there are five managing members and they're all well connected."

"Who's in charge?" Mason asked.

"We don't know." And man, did that get under Charlie's skin. "They could teach the CIA a thing or two about being secretive. Hell, for all we know, someone from the CIA is running their entire operation. They're sending messages and recruiting members through social media. This isn't anything new, criminals use coded messages sent through social media all the time. But even the U.S. Marshals' best tech guys can't track the origin or IP addresses to a specific location. And the marshals have the best tech guys in the country working for them. We're assuming there's big money behind them, but we can't find any paper trail to track. Eagan was the only connection we could make to Faction Five. It was almost like he was leading us straight to them . . ." Charlie trailed off. "Wait. Do you think that's what he's doing?"

"It's hard to say." Mason checked his rearview mirror and switched lanes. "Kieran isn't just street smart. He's got a damned near genius IQ. He gets bored easily and he lives to push the boundaries. I can't see him supporting any sort of crime syndicate unless he was directly benefiting. Or running the entire show."

"Do you think . . . ?"

"No." Mason squashed her question before she even got the chance to ask it. "He's not like that. He smuggles diamonds out of the DRC because that's what he's good at. He's not interested in conquering the world. Just fleecing it."

"He does realize that he's supporting terrorists by dealing blood diamonds, right?" Not that she expected him to have a conscience about what he did for a living, but Charlie always wondered how anyone could turn a blind eye to the atrocities associated with the black-market diamond trade.

"That's not how Kieran sees it." Mason gave a sad shake of his head. "Or at least, it's what he tells himself to justify what he does. It's a different game from when my dad started thirty years ago. But Kieran tried to ignore the antihumanitarian aspect of what he does. He's out to prove a point: that despite the increased rules and regulations, he can still game the system. He can still put one over on the people who want to shut him down."

Whether Eagan wanted to ignore the harm diamond smuggling did or not, what mattered was that he was currently involved with an up-and-coming syndicate that could cause some real and serious problems. Unchecked criminal activity and corruption needed to be stopped before it ran rampant. The task force's job was to shut Faction Five down before that—or anything worse—happened.

Charlie let out a slow breath. "Well, hopefully we get the chance to see what he's up to."

The drive passed quickly once they'd started to talk. Charlie was so wrapped up in her thoughts she hadn't paid much attention to where they were headed. Mason pulled up to an older but tasteful town house on the outskirts of the city and cut the engine.

"Let's get inside," Mason said. "I'll text Carrera and

have him meet us somewhere safe. We've got to figure out our next move, and fast. Kieran could call immediately, like he said, or leave us dangling for weeks."

Charlie hoped it wasn't immediately. She'd gotten in way over her head thanks to her hot temper and reluctance to give Mason any control. It was a mistake she wasn't going to make again.

"Can we get some dinner?" she asked. "I haven't eaten today."

"Me either."

Charlie rounded the car and she felt the weight of Mason's stare on her. Not entirely unpleasant, it suffused her with a delicious warmth and caused a riot of butterflies to take flight in her stomach. This morning, she'd been prepared to kick Mason Decker off her task force. Now, she'd be working much closer with him than she'd ever planned. Maybe that wasn't necessarily a bad thing.

Chapter Seven

"How about this one?"

Mason slid the diamond across the table to Charlie. She picked it up and examined it under the jeweler's loupe, pulling her bottom lip between her teeth as her brow puckered. Over the course of the past few days, Mason had learned that when Charlie Cahill threw herself into something, she did it 100 percent. Perfectionism at its best.

"The cut is okay . . ." she began. "Not very good, though. I'd give it a three on the AGS scale. Color's light. Not great. And the clarity is . . ." She pulled her lip between her teeth again. She looked up at him. "Included?"

Mason smiled and nodded. "That's right."

"The clarity's included," she said with more confidence this time. "I'd score it an eight. All in all, this isn't a very valuable stone. It's maybe worth five or six hundred dollars, tops."

Mason beamed. "I agree. It's not worth much." He'd been drilling the American Gem Society's diamond grading standards into her brain for the past couple of days. His dad had taught him everything there was to know about scoring gems when he was just a kid. Now, he got to impart that knowledge to Charlie. If she was going to convince Kieran—and anyone he sold to—that she was a professional, her con game was going to have to be tight. She'd have to know at least as much as Mason did about scoring gems.

"Okay, how about his one?" He slid another diamond over to Charlie.

She gave this diamond the same close, quiet consideration as she did the last. Mason examined Charlie with the same intensity. She fascinated him.

True, after the debacle at the prison, he'd been ready to throttle her. The last thing he'd wanted was to be saddled with someone so green. But over the course of a few short days, Mason realized something about Charlie. She took what she did very seriously. Dedication didn't even begin to describe her work ethic.

"Oooh, this is a *good* one." He smiled at her excited tone. "Excellent cut. At least a one. No color. Probably a . . ." Her mouth drew into a pucker and Mason's gut clenched. That expression was distracting as hell. "Hmm. Probably a one."

"I'd give it a point five, actually."

She looked up from the loupe and her full lips quirked in a half smile. "I didn't want to be too generous."

Mason chuckled. "What about the clarity?"

She brought the magnifying glass back up to her eye. "I'd say very slightly included. Almost flawless. VS-one?" Her tone was unsure.

"Don't ask me." Mason's gaze met hers. "You're the expert, remember?"

Her chin bucked up a notch. Mason had never realized how attractive assertiveness could be. "It's a one."

She waited for confirmation, but her confident expression didn't falter. Mason doubted anyone face-to-face with her in a trial could stand strong under that unwavering gaze. She didn't give anything away. It made Mason want to crawl inside her head and hear every single one of her thoughts. "It's a one." She was spot-on with this stone. "What's it worth?"

Charlie examined the diamond one more time. "Between fifteen and twenty thousand. I probably wouldn't pay more than eighteen."

Her intelligence and confidence might be the most attractive things about her. And that was saying a lot considering her luscious curves, full mouth, and thick, lustrous hair. *Whoa.* Mason gave himself a mental shake. This was work. He shouldn't be thinking of Charlie in any way other than two professionals collaborating. She looked at him expectantly. Damn. It was tough to think of anything when she focused her undivided attention on him like that. Remembering to take a breath was a feat.

"Eighteen and a half," he said. "No more than that, though."

Charlie smiled. "Highballing?"

"A little." Charlie passed the diamond back to Mason and he put it in the case along with the others that were on loan from a local jeweler. "Here's the thing," he said. "Buyers—no matter if they're on the right or wrong side of the law—are going to lowball you. The legitimate jewelers are actually worse."

Charlie leaned across the table toward him, her arms folded on the surface. Her undivided attention quickened his blood. A rush of exhilaration he usually only felt when he took down the bad guys. Dangerous. Unsettling. Exciting.

Goddamn.

"That doesn't surprise me. They want to make a good profit. But you can't lowball an expert."

Mason's smile faded. "Or bullshit a bullshitter."

Charlie's head tilted as she studied him. "Kieran."

The past few days had been dedicated to educating Charlie on how to properly grade and scale a diamond. They hadn't talked about the black-market diamond trade. Mason had been avoiding the subject. Anything to separate his life now from the one he'd been brought up in. He couldn't put it off forever, though. "Exactly."

"How do you suggest I deal with him?"

From the way he'd behaved at the prison a few days ago, Mason figured it wouldn't take more than a few flirty smiles from Charlie to distract Kieran. His jaw clenched and he forced it to unhinge. Kieran's professional interest in Charlie was bad enough. His personal interest in her had set Mason on edge. "He'll expect you to be confident. A little cocky, even. You act for even a second like you're unsure and he'll know something's up."

"Fair enough."

Charlie's expression became more contemplative. Mason found himself wishing she'd pull her bottom lip between her teeth again. His own hands, splayed out on his dining room table, twitched with the urge to reach out and touch her. Mason shot up out of his chair and the legs scraped against the tile as it pushed out behind him. He raked his fingers through his hair and flicked the strands forward.

"Hey." Charlie's inscrutable stare burned through him. "Are you okay?"

No. Not even close. "Yeah. I'm fine. Just need to stretch my legs." Every hour spent with Charlie, every conversation they had, only managed to intrigue him more. It could be months—hell, a year—before they got anything out of Kieran. How could he possibly spend every day with Charlie and keep her at arm's length? He'd barely known her a week and already he found her damned near irresistible.

"Look. Kieran is . . ." *Charismatic, confident, good-looking, dangerous to the wrong people and a godsend to the right ones, funny, charming . . .* Hell, did he want to warn Charlie off or was he trying to set the two of them up? Mason blew out a breath. "Not what anyone ever expects. You're going to like him, Charlie. Everyone likes him. I just want you to be aware of it so it doesn't surprise you when it happens."

Charlie watched him for a quiet moment. The attention sent a lick of heat up Mason's spine and he took a few steps deeper into the kitchen to put a little distance between them. Silence stretched between them before she let out a soft snort. "Everyone might like him, but I'm not like *everyone.*"

Wasn't that the truth? Charlie was one of a kind.

"You'll like him." Mason forced his expression to remain passive, but what he really felt was grim as fuck. She'd like Kieran, and Mason knew it would be hard *not* to let it get under his skin. "And it's okay." It would get to Charlie too. It would pluck at her conscience and sense of justice. He didn't want that to get under *her* skin.

Charlie's lips pursed and her voice went low. "You think I'm going to blur the lines? You don't think I can do my job?" With every sentence her tone escalated. "You think I'm going to forget who he is and how he makes his money?"

"That's not it, Charlie." Mason needed to backpedal before they got into a fight. "This isn't about your integrity. I'm just trying to prepare you. Knowing your shit is only going to be half of it."

Charlie pushed her chair out and stood. Mason's gut tightened. He stayed in the kitchen, rooted to the

tile as she walked toward him. Closer. Closer. Too
damned close. Her floral honeysuckle scent wafted
over him and Mason felt the need to swallow more
than usual. He kept his hands at his sides, balled into
fists. His gaze met hers and he stilled.

"I can hold my own, Mason." Her husky voice was
like a caress and it brought chills to the surface of
Mason's skin. "Kieran isn't going to dazzle me."

Her confidence couldn't be denied, but Mason
knew better. "You can totally hold your own. I'm not
worried."

"Okay, good."

Her self-assured smile damned near blinded him.
With every passing day spent with her, he found himself
more dazzled. Maybe it wasn't Charlie that Mason
needed to worry about.

Charlie's stomach churned with nervous anticipation. She'd spent the past several days with Mason and
she looked forward to each new one more than the
last. Her first impression of him couldn't have been
more wrong. In fact, no matter what CBP and the
USMS had said about his problem with authority, she
found him to be intelligent, professional, well-versed,
and cultured. He knew more about the black-market
diamond trade than anyone Charlie had consulted
with when the task force initially formed.

Hell, he was a one-man task force himself.

For the past two days she'd done nothing but think
about the day they had stood toe to toe in his kitchen.
More like obsessed over it. He'd warned her she'd
grow to like Kieran. But instead of worrying over
Mason's admonition, all she thought about was him.
His tall, muscular frame. Hard expression. Entrancing

light green eyes, fringed by dark lashes. The line of his mouth, grim and yet so kissable that Charlie'd had to force herself not to lean in any closer to him than they'd already been. Close enough to touch.

And oh, man, how she'd wanted to touch . . .

Jeez, Charlie. Snap out of it!

A knock came at her hotel room door and she started. A riot of butterflies took flight in her stomach and lodged in her chest on their ascent. This was *work*, and her body had turned traitor, hormones raging out of control like she was a teenage girl about to go on a hot date. Electricity sparked between them whenever Mason was near. It was the sort of chemistry that went way beyond professional camaraderie. The sudden rush of adrenaline through her bloodstream sent Charlie's heart to racing. Her limbs trembled as she hustled to the door of her suite to let him in. A few deep breaths did little to calm her. *Great.* All she needed was for him to see her nervous and unraveled.

The Marshals Service had agreed it would be best to put Charlie up in a hotel rather than have her stay at her own place. Mason said he didn't mind Kieran snooping around where he lived—he was playing the double agent after all—but there was no way Kieran would believe that Charlie had decided to play both sides against the middle as well. She'd been set up with a suite at the Fairmont, along with a fake ID to match the name Mason had given her, and a fake credit report that listed her previous employer as Tiffany's as she'd claimed. So far, so good. Of course, they'd yet to pass Kieran's little test for them.

Don't stare at him. Don't stare at him. Don't *stare at him!*

"Hi!" Charlie greeted a little too cheerfully as she swung the door wide.

"Hey." Mason gave her a look as he strode into the room.

Charlie swallowed down a groan and closed the door behind him. "So, what's on the agenda for today?"

Mason's lips hinted at a smile and that sheepish expression nearly buckled Charlie's knees. "I thought we'd grab some lunch. Have you eaten?"

"Lunch?" For days Mason had been drilling information into Charlie's head. Lunch, dinner, not even a snack had worked into the equation until today.

Mason chuckled. "Yeah, you know, food. I'm hungry and I'm sure you're tired of being cooped up."

That was the truth. Since the day they'd left the prison Charlie had been two places: her suite at the Fairmont, and Mason's place. She was practically climbing the walls. "Lunch sounds great."

"Good." His eyes sparkled in the midday light and Charlie stood, transfixed. Mason turned and headed for the door and she barely noticed until he cleared his throat. "Ready?"

Charlie snapped herself out of her stupor and grabbed her purse from the desk. "Yep. Let's go."

"In and Out Burger, huh?" Charlie took a long sip from her straw. They sat in the parking lot and ate in Mason's car. She put her cup in the holder near the gear shifter and reached for her fries on the dash.

"You're probably used to fancy corporate lunches, right?"

Charlie laughed. "Hardly. I live on takeout. Working as a public servant doesn't exactly net me a lot of five-star cuisine."

"I grew up on five-star cuisine," Mason remarked.

Charlie turned to look at him. "Really?"

Mason's lips pursed. He took a monster bite of his burger and chewed in silence before washing it down with some Coke. "Jensen had champagne tastes."

It was true that Jensen Decker fit the gentleman-thief persona to a tee. Mason came across as such an everyman. Working class. Unpretentious. Not a frivolous bone in his body. "So not a lot of Happy Meals when you were a kid?"

Mason snorted. "No."

"Do you think Kieran will let us in?" Charlie knew that getting too personal with Mason was dangerous ground to tread. The more she learned about him, the more she grew to like him on more than a professional level. She needed to keep the conversation steered toward work. Work, work, work. *Holy crap.* Even sitting in his car, wolfing down a burger, the man exuded sex. She needed to keep it together before she started to drool.

"You mean, do I think Kieran will trust us enough to give us intel on Faction Five?"

"Yeah."

Mason set his cup back in the holder as though trying to buy a little time before he had to respond. "I think he wants to trust me." Charlie wondered at his tentative tone. "But we've always stood on opposite sides of the road. Trust isn't something easily given in our—*his*—world. But I'll get it."

Our. Charlie hadn't missed the correction. Her own doubt that Mason was too close to Kieran to successfully do the job crept up on her and she forced the worry away. If she could handle this, so could he. She needed him to get close to Kieran Eagan. He was the only connection she had to Faction Five.

"*We'll* get it." They were a team after all. Mason needed to acknowledge that.

His eyes met hers. "We'll get it."

"Teamwork."

Mason gave her a wan smile and shifted in his seat. She knew that he preferred to work alone, but they were in this together now. He took another bite of his burger and Charlie did the same, letting lunch take precedence over conversation. She didn't mind the silence. It wasn't uncomfortable or awkward.

"You're doing really well, you know." Mason's deep voice coaxed a bloom of warmth in the pit of Charlie's stomach. "With the diamonds."

Charlie's competitiveness bordered on obsessive sometimes. Probably what made her such a good trial lawyer. Her need to win—to impress—drove her ambition. And lately, she'd found herself wanting to impress Mason. For some reason, his approval and his admiration mattered.

Charlie reached for her cup at the exact moment Mason reached for his. Their hands touched, fingers gliding against each other. The heat from his skin was like a brand. Charlie's breath caught in her chest and she froze. His touch lingered for a beat too long, the pads of his fingers sliding against the tops of hers as he pulled away. An exhilarating rush started low in Charlie's stomach and traveled outward through her limbs. Every inch of her tingled. Mason pulled away and still Charlie didn't move. Her lids drooped. God, she wanted him to touch her again. Craved the contact.

Mason cleared his throat. "Close quarters." His tone grated. Gruff. "Sorry."

Charlie's chest hollowed out. She didn't want his apology. Their fingers touched. It wasn't like he'd rubbed his bare ass against hers. Still . . . there had been something decidedly illicit about that contact.

Taboo and exciting. And at the same time, intimate. She sucked in a breath and held it for a moment before letting it out.

"It's okay." Her own voice sounded hollow. Small. Annoyance replaced the electric energy that coursed through her. Annoyance at her own reaction, that something so innocent could affect her so intensely. The fact that she wanted to touch him again. Silence stretched between them once again but it no longer comforted Charlie. Damn it. "So. . . . What's on the schedule for after lunch?" The moment was ruined. They might as well get back to business.

"More diamond grading."

Mason kept his gaze straight ahead. Tension tightened the definition of his muscles. Charlie wondered at the sudden change. Had it really been so awkward—so awful—to touch her? *Awesome.*

"Sounds good. I mean, we need to be prepared. Kieran could get in touch with you at any time and I want to be ready."

"Me too." Mason stuffed the wrapper from his burger and the empty fry container into the paper bag. He turned the key in the ignition and the engine roared to life. "Ready?"

Charlie stuffed the rest of her burger and fries into the bag as well. Her appetite was officially gone. "Sure. Back to work."

Work. This was a job and *nothing more.* The more she reminded herself of that, the better.

Chapter Eight

Ever since their awkward moment in the car a few days ago, Mason had tried to keep his interactions with Charlie as professional as possible. Mostly because since that day, she'd treated him with nothing more than polite professionalism. Total boost to the old ego. But with each passing day—hell, each passing minute—Mason found himself thinking of Charlie more and more. And wishing things had gone differently the other day during lunch. How had he wanted it to play out, though? When his fingers had brushed hers, it was all he could do to keep from taking her hand in his. That would have been stupid, though. They had a work relationship. Period. It could never be anything more than that.

He couldn't help but wonder what it would be like to have something real with Charlie though.

He put his fist to Charlie's hotel room door and called through the door, "Kieran called. We're on." The door opened a crack. Mason stood out in the hallway waiting for Charlie to open the door the rest of the way. "Are you going to let me in or are you going to make me stand out in the hallway and talk to you through the little crack in the door?"

Charlie's full lips gathered into a pucker and Mason suppressed a groan. For a solid week he'd had to endure that adorable—and sexy—expression as he gave Charlie a crash course on how to be a proper black-market diamond broker. Most of the time he couldn't decide if he was turned on or exasperated by her feisty attitude. Probably a little bit of both.

Sick.

And not exactly behavior befitting a professional. Then again, Mason was technically only temporarily employed by the USMS for this operation. Maybe his professionalism didn't matter a whole hell of a lot.

"Sorry," Charlie said after a moment. She opened the door wider, though still barely wide enough for Mason to fit through. "Come in."

Aside from being bossy and opinionated, Charlie Cahill was a freaking *slob*. The hotel room looked as though someone had partied pretty damn hard over the past week. Clothes strewn everywhere, room service trays on the bed and table, decorative pillows littering the floor of the tiny living room area of the suite . . . It entertained the shit out of him to see someone who was so obsessively organized in her professional life, living so disorganized in her personal one.

The door closed behind him and Mason took a seat on the small couch. Charlie looked as though she were about to crawl out of her skin. Her hair was pulled back into a messy ponytail that didn't quite hold all of the strands of her wavy strawberry-blond hair and she was dressed in workout pants and a loose tee that showcased the luscious round curves of her body. Mason forced his gaze from the ample swell of her breasts and cleared his throat. This was business, not pleasure.

He just hoped Kieran would go into this with a similar attitude, or Charlie would prove to be more of a distraction than he'd first thought she would be.

Damn.

She paced from one end of the room to the other. Back and forth, back and forth. She let out an exasperated gust of breath and Mason smiled. He sort of loved to push her buttons. It was so damned easy to do.

"Well?" Her eyes grew wide. "Are you going to tell me what's going on or what?"

"He wants us to fence something," Mason said with a sigh. "Thirty carats of cut and polished stones."

"That's easy enough." Charlie's tone lacked confidence. "Right? I mean, we can pretend to fence the stones to an undercover agent. We'll use our own money and people, and as far as Kieran knows, we conducted a successful business transaction."

In a perfect world, that's exactly how it would go down. Mason knew that Kieran would make sure it wasn't so easy. "Not quite. Kieran is choosing the fence. I'm assuming it'll be someone who's a tough sell. And he's not providing us with any authenticating certificates, which means he either wants us to forge them ourselves, or try to sell the diamonds without them."

Charlie blew out a frustrated breath. "We can get certificates," she said. "But if he wants to make it a challenge, I'm betting he's going to want us to unload the diamonds as-is."

"That's my guess," Mason said. "I'm sure we'll find out more when we meet him this afternoon."

"This afternoon?" The barest hint of panic infused Charlie's tone. Mason needed her calm and focused if they were going to pull this off. "So soon?"

"It's not like he's going to give us time to prepare," Mason said. "This is a test, Charlie."

"I know that. It's just . . . shit." She resumed her anxious pacing. "I don't know if I'm ready for this."

"It doesn't matter if you are or aren't," Mason replied. "You don't have a choice."

"I don't want to do this." Charlie's continued pacing was beginning to make Mason dizzy. "I want out. Tell him I changed my mind. That I'm worried about getting arrested. That I decided to take a job at a grocery store or something. I don't care. Just get me out of this."

Apparently, Charlotte Cahill didn't respond well to living in captivity. What happened to the cool and collected woman he'd squared off against in the conference room a few weeks ago? "You should have thought about what might happen before you walked into that visitors' room like you were untouchable."

"Me?" Charlie stopped midstep and rounded on Mason. "You were the one who changed plans without telling a single goddamned soul. If anyone acts like they're untouchable, it's you. I wouldn't have been there at all if I hadn't had to march down there to fire you."

Their entire week had been spent cramming. Tension had vibrated between them the entire seven days, and not the unpleasant kind. Mason was attracted to Charlie. To her mind, her wit. And her body, which made him want to drop to his knees and say a prayer of gratitude. But apparently that heated attraction cooled with the realization that shit was about to get real. And the stress wasn't going to let up anytime soon. In fact, it was only bound to get worse. Charlie had swung back to full antagonist mode. Maybe arguing was an attorney's wheelhouse?

"I'm not going over this with you again." Mason had more important things to worry about than winning a fight with Charlie. "What's done is done and there isn't a damn thing that's going to change it. You're *in this*, Charlie. Period. There's no backing out. No quitting. Unless you want to kiss your precious little task force and Faction Five good-bye, you've got to do this whether you want to or not."

Charlie turned away. She took a deep breath and exhaled. The second breath came smoother and by the third, she'd calmed. Mason waited until she turned to face him once again. Her expression was easy, the crease gone from her brow. Her blue eyes locked with his, as cold as a winter stream.

"I'm not quitting." Her tone rang with conviction. "I'm ready. What do I need to do?"

"First of all, you're not doing this alone. *We're* doing this. We're meeting Kieran at Quince in two hours. Let's get through that first. One obstacle at a time. You can't overthink any of this. It's just another day at the office, okay? Pretend like you're going to any other meeting and you're the badass bitch in charge."

Charlie's full mouth quirked in a grin. Heat pooled low in Mason's gut as he took in the sight of her—disheveled, determined, fierce, and goddamned beautiful. She didn't even know it. Had no idea the effect she had on him—on anyone. He'd seen Kieran's gaze spark with interest at the prison. And why wouldn't he be interested? Especially if he thought there was any sort of relationship between Mason and Charlie. Kieran always had to win. Damn it. Mason was going to have his hands full with Charlie at his side.

"You think I'm a badass bitch?" Charlie's grin widened. Her sultry tone reached out to stroke down Mason's spine in a pleasant shiver.

Charlie's joy was contagious. His own smile threatened. "I think you can hold your own."

Doubt crept into her gaze. "What if I can't?"

"Remember rule number one of the con game: Fake it till you make it. There's no room for doubt, Charlie. You've got to own everything you say. Everything you do."

She nodded. "Got it."

Mason settled back on the couch. "Good. Now, go get ready. We're wasting time."

Charlie started out the week berating herself for getting into this mess. Wishing she'd kept her cool and hadn't let Mason's inability to follow the rules get under her skin. Regretting that she hadn't gone to Carrera, to anyone else on the task force, to let them know that Mason had headed to the prison. Anything that would have kept her out of the situation she currently found herself in. But each day spent with Mason, she'd begun to forget about her monumental mistake. Instead, she'd fixated on his gorgeous eyes, the deep timbre of his voice, the ripple of pleasure she felt every time he smiled at her. She found herself wanting to impress him. To show him she was a woman who didn't back down from a challenge. By the end of the week she'd felt more than prepared for anything Kieran Eagan threw her way. But Mason's announcement that they were finally moving forward knocked the air from her lungs. Time to sink or swim. There was no going back. All she could do now was focus and try not to let Mason and the rest of the task force down.

She took one last appraising look in the mirror. Mason had said that people in the diamond smuggling business lived for the thrill and easy money. Charlie didn't exactly live on a champagne budget, but she'd hung out with enough of her parents' wealthy friends to know how to fake it. Luckily, she didn't skimp when it came to her clothes and makeup budget. She might not be living in the lap of luxury, but she could sure as hell make herself look like she did.

Charlie drew a deep, cleansing breath. The past week had put her through the wringer and not only because of the very precarious position she'd put herself in. With every day that passed, Mason became more of a distraction. He infuriated her more than any man—any person—she'd ever met, and even so, she found herself wondering what it would feel like to kiss him, every time her gaze wandered to his full, delicious mouth.

Whoa, girl. Dial it down a notch.

Even now, with her nerves raw and her stomach nothing more than an ocean of churning acid, she couldn't quit thinking about how amazing he looked in his crisp slacks and dress shirt that hugged every tight bulge of his body. The combination of his rough exterior and the elegant clothes was almost too much to handle. Did he even realize how freaking hot he was? Seriously, Charlie had to work not to pant every time he walked through the door.

And now she was stuck with him for God only knew how long. Partners. She was pretty sure she'd spontaneously combust long before they were able to identify any of the members of Faction Five.

At least she'd die with a smile on her face . . .

Charlie emerged from the bathroom ready to roll. Well, as ready as anyone could be in her situation. Walking the walk was one thing. Talking the talk . . . ? With her nerves as raw as they were, she'd be lucky not to sound like a blabbering idiot the second she opened her mouth. She didn't think she'd been this nervous when she'd tried her first case.

"Do I look like a badass bitch black-market diamond broker?"

Mason looked up and his jaw hung slack for the barest moment before he snapped it shut. A rush of warmth raced through Charlie's veins and pooled in her muscles. His eyes were hypnotic, so beautiful that they took her breath away. And when his gaze focused on her, it was all Charlie could do not to tackle him right in the middle of her hotel room.

Focus, Charlie. There was no room for misplaced lust when trying to convince a wily diamond smuggler you were on his side. Besides, she couldn't imagine a scenario in this universe or any other where a man like Mason Decker would actually want her. Their relationship was antagonistic at best, and she didn't see it getting any smoother.

"You look like you mean business."

Charlie wondered at Mason's tight tone. "But not like a lawyer, right?"

He snorted. "Not like any I've ever seen in court."

Was that a compliment? Mason was too tough to read. Charlie smoothed a hand over the precise finger waves she'd made in her hair. Her gaze wandered from the deep plunge of her crisp lavender dress shirt that showed more than enough cleavage, to the short black pencil skirt and black stilettos. "I didn't think I should wear a suit, but I figured Eagan would expect me to look like someone who brokered multimillion-dollar sales."

Mason's gaze further darkened. What in the hell had she done to upset him now? At times Charlie felt as though nothing she did would make him happy. How were they supposed to work together if all he felt for her was disdain?

"You look perfect." With his grumbled response, he

pushed himself from the couch and headed for the door. "Kieran isn't going to know what hit him. Let's go."

Again, Charlie wasn't sure if Mason was giving her a compliment or taking a shot at her. The warmth that had settled in her belly flared into an indignant fire. She'd show Mason that she could totally hack the con game. She'd play the part so goddamned well it would make Kieran Eagan's head spin!

She was going to salvage what she'd almost ruined. Charlie refused to lose.

Seeing Eagan so blatantly confident only made Charlie more determined to play her part and use him to bring Faction Five down. He waited for them at Quince, already seated at the posh table with a glass of red wine in hand. Charlie forced her gritted teeth into a pleasant smile as they approached. Beside her, Mason let out a slow, measured breath.

"I hope you don't mind." Kieran stood to pull out Charlie's seat. "But I've already ordered appetizers."

The man was selling blood diamonds and his biggest concern was whether or not they'd be put out by his choice in appetizers? Charlie wanted to throw up all over the fancy tablecloth. Or better yet, right in Kieran's lap.

"I'm sure whatever you ordered is fine." Charlie kept her tone pleasant. She wanted to give herself a pat on the back. She didn't sound even a little disgusted with him.

"I had the sommelier recommend a bottle of cabernet as well."

Mason snorted. Apparently he wasn't impressed. "You know you're not working an angle, right? There's no one here to impress."

"Speak for yourself." Kieran flashed a rakish grin. "Besides, it's not you I'm trying to impress, Mason."

Charlie caught Mason's scowl from the corner of her eye. Kieran, on the other hand, seemed pretty damned pleased with himself. His flirtatious banter didn't mean a goddamn thing to Charlie though. He could flirt himself to death for all she cared.

"We didn't come to eat." Mason settled in the seat directly across from Kieran. "We came to do business."

"This is part of business," Kieran said. Charlie had to give it to him. Kieran was smooth. "You know better than anyone that no one meets in shady back alleys anymore." He winked at Charlie. "But if you want, I'm sure we could find some real shitholes to hang out in."

Mason signaled for a waiter and ordered a whiskey straight up. The tension practically vibrated off of him. Charlie was starting to think that it wasn't her inexperience that was going to screw this operation up. Mason's history with Eagan—and his inability to play nice—would probably get the job done long before she had a chance to tank anything.

"Speaking for myself, I prefer a civilized lunch to a back alley any day. Thank you for the invite, Kieran." The pleasantries left a bitter tang on Charlie's tongue, but she swallowed it down. Pretending to enjoy Eagan's company was a fair trade for taking down Faction Five. "I understand where Mason is coming from, though. It's been a long week."

"Where are you from, Charlie?" Kieran asked. "Not from around here since you're staying at the Fairmont."

Well, Mason had been right about one thing: He'd been checking up on them. Her cover was tight, though. Carrera and the FBI had done a good job of fabricating all of the documentation to back up her fake persona. It was up to Charlie to sell it, however.

"New York, originally. I worked in Miami for a few months after that and then headed to the West Coast three years ago. I've got a place in Seattle, but I do a lot of business in California. I'm thinking of renting something either here or in L.A. Depends on how lucrative our relationship turns out to be."

Kieran graced her with a seductive grin. "I'm hoping our relationship turns out to be fruitful in more ways than one, Charlie."

He really was the total package. Charming, handsome, witty. It was no wonder Jensen Decker thought of Kieran as a son. The two were carbon copies of each other. Her gaze slid to Mason, who continued to brood beside her. It was hard to believe he'd been cut from the same cloth as his father. The two couldn't be any more different. And despite Mason's vow to uphold the law, there was a rivalry between him and Kieran.

"Make me some serious money and I'll be a happy girl," Charlie responded.

"I'm going to make you rich," Kieran promised. "You too, Mason. But I have to know I can trust you first."

"That's why we're here," Charlie said. "And we're ready. Just tell us what you want us to do."

Kieran bestowed another wicked smile on her. "Great. Let's play."

Chapter Nine

Mason was ready to crawl right out of his goddamn skin, and they were barely done with the appetizers. He wanted to be annoyed with Kieran. Angry at him for getting involved in something that had put him on an entire task force's radar. He'd always been arrogant, overconfident, someone who pushed the boundaries. Mason just wished he hadn't pushed so damned hard. And more than anything, he wished Kieran would stop looking at Charlie as though she was more delectable than the rich abalone their server had just placed in front of him.

Mason watched as Kieran worked his considerable charm on Charlie as he discussed wine, their meals, art and culture. The king of the black-market diamond trade. Slipping through federal and international law enforcement's fingers time and again. Feared by his enemies and allies alike. Rich and ambitious. Thrill seeker. Risk taker. Deadly and dangerous. Worldly and charming. Wine snob.

Gag.

Mason might not be rolling in money, but he was just as worldly and cultured as Kieran. He simply never felt the urge to flaunt it. If he had to listen to Kieran ramble on for another second, Mason was going to stab himself in the ear with his butter knife. He bragged until Mason wondered if he was going to stop to take a breath. Kieran smiled and made small talk and behaved civilly. Mason found himself hoping that Charlie would see through the bullshit.

But not because Mason was jealous of the attention she paid to Kieran.

Mason's mood took another sharp nosedive. He'd barely said a handful of words since they sat down. There was no need to. Charlie had taken charge of this meeting like she had that very first briefing. There was nothing meek or unsure about her. She was fucking spectacular.

She'd memorized every last detail about the diamond trade. Every word spoken exuded confidence. Mason doubted that Kieran even suspected he was being managed. In fact, he seemed even more dazzled by Charlie. More intrigued. The son of a bitch just couldn't help himself, could he?

"Mason? Did you hear me?"

He broke himself from his reverie and turned his attention to Charlie. "What?"

"I think we lost him somewhere around the ballet. Culture wasn't ever Mason's thing."

Please. Mason had been more cultured at eight years old than Kieran was now. His dad had surrounded Mason with culture from day freaking one. Kieran had been clueless until he'd come to live with Jensen and Mason. The gentleman-thief angle Kieran worked was getting old. Fast. "It's not the culture that bothered me," Mason replied. "It was the hypocrisy."

Charlie's gaze widened as though she couldn't believe he'd press his luck with the insult. Kieran chuckled and took a sip from his wineglass. "Back to dirty back alleys and unwashed, uncouth criminals, is that it?"

Mason shrugged. He knew that Kieran tried to be a moral criminal, if there was any such thing, but it didn't change the fact that he thumbed his nose at the law. For Mason, the law was everything. Maybe that's why his annoyance had steadily crested since seeing Kieran. It bothered him that Kieran had chosen to follow in Jensen's footsteps when he was capable of so much more.

"Didn't you know you're supposed to dress for the job you want, not the job you have?" Kieran continued.

Mason smirked. "So, you want to be an investment banker?"

Kieran broke out into robust laughter. "I missed you, brother."

Brother. That association had cost him dearly in his professional life. The stigma of his familial associations had haunted him throughout his adolescent and adult life. It wasn't Kieran's fault any more than it was Mason's, though. They'd both chosen their paths a long time ago. No point lamenting it now.

"Prove it." Mason leaned forward in his seat. "Hook us up."

Kieran wiped at his mouth with the pristine white napkin and set it gingerly on the table. "You never did like to beat around the bush, did you, Mason? I could have used you in India last year, you know. With muscle like you at my back, I doubt anyone would try to fuck with me. You should see your expression right now." He gave Charlie a gentle nudge. "Have you ever seen a more intimidating stare?"

Charlie turned her contemplative gaze his way. Her mouth softened and turned slightly upward at the corners. "He's scary," she agreed. "I wouldn't mess with him. Why do you think I take him everywhere I go?"

Kieran leaned in toward her conspiratorially. "I hope not *everywhere*. How will I ever get you to myself otherwise?"

Mason fought the urge to reach across the table and wrap his fist around Kieran's overpriced silk tie. If he didn't quit flirting with Charlie, he was going to be picking his ass up off the floor.

"Charlie and I are partners." Mason tried like hell to keep the annoyance from his tone. He needed to win Kieran's trust and that wasn't going to happen if he didn't quit acting like a hardheaded asshole. Charlie wasn't his to protect or anything else. He didn't even really know why in the hell it mattered so much. "We're ready to get to work and make some money."

"It's true," Charlie added. "We're both ready to get moving."

"Lunch first." Kieran turned his attention to the plate in front of him. "Business later."

Good God, he was going to bore Mason into an early grave if he didn't get this damned lunch over with. "Fair enough." At least he had a seventy-five-dollar steak to look forward to. And he'd be damned if Kieran didn't foot the bill for it.

Lunch passed in a blur. Mason checked out as Kieran rambled on and on about how goddamned wonderful he was. How anyone ever actually bought any of Kieran's bullshit was beyond him. He wondered if the other diamond smugglers mocked him behind his back. Because no one would dare insult him to his face. Not the great Kieran Eagan.

"Lunch was delicious," Charlie said. "Thank you." It was obvious that she was playing to his ego, and whereas it made Mason want to lose the lunch he'd just forced himself to eat, Kieran couldn't seem to get enough. "I think it's time we discussed business, though. Don't you?"

Kieran let out a long-suffering sigh, as though he was dreading this part. *Right.* He slid a black velvet pouch across the table toward Mason. Mason palmed the pouch and pulled open the drawstring before tipping the contents into his hand. Two diamonds, at least fifteen carats each tumbled out. Charlie leaned in to examine them without drawing any attention to their table.

"Beautiful," she said with honest appreciation.

Upon a superficial inspection, the diamonds did indeed seem flawless. The cut was top-notch, though until he could examine them more closely, Mason couldn't be sure about the clarity. They'd fetch a few hundred thousand from the right buyer, no doubt about it.

But their beauty was nothing compared to Charlie. She was goddamned radiant. Fresh, dewy skin, supple lips, curves that begged to be touched. Mason had barely been able to keep his hands off her all day. The more time he spent with her, the closer he wanted to get. And that was a huge fucking problem. Especially since Kieran had begun to look at her with the same interest and hunger.

"Origin?" Mason gave himself a mental shake and stuck to *business.*

Kieran cocked a brow. "Does it matter?"

"You know it does," Mason replied. "A buyer isn't going to want a stone from just anywhere if they're prepared to pay top dollar for something that's coming straight out of the DRC."

"You're right." Kieran picked his glass up by the stem and gave it a swirl. He watched with fascination as the dark red legs of the wine trailed slowly down the insides of the glass. "They were taken out of the Congo less than six months ago. Already cut and polished when I acquired them."

Strange. Kieran preferred to deal in raw gems. He smuggled them out of the Congo and transported them to India, where they were cut and polished. Kieran considered what he did a work of art. He didn't sell anything that wasn't as close to perfect as it could get.

Mason met Kieran's gaze. "And the buyer?"

Kieran smirked. This was where the game would get interesting. Kieran wanted to watch Mason jump through hoops in order to prove his loyalty. He wasn't going to make this easy and he'd be sure that whatever happened provided him with the maximum entertainment.

"The buyer is in L.A. Should work out well for you, Charlie, since you're thinking of setting up shop there. You can check out the real estate market and kill two birds with one stone."

Har, har. Charlie graced him with obligatory laughter that Mason didn't feel compelled to provide. He'd never been charming. Or fun. Or laid-back. If his part in all of this was to be the straight man, he was okay with that. It beat pretending to be some silly asshole.

"The fence is expecting us or you?" Mason asked.

"Me, of course," Kieran said. "But it's important to know the people you do business with are comfortable rolling with the punches."

Which meant the odds of getting the buyer to relax enough to complete the transaction would be slim to none. "And I don't suppose you're going to give him a heads-up to let him know you're not coming?"

"Who says I'm not coming?" Kieran's amused tone did nothing for Mason's temper. "How can I keep an eye on you from here?"

"Like you don't have spies everywhere," Mason remarked drily.

"True." Kieran leaned back in his seat. "But what's the fun in watching from the nosebleed section?"

Of course he'd want a front-row seat to this stupid little test. "How are we traveling?"

"Flying," Kieran said.

Getting the diamonds past TSA shouldn't be a problem. Two stones weren't enough to raise any eyebrows, and most agents were more concerned with sharp objects and whether or not people were traveling with more than a couple ounces of shampoo in their carry-on bag. No one gave a shit about a couple of gems in your carry-on.

"It won't be a problem."

"Not if you're as connected as you say you are," Kieran countered.

This wasn't just a test of loyalty and trust. Kieran loved games. He'd have them running the goddamn gauntlet. Mason was going to have to be on his toes from this moment on, because Kieran wasn't going to give him a single inch.

"When is the buyer expecting us?"

Kieran's smile widened. "Tomorrow."

Tomorrow? Charlie swallowed down the argument she wanted to make for his spur-of-the-moment job. Of course, he'd throw down like that, making them wait an entire week to hear from him, only to have him thrust them right in the thick of things without even a moment's notice. There wouldn't even be time to cut through the red tape necessary to make arrangements with Carrera and the rest of the task force. It made Mason's actions last week more understandable, though. He'd known Kieran would be ready to hit him with a curveball and so he'd beat him to the punch.

Smart.

Charlie never should have underestimated him. His history with Kieran aside, Mason really was the best person for the job.

"Tomorrow's a little last-minute, don't you think?" Mason had dominated most of the business talk, but Charlie needed to show that she was an equal partner in this. "What if we can't get a flight out?"

"Flight's already booked." Charlie wanted to slap the smug expression off Kieran's face. "The flight info will be e-mailed to you both shortly."

"Hotel?" Charlie ventured.

"Also booked."

The wily son of a bitch had thought of everything. And kept total control of the situation. It would effectively isolate Mason and Charlie from their support system. Just another part of his stupid test.

"When and where are we meeting the buyer?"

"Oh, come on, Charlie." Kieran chuckled. "You can't expect me to show my hand all at once. Preparation is so *boring*."

The fork sitting next to her plate was just begging to be stabbed into the fleshy part of Kieran's thigh. Charlie lived for preparation. Not being able to do her homework prior to heading to L.A. was bound to send the control-freak aspect of her personality into a frenzy. Anxiety crested within her and she drew in a slow breath to calm her racing heart. She could do this. No way would she let a Kieran Eagan get the upper hand.

"I suppose you're right," she practically purred in response. Kieran's mouth quirked in a half smile. At least he was easy to distract. "This should be fun." About as fun as a trip to the dentist.

Kieran leaned in close and dropped his voice to an intimate level. "I fucking can't wait to get into a little trouble with you, Charlie."

Kieran Eagan was the total package: good-looking, charismatic, rich, with a decent sense of humor and a fair amount of class. And he did absolutely *nothing* for Charlie.

"Looking forward to it," she said with a slow smile.

The server came with their check. Kieran pulled out several bills from his wallet and slid them into the little leather folder. He liked to show off, to flaunt his wealth and what he had. It was a good thing too, because his ego was going to be one of the things that would help her to take Faction Five down.

"Thanks for lunch." Charlie could play to his ego for as long as it took to nail his ass to the wall.

"Anytime," Kieran said in his smooth, silky tone. "Maybe next time I can talk you into dinner?" Mason grumbled under his breath and Charlie forced a smile. "Don't get jealous, Mason, you're invited too."

Mason didn't find him half as cute and amusing as Kieran did himself. "Where do we meet you tomorrow?"

"United terminal, four o'clock." His lips drew into a contemplative pucker and he said, "Better make it three. Who knows how backed up airport security will be."

The glint in his eyes told Charlie that they'd be in for it tomorrow. *Great.*

"We'll be there," Mason said as he stood from his chair and Charlie followed suit. "Thanks for lunch." He pushed out the words as though it caused him pain to thank Kieran for anything.

"See you tomorrow." The smirk didn't leave Kieran's lips though his gaze hardened almost imperceptibly. Again, Charlie wondered at his history with Mason. She didn't think it was entirely antagonistic. More to the point, she sensed the two regretted the way things were between them. As though they wished they could be close but knew the lives they led made it impossible. That worried Charlie. Could she count on Mason to do his job if he was so conflicted?

Charlie waited until they were out of the restaurant and in Mason's car to talk. She buckled her seat belt. "Well, how'd I do?"

Mason reached over and put a finger to her lips. The contact was electric and caused waves of heat to undulate over her skin. Her heart raced in her chest and her head swam as Mason slowly pulled his finger away. Such simple contact, and yet it drove her absolutely wild. Kieran could learn a thing or two about real sex appeal by studying Mason for a few hours.

"I think Kieran realizes that you know your business now. Of course, he doesn't know your sales history like I do."

Were they supposed to be in character still? Charlie had hoped that once they left the restaurant, she could let her guard down. Did Mason think that Kieran had bugged their car? Goddamn it. If he was truly as smart as Mason gave him credit for, it would make sense. But was there nowhere that Charlie could have a moment's peace and drop the damn façade?

"Tomorrow will be smooth sailing," she said. "I'm not worried in the slightest."

"Don't forget," Mason said. "It's a test. You have to bring your A-game."

"I will," she assured him. "You too."

"Kieran has nothing to worry about." Mason buckled up and turned the key in the ignition. The engine roared to life. "I'm in this for the long haul."

He reached to the dash and turned up the radio. The old-school hip-hop filled the interior of the car to the point that Charlie could barely hear herself think. She looked over and her eyes met Mason's. His brow was pinched, every inch of his handsome face lined with concern.

Nowhere was safe. From here on out they were under the microscope. One false move and Kieran would put them both in the ground before they ever had the chance to call in reinforcements. For the millionth time Charlie wished she'd trusted Mason enough to not have rushed in on him at the prison that day.

She was in way over her head and they both knew it.

Chapter Ten

Charlie's heart beat a mad rhythm in her chest. Was twenty-nine too young for a massive heart attack? Mason, however, was the very epitome of calm as they waited in the TSA line. Kieran was somewhere ahead of them, having magically breezed through the screening area without anyone batting so much as a lash.

So much for security.

The line moved and Charlie stepped up behind Mason and put her carry-on on the conveyor belt along with the plastic tub that held her shoes and cell phone. She watched as he stepped into the body scanner and let out a sigh of relief as the light turned green and he was allowed to walk through.

"Sir, I'm going to need you to step to the side, please."

Shit. Charlie's heart beat so quickly she was afraid it was going to disconnect from her chest entirely. Heat rose to her cheeks and she was sure her face turned bright red. Apprehension twisted through her as she stepped into the body scanner and put her arms in the air, all the while watching as a TSA agent waved a wand around Mason's body before declaring that he was going to have to be searched. What? Why? The scanner cleared him. What in the hell was going on?

"Ma'am? Can you step to the side, please?"

Oh God. Charlie took several deep breaths and willed her racing pulse to slow.

"Um, sure."

She could barely keep her eyes from Mason as she stepped to the side of the line. His duffel bag was taken from the conveyor and searched while he was patted down. Charlie swallowed down the fear that congealed in her throat and focused her attention on keeping her breathing level and her limbs from shaking. She'd never be able to fly again after this. She'd be road-tripping it from here on out.

Goddamn Kieran and his games.

She had no doubt the bastard had tipped someone off in order to test their mettle. See how they handled the pressure. She wanted to test his mettle by laying her knee into his crotch.

Why wasn't Mason panicking? He had almost a half million dollars' worth of illegal diamonds somewhere on his person, for Christ's sake! Charlie felt like her stomach lining was trying to abandon ship as she was haphazardly patted down. Mason hadn't even broken a sweat and they were practically strip-searching him.

"Ma'am. I said you can go ahead and go."

Charlie looked at the TSA agent. "Oh, sorry. Thanks." She walked on legs that felt more like noodles than anything solid, toward the conveyor belt, and grabbed her shoes, phone, and carry-on. Mason wasn't getting off as easily, however. Two TSA agents conversed in low voices as they searched his bag yet again, as well as his person. If they failed Kieran's test—a test that he'd made damned near impossible to pass—they'd be screwed. She could kiss the task force and Faction Five good-bye. *Damn it.*

Charlie slipped on her shoes and stowed her phone in her bag. She walked slowly away from the screening area while keeping Mason in sight. If she waited for him it might draw more suspicion. If she took off, he'd think she was ditching him. She had no idea how to behave. It's not like she was a seasoned criminal. Her job was to put the criminals in jail. Talk about walking a mile in someone else's shoes . . .

"Sir, you can go."

She barely heard the TSA agent's words to Mason, but the relief she felt caused her pulse to pound hard in her ears. She let out a shaky breath and waited for Mason to catch up to her before they headed toward their gate together.

"You look like you're about to swallow your tongue." Mason chuckled as he fell into step beside her. "You okay?"

"No." Charlie let out a nervous bark of laughter. "I feel like I'm going to pass out! How did you get past security? They patted you down so thoroughly they could have found a spec of dirt in your pocket!"

Mason flashed a confident grin. "I'm Jensen Decker's son." His dark tone belied his cheery exterior. "You don't think I learned a thing or two growing up?"

Charlie had never been so thankful that Mason was his father's son. "What did you do with them?"

His grin widened. "I don't have them. You do."

"What?" Charlie searched her pockets. True, her pat-down had been superficial, but how could she not know that she'd had the diamonds all along? She searched the pockets of her skinny jeans, knowing she would have felt it if Mason had tried to slip something inside. Empty. She stuffed her right hand into her jacket pocket and her fingers found the cool stones.

"Oh my God." She gave him a wide-eyed look. "How did you do it? When did you do it?"

He winked. "You've got a half million dollars in your pocket. Don't lose them."

Charlie's step faltered. All along she'd had the diamonds and hadn't realized it. Tricky. And damn risky. "I could have been arrested! Not that it would have mattered, but still."

Mason chuckled. "TSA doesn't care about the stones. If we were traveling out of the country it would be a big deal, but what does airport security care if you've got a couple of diamonds in your pocket? I knew that Kieran would want a little heat on me. He probably tipped them off that I was smuggling drugs or something they really cared about. He didn't want us caught, he just wanted to see how I'd react under pressure. I gave you the diamonds because women have a tendency to not receive as much scrutiny. TSA was looking for something on my person. I didn't want them to find anything."

There was so much more to Mason Decker than met the eye. Charlie couldn't believe how off her first impression of him had been. She'd thought of him as a bully. Annoyingly stubborn. Arrogant and opinionated. Stupid. Over the past week she'd come to realize that he wasn't any of those things. Not by a long shot.

They got to the gate just as the flight began to board. Charlie said a silent prayer that they'd be out of the airport and in the sky soon. The sooner they got this over with, the better. Kieran enjoyed watching them jump through his hoops, and Charlie hated giving him the satisfaction.

Kieran was already seated when they boarded the

plane, his trademark smirk affixed to his handsome face. "How'd it go?"

"Fine," Charlie replied. "No issues on our end whatsoever."

Kieran quirked a brow. "Really?"

Charlie smiled. The only thing allowing her the pleasant expression was imagining him rotting in a jail cell. "Really."

"Looks like you haven't lost your touch, Mason," Kieran said with a smirk.

Mason grumbled something under his breath as he stowed his duffel in the overhead compartment. He took Charlie's suitcase as well and placed it next to his.

"I think you underestimate Mason." At least one thing Charlie said to Kieran was 100 percent true. "He's much better at this than you give him credit for."

"Obviously," he said with feigned humility. "Maybe I should listen to Charlie more often. What do you think, Mason?"

Kieran was trying to bait Mason and he knew it. But he didn't play into the goading. Instead, Mason hiked a casual shoulder. "I listen to her. Why wouldn't you?"

Charlie gave Kieran a smirk of her own as she settled into the window seat. The first-class accommodations weren't a surprise. She didn't expect Kieran to travel any other way. Mason settled in beside her, his posture stiff. It could've been that having Kieran sitting behind him put him on edge. Or maybe he was feeling residual nerves from his encounter with the TSA agents. Either way, his demeanor changed the second they stepped into the airplane, and it piqued Charlie's curiosity.

"Who wants champagne?" Kieran leaned forward and spoke between the two seats.

Charlie glanced at him from over her shoulder. "It's five o'clock somewhere, right?"

"Exactly."

The flight attendant made her way down the aisle and stopped at their seats. "Can I get anyone anything? Mimosa maybe?"

"Whiskey," Mason growled.

"On the rocks?"

"Straight up," he said. "Actually, make it a double."

Something had Mason on edge and Charlie couldn't help but wonder what. And more importantly, would it affect how the rest of the day went down? She couldn't afford for him to lose his cool. Especially since he was the only thing keeping her own nerves from fraying into tattered shreds.

Kieran chuckled as though privy to some inside joke. Charlie cast a sidelong glance Mason's way. He sat ramrod straight in the seat, his gaze forward and his hands gripping the armrests. Was he afraid to fly? Charlie couldn't picture anything frightening Mason Decker.

Jesus. They might as well be flying in a goddamned coffin. Had Kieran gone out of his way to make sure they'd be flying in the tiniest fucking plane the airline could find? The walls closed in around him until Mason didn't think he could draw a deep enough breath to fill his lungs. Heat swamped him, his heart began to hammer in his chest, and his muscles grew taut. Where in the hell was the flight attendant with his drink? He'd never make it to L.A. unless he was on the verge of fall-down drunk by the time the plane took off.

"Hey. Are you okay?"

Charlie leaned in close. Mason took a deep breath of her fresh floral scent and held it in his lungs. He calmed, and the tightness in his chest loosened by a small degree. He could get through this flight, right? Hell, it was only an hour and a half. He'd taken road trips longer than that.

"Yeah." The word didn't seem to want to work itself past Mason's lips.

Charlie's drew into a pucker as she studied him. "You look a little pale."

The concern in her tone caused Mason's gut to clench. He didn't want her concern. He didn't want her to think that he was some ridiculous pussy who couldn't bear to be boxed in. Mason hated showing any weakness. What would her opinion of him be if she knew he was slowly unraveling?

Mason heard Kieran shift behind him. *Great.* The motherfucker wouldn't waste an opportunity to peel back his layers and expose him. "Didn't you know that he's claustrophobic, Charlie?" Kieran chuckled and it was all Mason could do not to turn around and pop him in the chin. "Mason and tight spaces don't get along."

Charlie's brows furrowed as her gaze met his. His gut sank at the pitying expression. "Take the window seat," she said. "It'll help."

"I'm fine." Mason pushed the words from between clenched teeth.

"You're not fine." Her expression became stern. "It's okay, I hate the window seat anyway. It makes me nervous to see how high up we are." She averted her gaze. "I'm not a very good flier."

Sure. No doubt she made the concession to try to make him feel better about his own pathetic state. Mason couldn't deny that he'd feel a hell of a lot better if he could see the expanse of sky and land beneath him, though. Anything to make him feel less closeted up.

"We're switching seats," she declared. "No arguing."

Bossy. But Mason wasn't about to argue. "Whatever," he muttered. "If it'll make you feel better to sit in the aisle seat, we can switch."

She gave him a soft smile that constricted his chest. "Thank you. I appreciate it."

Kieran sat back in his seat with a flounce. His disappointed scowl made Mason feel a little better about being thrown under the bus. No doubt he'd expected Charlie to chide him for his weakness, or maybe join Kieran in giving him shit about it. Anything that squashed Kieran's plans made Mason's day. It was bound to be a long damned twenty-four hours.

The quarters were close as he and Charlie switched positions. Her body rubbed against his, her lush breasts pressed tight against his chest. Mason sucked in a breath as he fought a groan. The softness of her body against his made him want to feel it again. And with a hell of a lot less clothes on the both of them.

Charlie tilted her head, revealing the long, delicate column of her throat. Her sweet scent wafted toward him with a swoosh of her almost shoulder-length hair and Mason filled his lungs once again. *Damn.* She was better at calming his nerves than a fifth of whiskey.

Kieran looked like someone had peed in his Cheerios, and Mason couldn't have been happier. Kieran obviously thought to trip him up at the TSA checkpoint as well as throw him for a loop by basically forcing him to spend a couple of hours locked up in a tiny metal tube. Mason had expected to be put through his paces. That didn't mean he had to like it, though.

"Here's your whiskey, sir." The flight attendant poured one tiny bottle into a plastic cup and set the other on the tray table. "That'll be twenty-two fifty."

Man, forget diamond smuggling. The real money

was in boozing up airplane passengers. Mason dug twenty five bucks out of his wallet and handed it over to the flight attendant. "Keep the change and keep them coming after takeoff."

She gave him a pleasant smile. "Will do."

"Don't overdo it, Mason," Kieran snarked from behind him. "Don't want to be off your game when we get to L.A."

He wanted to tell Kieran to take his cocky attitude and shove it right up his ass. So far, the only thing about this little test that was in the least bit challenging was sitting in this goddamned plane. Not for the first time, he was struck by the notion that it had all been too easy. He still had the flight to get through, though. A challenge he wouldn't complete without a little liquid courage. "Don't worry about me." Mason didn't bother turning to face him. "My game's tight."

Kieran chuckled. "We'll see."

The plane lurched as it taxied down the runway. TV screens embedded in the headrests of the seats popped on simultaneously as the preflight spiel began to play. Anxiety trickled into Mason's bloodstream as he tossed back the first whiskey in a single swallow. He stretched his neck from side to side. Rolled his shoulders. Unclenched his jaw. The video concluded and the TV screens went blank. It wasn't the flight that bothered Mason. He didn't give a shit about being rocketed through the sky at a million miles per hour. It was the tight space that made him want to claw his way out of his skin. He poured the second tiny bottle of whiskey into the plastic cup and swallowed it down.

Charlie leaned in, so close that their arms touched. An electric rush sizzled over Mason's skin and he barely noticed the sound of the propellers as they came to life. "Teach me how to pick someone's pocket," she whispered close to his ear.

Her warm breath stirred the fine hairs at his temple. Mason's gut clenched. Her proximity made his head swim. She was a distraction that he couldn't afford, and yet he was beginning to believe that she was the only thing that was going to get him through this.

"What?"

The plane picked up speed and shot upward. Mason wasn't sure if it was the takeoff, or Charlie's whispered words that made his stomach flip and twist on itself.

"I want you to teach me how to pick someone's pocket." A sly smile tugged at her lips. "I want to learn how to be a con man."

The plane began to level off and Mason relaxed back into his seat. He kept his attention focused on Charlie and not the overhead storage bin that felt like it was pressing him to the goddamned floor.

He found himself wanting to smile at her. To be as charming and goddamned witty as Kieran. To do something—anything—to win her undivided attention. He quirked a brow. "Don't you mean con woman?"

"Sure." Charlie's bubbling laughter rippled through him. "I want to be a con woman."

"International black-market diamond broker isn't enough for you, huh?"

A wry smile curved her luscious mouth. Mason wanted to rub the pad of his thumb along her bottom lip. Feel its petal softness against his skin before he leaned in to taste her.

"How did you do it?" Her dark blue eyes sparked with curiosity. "I didn't even feel your hand in my pocket. I never would have known I had the diamonds if you hadn't told me."

"You still have them, don't you?"

Her eyes widened and she stuffed her hand in her pocket. She let out a relieved sigh as though she'd thought he'd taken them from her without her knowing. "Safe and sound."

Mason leaned in close and dropped his voice to an intimate murmur. "The trick is having a light touch."

Charlie's mouth softened, making it look that much more kissable. "How light?" She inched closer.

Mason wondered how much of their exchange Kieran had overheard, and he couldn't help but feel smug about it. "Featherlight," he said, low.

A bright fire lit in her gaze and Mason was swamped with heat. All it would take was a slight shift and he could put his mouth to hers.

Behind them, Kieran let out a snort. "A light touch and an airport full of distraction."

Mason slumped back in his seat. Bastard just couldn't help but insert himself into the conversation. God forbid the attention should be off of him for even a split second. Charlie turned to look at Kieran through the space between the seats. "What sort of distraction, specifically?"

"A nudge," Kieran said. "Sometimes a shove. Did Mason bump into you in line or knock you off balance?"

"Just after we got into line." She gazed at Mason through the corner of her eye and grinned. "He lost his balance and had to grab on to me for support."

Mason scowled. Some things never changed. Fucking Kieran couldn't wait to burst his bubble.

"I can teach you how to pick a pocket, Charlie." Kieran leaned in—close enough that no one in the surrounding seats would hear their conversation—and declared with insufferable confidence, "I can teach you whatever you want to learn."

"I'm sure you've both got a lot of skills to impart."

Her flirtatious tone caused Mason's gut to clench. He hated when she spoke to Kieran that way. As though she were actually interested in him.

"That's the truth." Kieran edged even closer. Why didn't he just jump over the seat and sit in Charlie's lap? "But I have a feeling that Mason's a little out of practice."

"Which one of you is the better card player?"

"Me," Mason said without hesitation. "And Kieran knows it too."

He had the good sense not to deny it.

"Good." Charlie reached into her bag and pulled out a deck of cards. "We've got an hour and a half until we land. Texas Hold 'em. Loser buys dinner."

Chapter Eleven

"Looks like dinner's on you." Charlie wasn't a world-class hustler but she knew a thing or two about poker. "I almost feel bad taking advantage of a clearly inebriated man for a free meal."

He wasn't that drunk, but Mason had certainly downed enough whiskey to loosen him up. With his walls down, he smiled more. His eyes burned with a bright fire when he looked at her, and she'd spent most of the flight with the forced air blowing down on her to keep her flushed cheeks from showing how he made her feel. He laughed. A deep, infectious rumble that peppered Charlie's senses like warm summer rain. His posture relaxed and the permanent furrow that marred his brow smoothed.

Drunk Mason wasn't so bad. Maybe she'd liquor him up more often.

The sense of ease that Charlie felt during the flight quickly evaporated the moment they arrived in L.A. Flying blind wasn't exactly her thing, and Kieran seemed to enjoy the game he was playing. The stunt at the airport this morning only proved that he was prepared to make the road ahead as difficult as possible for Mason. Charlie couldn't begin to fathom the history between the two of them, but she had no doubt it was turbulent.

Kieran flanked Charlie so that she walked between the two men. They were two sides of the same coin: good, bad, light, dark. Funny that Mason represented not only the goodness but the darkness, while Kieran was bad to the bone and lighthearted. She was fascinated by the juxtaposition and it worried her as well. It was dangerous to become too enmeshed with either one of them. Detachment was a necessity that Charlie wasn't sure she could master. At least where Mason was concerned.

"Here's our car."

Kieran pointed out a sleek town car waiting in a row of others in the pickup area. Charlie changed course a beat before Mason and crashed into him. She reached out and steadied herself against his broad, muscled chest. It was no wonder he'd slipped the diamonds into her pocket without her knowing. A simple touch distracted her to the point that Charlie didn't know which way was up.

She looked up to find Mason's gaze trained on her. A pleasant wave of excitement rolled through her and Charlie let out the breath she'd been holding. "Did I distract you enough that I could have picked your pocket right now?"

Mason's nostrils flared. He gripped her shoulders and leaned in close. "The way you look right now could distract a man from breathing."

Oh wow. Heat gathered low in her belly and Charlie felt the need to swallow more than usual. "I'll keep that in mind for next time."

Mason held her for a beat longer. Kieran cleared his throat to break the spell, and she wanted to turn around and kick him in the shin. Mason released his hold as the scowl banished the heat from his expression. He turned away and headed for the car, and Charlie could do nothing but stare appreciatively from behind.

Charlotte Cahill, assistant U.S. attorney, would never have been so brazen with a man like Mason, but Charlie Sinclair, diamond broker and law breaker, was braver. She took risks, flirted with dangerous men, and said what was on her mind. She could see how some agents became addicted to undercover work. Pretending to be someone you weren't produced a definite rush.

Kieran made sure to sandwich Charlie in once they were all seated in the car. He could've taken the front seat, but instead pressed his body against hers as he leaned in intimately. "I know a couple of great real estate agents in the city. You should let me arrange to have them show you a few properties."

He was the sort of man who loved to throw his weight around. Charlie had known guys like that her entire life. The last thing she wanted was to keep company with men who reminded her of her father. She got enough of his elitist attitude when they met up for drinks and dinner once a month.

"That might be a little premature," she said. "I'm not exactly a high roller yet."

Kieran glanced Mason's way. "If the two of you come through for me today, I promise to make you a very rich woman."

The words were a low growl close to her ear. If he'd been another man, Charlie might have been attracted. Flattered by the attention. But he wasn't. It didn't matter what Kieran said or did to justify his lifestyle. He stole. Cheated. Gamed the system she swore to uphold. He disregarded the law that she revered.

Charlie took the bad guys down. Period. And Kieran was one of them.

"Promises, promises." She gave Kieran's shoulder a playful nudge. "I have no doubt that both Mason and I will come through for you today. You'll have to hold up your end of the bargain now and send some of that money my way."

"We'll own the diamond market," Kieran assured her.

Charlie forced the most sensual smile she could muster to her lips. "I hope so."

Blech. Even pretending to want to make money off the exploitation of others made Charlie want to scrub herself down with bleach. She'd play Kieran's game, though. Flirt, stroke his ego—as long as that's the *only thing* she'd be stroking—to ensure it got her the win.

"Where are we headed?"

Mason had been fairly quiet up until now. He hadn't had nearly as much to drink as Charlie initially feared he had. She'd done her best to keep his mind off his claustrophobia with round after round of Texas Hold 'em. Kieran sure as hell hadn't done anything to help Mason. Instead, he'd belittled him. Would there ever be an end to their sibling rivalry?

"Still the consummate control freak," Kieran remarked. "Worried?"

"Not even you go into a situation unprepared," Mason said. "I don't mind playing your games, but I think it's only fair we know what to expect before we get there."

"I agree." Charlie angled her body away from Kieran and straightened. "I understand the need for discretion and that you want to vet us first. But throwing us into a situation totally unprepared isn't just bad for us. It's bad for you too."

Kieran shifted so he faced Charlie. He braced his

elbow on the seat back and idly teased a strand of her hair. "Don't worry about my reputation," he said in a low, sensual murmur. "It doesn't tarnish."

An anxious shiver raced down Charlie's spine. His gaze warmed as he continued to play with her hair. She didn't move. Didn't dare to breathe. He was in charge and she had no choice but to go with the flow.

"Knock it off, Kieran," Mason growled. "Everyone here knows their place. If you want to keep me in the dark, fine. But there's no need to jerk Charlie around. She doesn't owe you anything."

Kieran raised a brow. "Oh no? Am I not about to set her up for life? I think a fucking thank-you might be in order."

They sure as hell bickered like brothers.

"It is," Charlie quickly agreed. She wasn't about to let the two get into a fight at this point. "And I'm incredibly grateful." She glanced Mason's way. "We both are."

Kieran's demeanor didn't soften. Instead, his lips thinned and his gaze cooled. He continued to fiddle with her hair as he focused his attention on some far-off point. "How did you meet Mason?" he asked. "I don't remember if you told me the story or not."

Fear skittered through Charlie's veins. She and Mason had come up with a passable cover story, but she hadn't had much time to rehearse it. "Mason arrested me." Charlie swallowed through the dryness in her throat. "Six months ago. I tried to fence seventy-five thousand in emeralds to two undercover agents. Mason was one of them."

Kieran leaned in closer and put his mouth to her ear. "Why aren't you in jail right now?"

Charlie shivered. "The evidence was misplaced."

"Convenient." His fingers threaded through her

hair and Charlie forced herself not to cringe away from the contact. "What happened to the emeralds?"

"Mason gave them to his father," she said on a breath. "At the prison last week when we met you there."

"Are you the reason he flipped, Charlie?" Kieran pulled away to look at her. "Did he throw all of his convictions to the wayside for you?"

Kieran still had doubts. It was written all over his face. She heard it in the tenor of his words. Felt it in the tension that vibrated off him. She had no idea what he wanted to hear. What could she say that would put him at ease once and for all?

"It's not like that," she said. "Mason saw an opportunity for a lucrative partnership and he saved my ass. I owe him."

Kieran abandoned her hair and brushed the pad of his thumb across her cheekbone. "I suppose you do."

God, she hoped they made it out of this alive.

Mason's control hung by a damned-near invisible thread. Healthy—if not a little antagonistic— competition had always been a part of his relationship with Kieran, but this was different. Charlie was different. He didn't like the way Kieran looked at her. The way his voice went low when he talked to her. Charlie could hold her own, Mason had no doubt, but that didn't make him any more comfortable with Kieran's come-on.

With Charlie's back to him he couldn't see her expression. Had no idea if she was keeping it together or not. Kieran wanted Mason to watch their exchange. To see him touch her, to show her exactly who was in charge. And despite the fact that Mason knew their lives were safe with Kieran, the world he brought them into was anything but. Threats lurked around every corner. Whoever Kieran was taking them to meet could be a volatile sociopath. Mason didn't want Charlie anywhere near that shit.

Having the responsibility of someone else's safety thrust upon him frayed Mason's nerves. He wanted to work alone for a reason, but he could have at least handled it better had he been saddled with another agent. Seasoned and capable. Charlie had a good head on her shoulders. She was cool steel under pressure. But she had no direct experience with the violent world she'd been suddenly immersed in.

He'd never forgive himself if something happened to her. But he'd sure as hell make someone pay if she got hurt.

"Charlie doesn't owe me," Mason said. Kieran pulled away, that goddamned smirk plastered on his smug face. "I saw an opportunity and I took it, plain and simple."

"After years of walking the straight and narrow . . ." Kieran mused. "And she's the one you jump the fence for."

Kieran's ego had never bothered Mason much. It came with the territory when you grew up with Jensen Decker as your teacher and father figure. When his dad was off running a con, smuggling gems into the country or fencing forged paintings all over Europe, Kieran had been the only family Mason had. Hell, despite their differences, he still was. He could forgive Kieran for a lot of things. Working his charm on Charlie wasn't one of them.

"I told you," Mason said. "I didn't do anything *because* of her. Customs had been trying to get their hands on her for months. I needed someone with the necessary contacts to get me where I wanted to be."

Kieran's brows shot up into his hairline. "And where is that?"

"In that visitors' room with you."

Kieran scoffed. He flounced back in the seat. Mason let out a breath, grateful Kieran had put some distance between himself and Charlie. "You could have just picked up a fucking phone, you know."

"Yeah." Mason allowed a chuff of laughter. "Because I've got you on speed dial. Even if I had looked you up, would you have believed that I was through with CBP and law enforcement? Or would you have turned your back on me before I even got the chance to explain?"

"You know that wouldn't have happened."

Mason cocked a challenging brow.

"Oh, fuck off," Kieran said with a wave of his hand. "I said I didn't trust you, not that I didn't want to have anything to do with you."

A twinge of guilt pulled at Mason's chest. He'd tried to put his past behind him. He'd cut all ties with his dad and distanced himself from Kieran. That association had been a shameful burden he'd carried for years. He couldn't change the circumstances of his upbringing though. Or the people he'd been raised with. They were family. Kieran wanted to believe that Mason had come back to that family. And Carrera had ensured that by bringing Mason into this mess he'd tear that family apart once and for all. Again Mason wondered, was his endgame worth what he'd lose in the process?

"After tonight," Mason said, "maybe we can put that doubt to bed, too."

"That's the plan." Kieran's eyes sparked with mischief. "Time to prove your mettle, brother."

Brother.

Each time Kieran said the word, Mason felt his

past—and the burden of guilt for his actions—creep up on him. There was no way he'd come out the other side of this unscathed. He only hoped that he could keep the damage to a minimum.

Mason took in his surroundings as best he could in the encroaching twilight. The car negotiated the crowded streets of the strip, past affluent storefronts and popular nightclubs that hadn't even begun to heat up for the night. Mason knew better than anyone that just because they'd be in the company of money tonight didn't mean they'd be with upstanding, law-abiding citizens. Looks could be deceiving. Just because someone owned a million-plus-dollar house and drove a Bentley, it didn't mean they walked the line. Most criminals were wolves in sheeps' clothing. They blended in, pretended to be something they weren't. Only the people they did business with saw their true colors. This wasn't going to be a cakewalk by any stretch of the imagination. Mason could hold his own. He'd grown up in this dog-eat-dog world. It was his worry for Charlie that stretched his muscles taut and caused the acid to churn in his gut.

He had to believe that she could handle this for both of them. Otherwise, he'd put an end to it before it even really began.

They drove for several more blocks before the car pulled up to a trendy, high-end strip club. The sign read FIORE, and from the line of people waiting to get inside, Mason figured it must be one of L.A.'s hottest venues. No doubt the owner was as crooked as a rail fence, too.

"Ready?" Kieran's grin stretched ear to ear. Mason gave him a look and he shrugged his shoulders. "What? You're here for business. I'm here for pleasure."

Mason had yet to make eye contact with Charlie.

The interior of the car had grown steadily darker as twilight gave way to night. He'd do his damnedest to make sure this transaction was quick and painless. In and out. The faster they could get the hell out of L.A., the better.

"I'm not going in until I get a little background," Mason said. "Who's the buyer, for starters."

"Katarina Evgeny," Kieran replied.

Stellar. The crown princess of the Russian mafia. Kieran might as well have asked them to walk over burning coals first. The daughter of Sergei Evgeny was rumored to be demanding, spoiled, and ten times more ruthless than her father. She was in line to inherit his entire North American operation and had already made a name for herself with her own business ventures. Some legitimate, others so far south of the law, they might as well be in hell.

Talk about running the gauntlet.

For the first time since they'd gotten in the car, Charlie faced him head-on. Her brow furrowed with curiosity, and even in the low light, Mason could make out the worry in her bright blue eyes. He gave her a re-assuring smile, though he felt anything but reassured himself.

"She's got enough money to buy out every jewelry store on Rodeo Drive," Mason remarked. "Why in the hell would she want these stones?"

"The stones have an interesting flaw that makes them incredibly rare," Kieran said. "Plus, they have sentimental value."

That sounded sketchy as hell. "What sort of sentimental value?"

"She tried to trade a few crates of Dragunovs for the stones a few months ago. She wants a chunk of the change that the arms dealers are hauling in. The

African market is booming. Abidemi Bello, the warlord she offered up the sniper rifles to, told her that he wouldn't do business with a woman and that if she showed her face in his camp again, he'd give her to his men and have her clit cut off."

Mason's brows shot up into his hairline. It was a wonder the warlord had lived long enough to issue the insult. "And she didn't have his balls right then and there?"

"She put a contract out on him," Kieran replied.

Mason knew killing wasn't Kieran's thing. He avoided violence unless it was necessary. "How in the hell did you get your hands on the diamonds?"

Kieran answered with an enigmatic grin.

"This isn't a fence," Mason said slowly. "We're delivering proof of death and collecting an assassin's fee."

"Not quite," Kieran said. "I didn't kill anyone. I just managed to get my hands on the stones after Bello was already dead. The diamonds are ransom. Sort of. She offered up two million. I contacted her, told her my associate had the stones but wanted ten million."

Motherfucker. Kieran had done a damned good job of stirring up a hornet's nest. Mason and Charlie would be lucky to walk out of here with all of their fingers still attached if not wrapped in plastic. Flawless, the stones were only worth a half million. Because of their flaws, they'd be worth even less. For whatever reason, Katarina had offered up a fortune for practically worthless diamonds, and Kieran was demanding more money still.

"This isn't a test," Mason said. "You're pulling the goddamned trigger on us."

Charlie remained deathly silent. The almost indiscernible rise and fall of her chest was the only indicator that she was about to lose it.

"I need to know you can work under pressure,"

Kieran said. "I need to know that you can be ruthless. I'm not running small-time cons and fencing one-carat stones, Mason. The people I'm involved with expect nothing short of perfection. If you can't hack it, you're dead. You said you wanted in. If I can trust you to manage Katarina, I can trust you with what I'm involved in. That's the deal. Take it or leave it."

The situation had spiraled so far out of control that Mason couldn't even grasp how quickly they'd spun. He opened his mouth to tell Kieran he wanted no part of it when Charlie interrupted him.

"We can handle it," she said.

Well, fuck. Looked like there was no going back now.

Chapter Twelve

Charlie's eyes widened as the words slipped past her lips. *We can handle it?* Sweet merciful God, what was she thinking?

"I like your backbone, Charlie." Kieran's smooth words slithered over her. The valet opened the back door and Kieran turned to her before he got out. "Let's tear it up."

Charlie moved to climb out behind him. Mason snatched her by the wrist and pulled her back to him. "Stay close to me," he murmured close to her ear. "I'll run point, you're just here to authenticate the gems. Don't make prolonged eye contact with anyone. Be pleasant, be professional, but don't let your guard down. You can't be nervous or unsure, do you understand? I need you to be a rock once we walk through that door."

Charlie nodded. She couldn't speak past the nerves that congealed in her throat.

"I've got you." Mason's intense gaze bored into her. "I won't let anything happen to you. I promise."

His words of reassurance meant more to her than all

of the coaching in the world. "Okay." She locked her gaze with his. "I can do this."

He gave her a crisp nod in response and released the hold on her wrist. As she got out of the car, she hated to admit that she missed the comforting pressure of his grip. Mason promised to protect her and because of that, she wasn't going to let him down.

Charlie waited beside the car for Mason. His presence at her back gave her the courage to put one foot in front of the other as they met Kieran at the entrance to the club. A bear of a man in a tailored suit pulled the velvet rope aside to let them through. "She's waiting for you," he said to Kieran. "And just a heads-up, she's in a foul mood tonight."

That didn't sound good. Charlie had to assume that a badass mafia princess wasn't easy to get along with on a good day. She could only imagine what dealing with Katarina when she was in a bad mood would be like.

Stepping through the doors of Fiore was like walking into another world. One that only added to the fantasy persona Charlie had been forced to construct for herself. The air sizzled with dangerous sensuality. There wasn't a woman in the club who wasn't a specimen of physical perfection. Men and women alike sat at the bar, surrounding tables, and the bar that lined the main stage. No neon lights or lasers dared to mar the atmosphere. Instead, there was an old-school, burlesque tone to Fiore that sold the venue as a high-brow establishment. The only thing that stood out was the slow techno song that filled her ears. Charlie's gaze was inextricably drawn to the main stage at the front of the club, where a naked woman twined herself around a pole in a graceful spiral that held her rapt.

"Entertaining, no?" Kieran said close to her ear.

Charlie gave a noncommittal shrug.

Kieran's warm laughter sent a rush of adrenaline into her bloodstream. "We're in the VIP room. Come on."

Charlie didn't make a move until she knew that Mason followed. She kept her gaze trained straight ahead and was sure not to let her attention linger on any single person or thing. Did that make her look more suspicious? Less? Did she look like an uptight basket case?

"It's okay to loosen up a little." Guess that answered her question. *Crap.* She looked back to find an amused expression on Mason's face. "Keep your emotions under wrap. This is just another day at the office."

"Maybe for you." She knew what Mason meant, though. In court it was important to keep your expression passive. Unflappable. Jurors noticed even the slightest hint of worry or doubt. It was safe to assume criminals were just as observant, if not more so.

"Be that woman I met in the elevator," he said. "Be the take-no-shit badass who ran that briefing, and you'll be fine."

Easier said than done. She'd been in her wheelhouse then. With people who knew their roles and what was expected of them. They'd all been on the same team. Maybe that was the problem. She was still thinking like a prosecutor. She was a good guy and they were the criminals. What she needed to keep reminding herself was that here, in this world, she was a criminal too. She needed to see through the eyes of the people she'd been sending to jail. She knew the criminal mind-set. Hell, she'd spent years studying it. This was the sort of on-the-job training she'd never get in a courtroom. Charlie could use it. Learn from it.

That is, if she lived through it.

Another behemoth of a man in an expensive suit met them at the VIP section and escorted them down a long hallway to a private room. Charlie felt Mason bristle beside her, and she could only imagine that the tight, windowless space wasn't going to do much to keep him level and calm.

A door swung wide and the security guy stepped to the side to let them through. Kieran walked in, followed by Charlie. Mason knocked into her as the cold steel of a gun barrel pressed into her temple and she froze.

Please don't let me die in a strip club owned by the Russian mob. Her father's head would explode right off his shoulders.

"Kieran, you piece of shit." A smooth, sensual voice with a refined Russian accent broke the silence. "Did you bring my stones?"

"Charming as ever, Katia." Kieran spoke as though he didn't have a gun pressed into his head along with Charlie and Mason. "I didn't bring your stones," he added. "But my associates did."

Charlie scanned the room. The panic that overran her system made it tough to focus, but after a moment she zeroed in on the woman who spoke. Much younger than Charlie anticipated, and beautiful. Her cold, dark brown eyes narrowed and she smoothed a hand over her perfectly coifed chocolate-brown hair. Her attention fell on Charlie and then Mason. She paused for a moment as her gaze raked him from head to toe and her bright red lips spread into an indulgent smile. "Fine, then. Kieran's associate, give the stones to me and I'll consider letting you leave with you limbs intact."

Charlie had agreed to let Mason run point. He'd grown up in this world—had worked cases with people just like Katarina—whereas her own knowledge was superficial at best. Still, the urge to speak up, to put the other woman in her place, was almost more than

Charlie could resist. She hated entitlement. Especially when that attitude came from murderers and criminals.

"I'm sure there's a better way to conduct business." Mason took a step forward and Katarina's bodyguards converged on him. His arms were forced behind his back and he was slammed face-first against the nearest wall.

Charlie cringed at his grunt of pain. Kieran took a protective step toward her, placing her behind his right shoulder. She wanted to elbow him right in the soft spot of his gut. His chivalry was a bunch of bullshit. He had to have known this would happen.

Katarina let loose a string of angry Russian that made Charlie's ears burn. "You know *dick* about my business." She rose up from her chair with all of the pomp and circumstance of a queen. Her Louboutin heels clicked sharply on the floor as she crossed the room to where her goons had Mason smashed against the wall. She reached out and tousled his hair with the blood-red tips of her nails and leaned in close to whisper something in Mason's ear.

Charlie strained to hear, but even in the nearly soundproof room she spoke too quietly. Her red lips pursed before curving upward. She came around Mason's left shoulder so that she could look him in the eyes.

"Let him go."

The order was obeyed in an instant. Mason pushed himself away from the wall and straightened his shirt. Charlie moved toward him and Kieran took her hand in his to keep her in place. "He's a big boy, Charlie," Kieran murmured. "He can take care of himself."

That might be true, but it didn't put her any more at ease.

"So, Mister . . . ?"

"Decker," he answered. Katarina's mouth turned down as if the name had no significance. "Mason Decker."

It took a moment before her expression lit with recognition. Her smile grew and Charlie couldn't help but admire her sultry beauty. What had she whispered in Mason's ear? And why was she so suddenly willing to hear him out when only a moment ago she'd threatened to give him a permanent vacation from his limbs?

She jerked her head in Kieran's direction. "What's in it for you?"

He hiked a shoulder. "Finder's fee."

Katarina snorted. "And how do I know the diamonds are authentic?"

Kieran's eyes slid to Charlie. "That's what she's for."

The Russian mafia princess's attention wandered to Charlie as though she'd only now realized she was standing there. Charlie fought the urge to squirm under her appraising stare. "Who is she?"

"Charlie Sinclair, meet Katia Evgeny," Kieran said. "Katia is an old friend. And Charlie is a broker and an expert. I've vetted her personally. She'll know if the stones are legit."

"And I'm supposed to trust your word, Kieran?" Katarina's eyes went wide. "What do I care that you've vetted her? *I haven't*, and that's all that matters."

"Fair enough." Kieran's stance relaxed. "What do you suggest?"

She held out her hand to Charlie. *Holy mother of rocks.* The diamond ring she sported looked more like a golf ball resting on top of her finger. "What can you tell me about this?"

Katarina fucking Evgeny. Kieran might as well have sent them into North Korea to fence the diamonds. In no time at all, Sergei's daughter had managed to build her reputation as the evil dictator of Los Angeles. She certainly ruled the underground. Kieran had really fucked Mason over this time. But he had one up on Kieran. Not that he wanted to be anywhere on the mobster's radar. Still, he'd take any advantage he could get.

Mason's relief at no longer having his face pancaked against the wall was short-lived. Katarina had put Charlie on the spot by requesting that she prove herself before being allowed to authenticate the diamonds. Mason had given her a crash course in how to grade a gem, and though she'd been a quick study, Kieran hadn't given her enough information on the stones for Charlie to know exactly what sort of flaw she should be looking for. They could be practically unidentifiable to the untrained eye. In this case, the flaws in the stones were what made them so attractive to Katarina. Apparently, perfection bored her.

Charlie cleared her throat. Mason kept his stance relaxed, but the tension continued to creep up on him until his muscles burned. He swore to God if anything happened to her—if any of Katarina's goons laid a fucking finger on her—he'd burn this place to the ground.

"I'd be happy to take a look at your ring." Every word projected confidence. Not even a quaver to her voice. "Do you mind if I get my lens out of my bag?"

Katarina gave a flick of her wrist. "Alex."

One of the men reached out and snatched Charlie's handbag. He rifled through it before giving his boss the all-clear with a nod of his head.

She gave another flick of her wrist. Kieran had brought them before a queen tonight. One who didn't have any qualms about lopping off heads. Not one of the three of them had come armed. It was a mistake

Mason wouldn't make again. Not that it would have mattered now, but it would've been nice to have been given the opportunity to be a little more goddamned prepared.

Charlie retrieved the loupe from her bag. She glanced Mason's way and his chest swelled with pride that she didn't give any outward show of worry. She'd absorbed every bit of information he'd drilled into her over the course of the past week. Charlie was smart. Capable. There was no need for worry. She had this.

"May I?" Charlie reached out a hand toward Katarina, who graced her with an indulgent smile.

"Of course," she purred.

Charlie didn't miss a beat as she gently removed Katarina's ring from her finger. "Is there a possibility we could do something about the lighting? I'm used to working in much brighter surroundings."

Katarina's brows raised and it was as good as a shouted command. Within seconds additional lights were brought in and set up on a nearby table. "Sit." Katarina held out a welcoming hand to Charlie before her gaze wandered to Kieran and then to Mason. Her lips spread in an indulgent smile. "Everyone."

Charlie cast a glance over her shoulder. Mason was proud of her for going the extra mile not to appear to be any more uptight than she should be, given their situation. Hell, even criminals got twitchy when their lives were on the line. And there was no doubt Kieran had dangled them out in the wind. On a scale of one to ten, Mason's own anxiety had crested to about a thirty. The guns in his face had actually been a nice distraction from the small, windowless room they'd been shut up in. Maybe one of Katarina's henchmen wouldn't mind shoving his face into the wall one more time. You know, just to give him something else to worry about for a minute or two.

Charlie situated herself under the lighting. Mason sat down beside her and Kieran once again flanked her. The way he seemed to want to be stuck to Charlie like glue made the hairs on the back of Mason's neck stand on end. It was a little late for Kieran to play the chivalry angle, considering the fact he was the asshole who'd gotten them into this mess.

You could have heard a damn pin drop while Charlie held the loupe to her eye and examined Katarina's ring. Long moments passed. Tension pulled Mason's muscles taut. His mouth felt too goddamned dry, and he took stock of every single body in the room as he weighed their odds of making it out of there alive in the event that shit went south.

Not fucking great.

Charlie looked up. She pulled the loupe away from her eye and met Mason's gaze. Her brow furrowed, though she kept her expression passive. His gut knotted up as her lips parted. Something was wrong.

"Well?" Amusement tugged at Katarina's lips. "What is your opinion of my ring, diamond broker?"

Charlie inspected the ring once more. Katarina let out a dramatic sigh.

"It's . . ."

The quick, rhythmic tap of Katarina's long nails on the tabletop echoed Mason's racing heartbeat. "Yes?"

Charlie's gaze met Mason's once again. "It's fake."

Impossible. Mason couldn't imagine someone like Katarina wearing anything counterfeit.

The Russian fixed Charlie with an inscrutable stare. One brow arched delicately over a dark eye.

"It's remarkably well made." Charlie spoke with

confidence. Her voice didn't so much as quaver. "But it's not a diamond."

Mason exchanged a quick glance with Kieran, who looked like he was about to fall off his chair. Obviously he shared the same opinion: Charlie had fucked up and they were about to pay for her insult with their lives.

"Katia," Kieran began.

She broke out into low, rippling laughter. "You look as though you might piss your pants at any moment, Kieran. Relax. She's right. The stone is a fake."

Some of the tension eased from between Mason's shoulder blades and he willed the rush of his heart to slow.

Katarina relaxed into her seat and regarded Charlie. "Most would lie to me," she remarked. "Too afraid to anger me with the truth in case I'd been duped. Are you not afraid of me?"

"If I were in your position, I'd want the truth. I don't appreciate being patronized. I can't imagine that you do, either."

"I like you," Katarina said with a downward stab of her finger. "Women are rare in my business. It's refreshing to not be indulged for a change."

Charlie glanced Mason's way and smiled. The pride in her expression sent a rush of emotion through his chest. Was there anything she couldn't do? Seasoned attorney. Ballbuster. Strong. Assertive. Smart as a fucking whip. Tough. And now Mason could add con artist, gem appraiser, diamond broker, and undercover agent to that list. Charlie Cahill was one of a kind.

Over the past week, Mason's interest in her had begun to surpass that of simply professional. He scowled as Kieran leaned in to whisper something near Charlie's ear. She angled her head toward his and her lids drooped almost imperceptibly as a soft smile curved her lips. Mason wasn't the only one whose interest in Charlie went beyond the job. A sharp stab of jealousy speared through Mason's center. His gut burned and his throat ached as the urge to shove Kieran away from her overtook him. Another second of this bullshit and his head was going to fucking explode.

"Charlie's proven herself." Mason forced his attention to Katarina. "So how 'bout we get down to business."

Katarina responded with a tight-lipped smile. "Yes," she purred. "Let's."

Finally. Mason wanted their business settled so they could get the hell out of here. The more time he spent with Kieran—or rather, the more time *Charlie* spent with Kieran—the more he wanted to put his fist into the other man's gut, brother or not. Mason's headspace had been fucked up since the day Charlie pushed her way into that elevator. He hated being off his game. Hated not having control. He needed some goddamned fresh air and to see the sky above him. He needed—*shit.* Mason didn't know what the hell he needed. Whatever it was, he had a feeling that only Charlie could give it to him.

Chapter Thirteen

Charlie wanted to shout her elation. She'd killed it! A badass with a jeweler's loupe, she'd proven herself to one of the most feared heads of the Russian mafia and gotten kudos to boot. It shouldn't have felt so good to receive praise from a murderer and a criminal, but it gave Charlie a distinct rush that had gone straight to her head. She was drunk on her own ego and accomplishment. No wonder men like Kieran continued to chase bigger and more dangerous deals as their careers progressed. She'd never felt anything like it.

She might as well have been invincible.

"I can't resist a woman who isn't afraid to speak her mind."

Kieran's whispered words in her ear weren't altogether unpleasant. She appreciated the praise and boost to her self-esteem. But it wasn't Kieran's admiration that she wanted. No, her blood quickened in her veins when she imagined those words spoken low from Mason's lips. And it set her on fire.

From the corner of her eye she caught his scowl. Where Kieran seemed only to want to smile, Mason never broke from his furrowed brow and downturned mouth. Was he pleased with her for coming through with Katarina? It made her feel weak and pathetic to need that sort of attention from him. Maybe his reluctance to give it made her want it that much more. Did it matter? This wasn't the time or place to hash out her feelings for Mason. She needed to play her part, let Mason negotiate the deal, and get the hell out of here.

Katarina's gaze met Charlie's. "The stones?" Mason dug the black velvet pouch out of his pocket and handed it to Charlie. Katarina let out an amused snort and gave a rueful shake of her head. "You come to me with a ten-million-dollar price tag and carry them around like pocket change?"

"They're flawed." Mason shrugged with disinterest. "They're not worth anything to anyone but you."

"Yes." Katarina pursed her glossy red lips. "As you've made perfectly clear in your price."

"Ten million is a small price to pay for your pride and reputation," Mason pointed out. "Wouldn't you agree?"

Katarina's eyes narrowed. Charlie watched the power play with fascination. She'd never met a more ruthless or frightening woman than Katarina, yet Mason dealt with her as though he were on her level. Just as ruthless. Equally frightening. It shouldn't have turned her on, but a rush of warmth suffused her and settled low in her abdomen.

"Did he suffer?" she asked.

Mason didn't miss a beat. "Immeasurably."

Her lips curved into an indulgent smile. "Good."

Katarina snapped her fingers and one of her men took the small bag from Mason's outstretched hand as though she didn't dare sully herself by making contact. Once in her possession, she pulled open the drawstring and tipped the contents out into her hand.

The diamonds glittered like winter ice under the bright lights. Katarina studied them for a quiet moment before she handed them over to Charlie. "Tell me about them."

Katarina didn't ask anyone to do anything. She gave orders and expected them to be obeyed. Charlie set the diamonds on the table in front of her. Like when she'd examined the stone in Katarina's ring, she had no idea what to look for. Mason had done a good job of coaching her though, and she was confident that as long as she didn't try to pull one over on Katarina, she'd be fine. Kieran wouldn't sink them by offering up counterfeit stones, would he? After all, he was in it for the money as well. Charlie couldn't imagine that he'd put himself at risk in order to get some sort of twisted revenge on Mason for whatever it was they'd fallen out over.

Better get to work . . .

Charlie retrieved the first stone and examined it under the jeweler's loupe. The cut and clarity were actually quite good. Almost no color whatsoever. She would have guessed the stone would score a one on the AGS grading scale. Close to perfect and extremely valuable, if not for its flaw: a miniscule garnet embedded in the stone's center.

"Tell me, Mason." Katarina tapped her long nails on the tabletop. "How did you get the diamonds past customs?"

"I work for CBP," he said as though it were inconsequential.

Katarina said something to her entourage in Russian and they all had a good laugh over it. Charlie imagined that even if she'd said something completely dull she'd have gotten a raucous response from her men.

"You do surround yourself with the most interesting people, Kieran," Katarina remarked. "I could use a man like you on the payroll, Mason." She graced him with a seductive smile. "We should talk."

There was a little too much heat in those last words for Charlie's peace of mind. She forced her attention back to one of the diamonds in question. "I'm curious. Why go to so much trouble for flawed stones that have no real value?"

"It is our flaws that make us truly beautiful," Katarina replied. "The warlords know this. They covet certain flawed stones for various reasons. Some personal, some spiritual. Superstition abounds in Africa. I wanted these particular stones for their flaws."

And the warlord had not only denied her, but insulted and threatened her. Not a good idea, obviously.

"This stone has a garnet embedded in its center," Charlie said. She looked up from studying the diamond to find Mason's full attention on her. "An SI flaw. You can only see the inclusion when magnified, but it almost looks like a heart."

"A true blood diamond, no?"

The comparison left Charlie feeling a little nauseous. "Definitely." She set the stone aside and picked up the second diamond. Like its partner, the cut and clarity were nearly flawless. The stone was even more crystal clear than the first. It would have easily scored a zero on the AGS grading scale, save the garnet suspended near its center. This garnet, however, was slightly larger and split down the middle. A broken heart.

Charlie brought her gaze up to Katarina's. "One heart intact, the other broken. It's sort of poetic, don't you think?"

Something fired in Katarina's dark eyes. A depth of sadness that she kept hidden under her fierce exterior. "Exactly." She spoke again in Russian. A rolling wave of words that Charlie found beautiful and lyrical. Of course for all she knew, Katarina had just ordered her men to kill all three of them and dump their bodies in the ocean.

An eerie silence followed her words. She turned her attention to Mason, her jaw set. "Ten million is excessive. Charlie, what are the stones worth?"

"Not much," she admitted. "Like you said, they have no real value to anyone aside from collectors who would want them for the flaws. They're definitely worth less than the two million you originally offered for them."

Katarina threw a superior smirk Mason's way. "You can't possibly think I'll pay what you're asking."

Mason wasn't fazed. "You can't possibly think I'd go so far as to put myself on Bello's gang's hit list if I wasn't going to make sure it was worth my money."

Katarina gave a derisive snort. "You should have made your deals prior to making assumptions."

"You would have offered to give me the moon," Mason said. "And we'd still be where we are right now."

Katarina shrugged. "Eh. Maybe so. Either way, you must think I'm made of money if I have ten million dollars in cash to simply hand over to you."

"No one deals in cash anymore," Mason chided. "And I'm sure you have more than enough that you could wire me the funds and not even feel a pinch."

Again, Katarina couldn't argue. She glanced Charlie's way and smirked. "One of the downsides of being infamous. Everyone knows your business."

Charlie laughed. So far, her experience with the

people who dealt in the seedy underworld of blood diamonds hadn't been as unsavory as she'd anticipated. Katarina, despite her reputation, was someone that Charlie thought she might like under different circumstances. Of course, she wasn't so foolish as to think that everyone she'd encounter would be so personable. She suspected that Kieran preferred to do business with people who had like personalities. Which made her even more curious about the esoteric leaders of Faction Five. Who were they and how in the hell had Kieran become mixed up with them?

Kieran is *one of them.* In the short time they'd known each other, Charlie had begun to think of him almost as a friend. She toed a very dangerous line. One that she couldn't allow herself to cross. She couldn't afford to like Kieran. To feel anything for him. She couldn't let herself like any of these people. They were criminals and she was an assistant U.S. attorney. Black and white. There was no room for a moral gray area here. How had Mason done it? How had he walked away from this life—from Kieran—and those relationships so easily? Had he never been tempted to take the easy route instead of working way too hard for every dollar? He couldn't have made more than fifty thousand a year with CBP. Kieran's income had to be a hundred times that.

"I want the ten million, or I'm taking the diamonds and walking." Mason's words broke Charlie from her thoughts. "It's your choice, Katarina. Take it or leave it."

Charlie couldn't help but wonder how long Mason could play this game before his own lines became blurred. Or had they already?

* * *

Katarina could talk until she was blue in the face. There was no way in hell Mason was backing down. She had more than enough to pay the price he was asking, and he knew that she'd rather die than let the diamonds go. This was about pride, after all. His and hers. Of course, there was the possibility she'd just kill them all and take the diamonds. But above all, she was a business-woman. A damned good one. She was a practical killer rather than a ruthless one. Putting them down for no other reason than losing a game wasn't her style.

At least, Mason hoped not.

Their saving grace was Charlie. Mason doubted they would have gained Katarina's good graces without her. She continued to surprise him. To show him her strength. She was more than capable and a damned good actress to boot. Maybe too good. Mason was almost buying into the Charlie Sinclair persona. At the end of the day he had to remind himself that this was a J-O-B. She was behind the task force that held his career in their hands. Any interest he had in her needed to be put on the back burner, stat.

Katarina disregarded Mason once again as she held out her hand. "Charlie, may I?"

"Absolutely."

Charlie handed Katarina the stones as well as the jeweler's loupe. Silence descended once again as she quietly examined the diamonds. She let out a gentle sigh and slowly looked up to meet Mason's gaze.

"I'll pay your price," she said without an ounce of humor. With gentle care Katarina placed the stones back in the velvet satchel and pulled the strings tight. She held the bag close to her heart as she said some-thing under her breath about love and sacrifice in Russian. Whatever the stones reminded her of, Mason knew it was something deeply private. Kieran had known she'd pay any price for the diamonds—which made him wonder what sort of connections Kieran had to get that sort of intel.

Kieran removed a folded piece of paper from his jacket pocket and slid it across the table to Katarina. She sneered. "You've always been too goddamned arrogant for your own good, Kieran."

He answered with a good-natured chuckle. Kieran never worried about consequences. Neither did he ever go into any situation less than 100 percent confident he'd come out ahead. He stacked the deck in his favor time and again. As soon as they were free and clear, Mason was going to make him fess up as to how he'd known that Katarina would pay their price.

Had Kieran really wanted to test Mason and Charlie tonight? Or was this simply another one of his games?

With business all but conducted, Kieran rose from his seat. Mason followed suit and gave Charlie a slight nod to let her know it was time to go. Her posture relaxed and she let out an almost imperceptible breath. She'd done well tonight. He was proud of her. And he couldn't wait to say the words to her.

"Not so fast."

Katarina hadn't moved from her seat. A spasm of anxiety rippled through Mason as he exchanged a glance with Kieran.

"Kieran gets his finder's fee. Charlie, I'm sure, will collect her fee as well. They have nothing more to offer me," Katarina said. "However, I'm not done with you, Mason."

Shit.

What more could she want? The warlord who'd insulted her was presumably dead, and she held the prize he'd kept from her tight in her grip. Like Kieran and Charlie, there was nothing more Mason could offer her either.

"What more do you think we have to discuss?" He might be pushing his luck with his demanding tone, but Mason had been through playing games about twenty-fucking-four hours ago. He wanted to get his ass outside and take as deep a breath as the shitty L.A. air would allow him.

Katarina didn't give anything away in her expression. "A car will take Charlie and Kieran back to the hotel."

Mason's jaw clamped shut. The last thing he wanted was for Charlie to spend any amount of time alone with Kieran. And not simply because of the way he looked at her. "Whatever business you have to discuss with me, you can discuss with them."

Katarina's gaze hardened. "Do you want your ten million . . . or perhaps not?"

Mason's attention shifted to Charlie. If she was nervous, she gave no outward sign. Kieran, however, wore his suspicion plainly in his expression. Obviously, he hadn't anticipated Katarina wanting a private word with Mason. To be honest, neither had he.

"I'll meet you back at the hotel?" He turned to Kieran and gave a helpless shrug.

"Yeah." For the first time in a week, Kieran's tone grew serious. And for the first time in a week, Mason felt like he might be fucked. "We'll get settled in and meet you there."

He didn't dare give Charlie any reassurance. She was supposed to be able to handle herself. Katarina snapped her fingers and one of her men headed for the door. It swung wide and he waited out in the hallway for Kieran and Charlie to walk out in front of him.

If they all made it through the night alive, it would be a miracle.

The door closed behind them and the sound punched through Mason's chest. He turned to face Katarina, and a seductive smile spread across her crimson lips. "Now," she purred in her smooth accent, "where were we?"

Chapter Fourteen

"I had my doubts about you, Charlie. But you proved yourself tonight," Kieran said.

She'd done well. Too bad she was too damned worried about Mason to pat herself on the back for it. If anything happened to him, she'd be set adrift in a world—and with a man—she knew nothing about. Thoughts of her own safety took a backseat to her concern for Mason, though. What had Katarina wanted? Was he okay? What if Katarina decided to go back on their deal and killed Mason just to prove a point? The lack of control she had over the situation caused Charlie's stomach to churn. All she could do was play her part and wait. She climbed into the backseat of the car and settled in beside Kieran. She was antsy as hell and felt like throwing her guts up. And she had no choice but to play it cool like it was simply another day at the office.

There was definitely an ulcer in her future.

"Maybe now you'll stop trying to test me and let me in on whatever big deal you've got going on?"

"Just you?" A flirtatious smile tugged at Kieran's mouth. "What about your partner?"

He'd love it if Charlie turned on Mason, wouldn't he? "Both of us." She pinned him with a chiding look. "I thought that went without saying."

"What's the deal with you two?" The car pulled out onto the street and Charlie forced herself not to look back at the club. Mason was capable. He could take care of himself. "You're not fucking him, are you, Charlie?"

She'd learned enough about Kieran to know when he was trying to get a rise out of her. She met his gaze, the epitome of calm. "No," she said. "I'm not fucking him."

His eyes crinkled at the corners with amusement. "Good. I'd be jealous otherwise."

Charlie's chest tightened. She couldn't tell if Kieran was actually coming on to her or not. Again, he might be trying to get a rise out of her. More likely, he was deflecting. Making sure the conversation veered away from his current business dealings. Namely, Faction Five. Charlie infused her tone with skepticism, playing along with whatever game he played. "I'm sure you would."

Kieran reached out and smoothed her hair away from her face. "I'd be absolutely *green*."

"What do you think Katarina wants with Mason?" If Kieran could deflect, so could she. She'd keep the conversation focused on business, no matter his efforts to steer her in the opposite direction.

Kieran's gaze darkened. Charlie wasn't sure it was concern she saw in his eyes, but perhaps a little of that jealousy he'd mentioned. It wasn't over a woman, either. Charlie suspected that Kieran's rivalry with Mason spanned years and ran deep. They might not share the same blood, but they were brothers just the same. Sibling rivalries were often the worst kind.

"If I had to guess?" he began. "She's either offering him a job, or taking him to bed."

Embers of her own jealousy smoldered in the pit of Charlie's stomach. It had been obvious from Katarina's hungry gaze that her interest in Mason wasn't strictly professional, but Charlie'd hoped that the mafia princess would be smarter than to mix business with pleasure. "If it's a business relationship she's offering, Mason isn't interested." If she was being honest, she hoped he wasn't interested in *any* relationship with Katarina Evgeny, business or otherwise. "He won't screw us over."

Kieran leveled his gaze on Charlie. "Don't be so sure."

He still didn't trust Mason. At this rate, they'd never infiltrate Faction Five. "What's it going to take for you to trust us?"

Kieran fixed her with a contemplative stare. "Why do you trust him?"

Good question. Why did she trust him? Aside from him being recommended by Carlos Carrera, Charlie didn't know much about him. His work performance had been exemplary. In fact, his supervisor with CBP had been sad to see him go. Being good at his job didn't make him trustworthy, though.

"He could have let me go to jail," she said after a moment. Keeping to the details of her cover story wasn't as hard as she thought it would be. "And instead, he helped me out."

"You're beautiful." Kieran's hungry gaze roamed over her, making Charlie feel a little like a meal. "I don't know a man on the planet who wouldn't have helped you out."

Heat collected in the pit of Charlie's stomach and fanned out into her limbs. Kieran's compliment shouldn't have pleased her. She'd never thought of herself as attractive. She was a little too curvy, her personality a little too severe. "I doubt he took the risk because he thought I was good-looking." Did Mason think she was good-looking? Jesus, that was *so* not something she should be contemplating right now.

"I would have." Kieran dropped his voice to a murmur. "In a heartbeat."

Charlie wasn't going to let herself be affected by his words. "Liar."

Kieran chuckled. "Maybe." He shrugged. "Maybe not."

He leaned forward in his seat and said something to the driver in Russian.

"What did you say to him?"

"I told him not to take us to the hotel."

Charlie shifted in her seat. "Where did you tell him to take us?"

"Mélisse. I'm starving, aren't you?"

There was no way she'd make it through a casual meal as wound up and worried as she was. "What about Mason?"

"What about him?" It seemed Kieran couldn't turn off the playful vibe. "He can get his own dinner."

Was there anything that worried him? Not even Mason's safety?

Charlie had never been more ready for a day to come to a close. She'd made a conscious effort to soldier through dinner. It's not like she had a choice. She couldn't help but wonder if Mason was stuck in the same situation right now. A captive audience without a choice.

"How's the wine?"

"It's great." He knew it was, but Charlie suspected that Kieran wanted to hear her say it. To reinforce that he was suave and sophisticated. That his tastes were impeccable.

They'd already polished off the first bottle and were working on the second one. Charlie had thought that a couple glasses of overpriced chardonnay would calm her nerves, but she'd passed calm a mile or so back and was headed straight toward tipsyville.

"And dinner?"

He couldn't help but fish for compliments. You'd think he'd cooked her salmon himself. "Delicious," Charlie said with a smile.

Kieran watched her. The intensity of his attention compressed the air from Charlie's lungs and left her feeling a little shaky. Or maybe it was the wine. Either way, she was pretty sure that the best thing for her at this point was to finish eating and get her butt to bed.

They'd kept the conversation light throughout most of the meal. Charlie had almost forgotten that she was dining with a man who was on the radar of every law enforcement agency in this country and a few others. Kieran liked to showcase his sophistication, and the topics of conversation ranged from theater and ballet to music and art. He had Charlie beat on the high society chart. Not for the first time, she considered how much her dad would have loved Kieran if not for the whole international criminal thing.

"How did you get into the jewelry business?" Kieran twirled his wineglass by the stem. "Were your parents jewelers?"

"No," Charlie said with a laugh. "Why would you think that?"

"It's the sort of business that runs in families."

"Sort of like diamond smuggling?"

Kieran laughed. "Sort of."

"My dad's a lawyer." Some small measure of truth couldn't hurt. Kieran didn't know her real last name after all. "About as far from a jeweler as you can get."

Kieran regarded her. "What sort of law does he practice?"

Charlie sipped from her glass. "Corporate."

"So he's in it for the money?"

Kieran didn't mince words and Charlie wasn't going to downplay the truth. "Yep." She picked at her risotto, suddenly more interested in another glass of wine than getting food in her stomach. "That and the clout."

"How good is he at his job?" Kieran reached across the table and refilled Charlie's glass as though on cue.

Charlie brought the glass to her lips. "Very good."

"I doubt he was thrilled at his daughter's choice of profession, then."

Jeweler . . . black-market diamond broker . . . prosecuting attorney . . . They were probably equally heinous in her father's opinion. She took a good, long swallow of the crisp white wine. "No."

"But you think he'd respect you more if you brought home an impressive paycheck."

Wow. Charlie was beginning to think that Kieran might actually know her dad. "Probably." She couldn't seem to muster more than one-word responses. *Change of subject, please!*

"I can give that to you." The way Kieran promised her the world was seductive and a little slimy all at once. "I can give you the respect you deserve."

Charlie set her glass down on the table. Kieran was absolutely right. He just didn't realize how he was going to enable her to get it. She leveled her gaze to his and held it. "I'm counting on it."

The elevator doors slid open on the tenth floor. Mason let out a gust of breath as he stepped into the hallway and pulled the plastic key card out of his pocket. He'd been trying to get ahold of Charlie on her burner phone for the past half hour to no fucking avail. Why wasn't she answering? Where was she? Mason had damned near worried himself into an ulcer over it. Plus, he was tired, hungry, and so wound up that his head felt like it was going to spring right off his shoulders.

Katarina had proved to be quite a handful. Spoiled. Demanding. Exhausting. Horny as fuck. Oblivious to anyone *not* wanting her. Getting out of that club without damaging her precious ego had been a feat in itself. She'd offered him a job first. Then, her body. And when he hadn't expressed interest in either, she'd threatened to withhold payment for the diamonds and deposit his body in the nearest Dumpster.

It had taken more coddling than Mason thought he was capable of to let her down easy. He'd reluctantly admitted to her that his feelings for Charlie ran deeper than mere business acquaintances. Katarina had made the leap to assume that Charlie was interested in Kieran. And why not? Kieran was dangerous, suave, cocky, rich. Charming. The total package. At her core, Katarina was a romantic. A brokenhearted one. She sympathized with Mason's supposed unrequited love. In the end, she vowed to pay Mason every dime they'd agreed to and let him leave with an offer in parting. Her door was always open to him, should he change his mind.

He wanted to lay his fist into Kieran's gut for putting him in that position tonight.

Mason forced one foot in front of the other as he trudged toward his room. He rounded a corner and came to a complete stop not fifty feet from where Kieran had Charlie pressed against a door. Their mouths hovered less than an inch apart and Kieran's fingers were wound in the length of Charlie's shining, silky hair. They both turned and faced him at the same moment and the three of them stood there, staring in stunned silence.

What—the actual—fuck.

Kieran had the nerve to let loose a superior smile. Mason was going to pull the fucker's perfect, straight white teeth right out of his head. Charlie's eyes went wide. She ducked under Kieran's arm and hustled down the hallway to the spot where Mason stood rooted to the floor, as if she hadn't just been caught with her pants down.

Or at least she would've been if he'd shown up a few minutes later.

Seriously. *What the fuck?*

"What happened? What did she want?" Charlie searched Mason's face, her own pinched with worry. Her concern was a bitter gall considering what he'd just walked up on. He'd been worried out of his damned mind, wondering what had happened that she couldn't answer her phone. Of course she couldn't answer. Her hands had been too damn full of Kieran to handle anything else.

"Nothing happened." Mason forced his jaw to unclench, but it didn't soften the bite of his words. "She wired the money, I gave her the diamonds. End of story."

He wanted to tell Charlie something completely

different than the truth. That he'd bent Katarina over a table and fucked her so hard that neither one of them could walk straight. He wanted her to feel exactly what he felt right now. Like someone had just gutted him with a dull knife. Like he couldn't take a deep enough breath to fill his lungs. But she'd actually have to feel something for him in order to be hurt, wouldn't she?

Charlie's jaw squared. "It's been two hours. You're telling me that's all that happened?"

Mason didn't owe her an explanation. He didn't owe her a damned thing. "Yup."

Charlie glanced over her shoulder. Mason followed her line of sight to where Kieran leaned against the wall, watching them. The silence that stretched between them all grew more aggravating by the second. What a shitty-ass day. Mason was more than ready to put it behind him.

"I'm going to bed."

Kieran laughed. Arrogant asshole.

Charlie turned to face Mason, her brow furrowed. She brought her voice down to a murmur. "Don't you think we should talk about a few things first?"

Mason looked over her head at Kieran. "Nope." There were too many thoughts tangled up in his brain for Mason to hash any of this out tonight. His temper was hanging on by a thread as it was. He brushed past her, didn't dare look back.

Kieran continued to lean against the wall, arms folded across his chest. "Tough to satisfy, isn't she?" he remarked as Mason walked by.

Was he talking about Katarina, or Charlie? "Fuck you, Kieran."

Kieran's laughter trailed after him down the hallway. Mason stopped three doors down and shoved his key card into the slot. He pushed open the door and let it slam behind him, effectively drowning out the sound of Kieran's amusement.

Why in the hell had he ever agreed to this?

Mason stalked toward the bed. For someone who'd had no problem expressing her disdain for the criminal element, Charlie had sure cozied up to Kieran quickly. Jesus, he didn't even know why he was so twisted up about it. No, he *did* know. Because nice guys finished last. That's fucking why.

The blackout curtains were drawn over the windows, making Mason feel as though the walls of his room were closing in. He ripped them away and jerked open the sliding glass door that led out to the balcony, in order to let in some fresh air. It did little to clear his mind or slow the pounding of his pulse, but at least he no longer felt like climbing the walls.

"Your dad's going to shit a brick, you know that, right?"

Memories that Mason had spent years quashing resurfaced. Kieran had worn the same shit-eating grin that night as he did tonight. Too smug for his own fucking good.

"Which is why you're not going to tell him."

"Damn straight I'm not."

Mason watched Kieran count out the stack of bills. For the better part of two hours he'd been working the pool table, hustling unsuspecting jackasses who'd just cashed their paychecks for the week. Mason didn't want any part of it. He kept his distance from that shit. He was leaving for the academy in a few days and the last thing he needed was to get caught doing something underhanded with Kieran. It was bad enough he was Jensen Decker's kid. He didn't need any other dark marks on his already soiled reputation.

"He's gonna find out, though. I mean, no way can you keep your dirty secret forever."

Dirty secret? Jesus. "Since when is doing the right thing the wrong choice?"

"You tell me." Kieran chuckled as he folded the bills and shoved them in his pocket. "You're the one who doesn't want to tell Dad about it."

Dad. They weren't brothers by birth, but that didn't matter. After living with them for eight years, Kieran was as much Jensen's kid as Mason was. And Mason loved Kieran like a brother. But that didn't mean he could continue to condone Kieran's walking in their dad's footsteps.

"You don't have to keep doing this, you know." *Kieran chased the thrill just like his dad had done for years. Mason knew that thrill. He loved the rush of adrenaline as well. But he'd chosen to get his fix on the other side of the law.*

Kieran snorted. "What? Want me to be a cop like you?"

"I want you to not end up in jail." *Like Dad.*

"That's not going to happen," Kieran assured him.

"That's the thing," Mason said. "It will. It always happens. You think Dad ever thought he was going to get caught?"

Kieran's lips thinned and he averted his gaze. "I'm smarter than Dad."

Mason tipped the bottle of beer toward his mouth. "If you say so."

"You know what the worst part of this is?" Kieran asked. "It's that you obviously don't give a shit about me."

Once again, Kieran knew how to make everything about him. "This has nothing to do with you."

"You're cutting me out of your life."

Was he? Mason hadn't really considered that. "No, I'm not."

"You absolutely are." Kieran retrieved his bottle of Stella from the bar and drained it in a couple of swallows. "What do you think will happen once you put on that badge? We won't be hanging out, that's for damn sure. No one'll do business with me otherwise, and you'll have internal affairs up your ass on a daily basis." He signaled the bartender for another. "They'll make you turn on me."

Again, his overinflated ego molded Kieran's words. He obviously thought he'd be a big deal, make a name for himself within the syndicates. There wasn't a scrap of paperwork to connect Mason to Kieran. They were unofficially brothers. Kieran was a homeless, orphaned, street-hustler-in-training who'd managed to impress his dad. He'd become a part of their family, but as far as the state was concerned, Kieran Eagan might as well be a ghost.

"You know that'll never happen," Mason said.

"We'll see, brother," Kieran replied. "But don't forget, nice guys finish last."

Chapter Fifteen

Charlie wanted off this ride. She'd only been at it a week and the stress was starting to get to her. Her emotions swung on a pendulum. Her head ached. Her brain buzzed. And she was pretty sure she'd developed some nasty acid reflux.

There seriously weren't enough Tums in the world . . .

Letting Kieran down easily and getting rid of him for the night had been like trying to peel two pieces of duct tape apart. She'd finally managed to use too much wine as an excuse, and he'd reluctantly gone to his own room. Charlie let out a groan as she threw herself on the bed. She'd almost swallowed her tongue when Mason came around the corner and saw her and Kieran together. There was no way to put a positive spin on it. She knew what it had looked like.

But Mason had it *so* wrong.

Charlie pushed herself up from the bed and paced the confines of her room. Mason would interpret what he'd interrupted as a betrayal. She was sure his reaction to what he'd seen had nothing to do with any feelings he had for Charlie. Though she wouldn't deny that the notion of Mason being jealous of another man paying attention to her made her feel a little too warm and fuzzy.

This was about Kieran. Plain and simple. And the rivalry between them. Kieran was his Achilles' heel. The only chink in his armored exterior. Charlie needed Mason confident. Tough. The grim-faced hard-ass who didn't take shit off anyone.

How in the hell had she gotten caught in the middle of all this?

Screw it. Charlie wasn't going to spend the rest of the night wearing a path into the carpet worrying about what Mason may or may not have thought. She swiped her key card from the dresser and stalked out of the room. Her temper mounted with each step toward Mason's room. Who in the hell did he think he was? He'd dragged her into this mess and then had the nerve to be pissed when she was simply playing her part. He'd never shown an ounce of interest in her, and yet she'd spent the past week pining after him like some stupid lovesick girl. Mason Decker: the man, the myth, the legend. Charlie snorted. He and Kieran were exactly alike. Their egos wouldn't allow them to lose. And their personal battle was going to sink her investigation and her task force.

It was time to take back control.

Every ounce of stress she felt went into her fist as she pounded on Mason's door. Charlie waited. Waited. Brought her fist up and pounded again. Waited. Waited some more. And threw her foot into the door at the exact moment it swung wide.

The toe of her shoe connected squarely with Mason's shin. He let out a grunt and Charlie's hands flew up to her mouth. His brow crinkled with pain and anger and he drew in a sharp breath as he took a stumbling step back.

"Son of a bitch! Jesus, Charlie, what in the hell was that for?"

He deserved more than a kick to the shin for his shitty attitude, but Charlie wasn't about to tell him that. She pushed her way into the room and let the door close behind her. "We need to talk."

"Talk?" Mason's gorgeous eyes went wide. "You fucking kicked me."

"Yeah, well." She blew out a frustrated breath. "I didn't mean to kick you. What took you so long to answer the damn door?"

Again, Mason had the nerve to look shocked. "I was asleep. It's one o'clock in the fucking morning."

For the first time since barging in, Charlie realized she was standing face-to-face with a nearly naked Mason Decker. She took in the sight of his bare chest, packed with muscle, down the narrow taper of his waist, over the ridges of his abs, to the V that cut a path down his hips and disappeared into the waistband of his boxers. Her gaze lingered a little too long there and Mason cleared his throat. Charlie's head snapped up and she found his expression dark. His jaw formed a hard line.

Heat swamped her. Goddamn, he was hot when he was angry.

"I want to know what happened with Katarina tonight."

Okay, so it wasn't how she'd planned to start their conversation. It would have been better to begin by being a little less confrontational. Charlie didn't know how to handle herself around Mason. She'd never had trouble taking charge. Being assertive. Speaking her mind. But whenever he leveled his gaze on her, her mind went blank. Any ability to make well-thought-out decisions vanished. It was like she was twenty years old again. Flustered in the presence of a good-looking guy.

Pathetic.

His jaw flexed. "I already told you. Nothing."

Good Lord, he wasn't even fazed by his almost naked state. A flush heated Charlie's cheeks and she swayed on her feet. Maybe she had drunk a little too much wine . . . Would it kill him to put some damn clothes on?

"You were there for almost two hours," she pointed out.

Mason's gaze hardened. "I'm surprised you noticed. You seemed a little preoccupied yourself."

"What's that supposed to mean?" As if she didn't know.

Mason snorted. "You and Kieran were pretty damned cozy when I showed up. Isn't hooking up with a criminal you're trying to take down a violation of your pristine ethical code, Charlie?"

"Hooking up?" Her outrage was totally misplaced, but she couldn't help it. Mason had a way of setting her temper off. "I was *on the job.* How in the hell was I supposed to act?"

"I don't know," Mason mused. "Maybe like you weren't dying for him to get into your pants?"

Was he for real? The hard line of his jaw was begging for her palm. Kieran's room was at the opposite end of the hall, far from earshot, but Charlie still let her voice drop by a few decibels. "From the way Kieran made it sound, you were the one whose pants were getting into."

He cocked a brow and one corner of his mouth hitched.

Ugh! Charlie hated how she became an inarticulate fool the second she entered into an argument with Mason. She couldn't even form complete—not to mention coherent—sentences. His cool, self-possessed attitude drove her up a wall. Even angry and almost naked, he was practically unflappable.

She fixed him with a stern stare. "You know what I mean."

His expression didn't change. "Do I?"

Infuriating! "What did she want, Mason?"

He leaned in close. Charlie took his crisp, masculine scent into her lungs and held it for a moment. How dare he smell so good when she was trying to be mad at him?

"She offered me a job."

Charlie tipped her face up so that she could look at him. "Is that all?"

Mason shrugged.

Anger churned in Charlie's gut. Frustration clawed at her. Desire bloomed in her chest, so hot and thick that it choked the air from her lungs. She hated herself for wanting him. For feeling so out of control whenever he was around.

"You still answer to me." Charlie bucked her chin up a notch. "I'm still your boss."

Childish? Absolutely. But it beat admitting she was beyond attracted to him. Anything was better than that.

"Is that what you were doing with Kieran in the hallway earlier?" Mason's brow quirked. "Showing him who's boss?"

"I—he—you were—" She wanted to kick him in the other shin, just to release some of the tension that bound her muscles tight. "What in the hell was I supposed to do?"

"Maybe not drape yourself all over him, for starters."

The insinuation that she'd been all over Kieran and not the other way around sent Charlie's anger into a tailspin. "See it however you want, Mason. All you're

doing is deflecting so you don't have to answer my
questions about Katarina."

"Maybe." Sweet fiery hell. His unapologetic attitude
galled her more than anything.

Charlie squared her shoulders. "You should have
checked in."

"I did," Mason said without an ounce of inflection.
"Several times."

"No, you didn't."

His eyebrows arched curiously over his bright green
eyes. A silent challenge. "You probably didn't see the
missed calls since you were sort of occupied."

She hadn't checked her phone. Kieran had dominated their conversation during dinner and afterward.
He hadn't given her the chance to take a deep breath—
or even a quick bathroom break, for that matter—
before he'd ushered her up to their rooms and tried
to put the moves on her.

"I didn't see any missed calls from you." Petulance
wasn't going to win the argument, but she had to do
something to salvage her battered pride.

He took a step closer. "I don't doubt it."

How was he able to maintain that insufferable calm?
Charlie was ready to climb right out of her skin. She
wanted to shout, to let her temper explode. It seemed
the angrier she got the more level he became. It drove
her out of her mind, bat-shit insane.

Mason closed the space between them until mere
inches separated them. The heat from his body perme-
ated Charlie's thin blouse and she sucked in a breath.
"I don't *ever* want to see his hands on you again."
Mason's voice lowered to a dangerous growl. "I don't
want him within touching distance of you. Do you
understand me?"

No. Not even a little bit. Charlie's jaw set as she

made the decision to press her luck. "Why? What'll happen?"

"Without Kieran, you'll lose your precious task force and any hope of getting your hands on Faction Five, for starters." Mason's gaze darkened as he bent his head over hers. "Because if he so much as brushes against you again, it'll be the last thing he *ever* touches. Get me?"

If ever Mason had sounded like a world-class asshole, it was right now. He had no control over his own raging temper or the words that flew so carelessly from his mouth. Kieran had crossed a line tonight. He'd made a move on Charlie, and you could guarantee the son of a bitch had done it to spark Mason's jealousy. Kieran didn't lose. Ever. Even if that meant stomping all over his own family in the process. Mason had been down this road before with him. And none of them would be okay when they got to their destination.

Charlie's deep blue eyes widened at his words. Part shock, part indignation, and 100 percent outrage. His childish display had done nothing more than push her away. Rather than tell her how he felt about her, he treated her like a possession. Something he had the right to control. Women like Charlie couldn't be controlled. It was what Mason liked best about her. Instead of telling her that, he'd buried his admiration under the guise of his selfish, sudden, Neanderthal mandate.

Smooth.

"Get you?" Charlie's eyes went wide. Her cheeks flushed crimson, and fire lit in her eyes. "I don't even understand you! Whatever you *think* you saw out there, Mason—"

"I know what I saw." Charlie took a step backward

and Mason closed the gap. She wanted to distance herself from him, when she'd been chest-to-chest with Kieran earlier? Jealousy flared white-hot in Mason's chest. "He wants you." No question about it. "It just sort of shocked me to see firsthand that you wanted him too."

Charlie took another step back. He stepped forward. She wasn't scared, and her expression no longer blazed with fire. Instead, she dared him to come after her. The challenge sparked in her gaze and Mason accepted, and then some, as her back met the wall and he caged her in with his arms just as Kieran had earlier in the night.

Charlie tipped her head up toward him. Mason's gut clenched and his cock stirred at the sight of her, disheveled, angry, her mouth parted and her full lips practically begging to be kissed. Had she begged Kieran for the favor? The thought of her saying anything to him in her smoky tone, her eyes full of heat, made Mason want to march down to Kieran's room and put the son of a bitch in a choke hold.

"You think I want Kieran?" Her tone slid over him in a sensual caress that made Mason want to moan. "You must be as blind as you are stubborn if you think that."

His response was nothing more than a ragged whisper. "I know what I saw."

Charlie came up on her tiptoes. She put her mouth to Mason's ear and his gut clenched with lust. "You don't know *anything*, Mason."

Her sultry voice was a lick of heat down Mason's spine. His nostrils flared, his senses were awash with her scent, the heat of her body, her words, her proximity. Mason shouldn't want her. He shouldn't give a single shit about what—or who—she did. He should put as much distance between them as possible. Send her back to her room and make sure she didn't come within ten feet of either him or Kieran after tonight.

Mason crushed his mouth to hers. Relief washed over him. Finally giving in to what he wanted was like guzzling a gallon of water after a month in the desert. Charlie's arms wound around him. Her nails scraped the hair at the nape of his neck. Her breath became his as their mouths slanted, both of them desperate to deepen the kiss. He pressed his body against her and his hips gave an involuntary thrust. A low moan gathered in Charlie's throat and the sound hardened his cock to stone.

He wanted Charlie. And not because he knew Kieran wanted her. Not because he needed to take something from the man who'd been his brother. The man who'd taken his own father from him. And not for Mason's own stupid pride and ego. He wanted Charlie because the thought of not being with her, not seeing her, not hearing her voice, filled him with dread. He wanted her because he couldn't picture another day that didn't have her in it. He wanted her because she was the most beautiful, intelligent, brave woman he'd ever met. He wanted her because he didn't feel so goddamned empty when she was around.

He wanted her for the simple reason that he'd never wanted *anyone* with the same scalding intensity that he wanted her.

Mason let out a low groan as his hands wandered to Charlie's hips. He broke their kiss and spun her so that her back molded to his chest. He plucked at the buttons of her shirt, his fingers fumbling in his haste to get it off of her. She pulled her arms out of the sleeves and the garment fell to the floor with a whisper. His mouth found the juncture where her shoulder met her neck and Charlie shuddered. Her reaction spurred him on, and Mason let his open mouth, his tongue, explore the sweetness of her skin. His teeth grazed her delicate flesh. He reached up and cupped the generous swells of her breasts through the thin satin of her bra. Her nipples hardened under his fingertips. Charlie sucked in a sharp breath. Their bodies melded together and he ground the length of his erection against her ass. He needed to get her naked, to strip her down and devour every inch of her.

"Mason . . ."

He didn't want her to think. To let logic take hold. She'd try to see this rationally and she'd stop this before they even got started. "Let me have this, Charlie." His mouth met the delicate flesh below her ear. "Let yourself have it." Hell, Katarina could have killed them both tonight. Life was too damned short to go without. He kissed her throat. Her jaw. Her temple. "I think we've earned it."

She sucked in a sharp breath as his thumb brushed over the peak of one nipple. "We have." The low, husky murmur of her agreement quickened his blood. "And then some."

Since day one, Charlie had managed to get under Mason's skin. Bit by bit she'd burrowed so deep that she'd become a distraction. He needed to work her out of his system. Win a little of his focus and composure back. Giving in to his desires was the only way to regain his control over the situation. It was in both of their best interests that he was at 100 percent.

He hadn't just earned this. He *needed* it.

And it sent him over the edge of his restraint to know she needed it too.

Mason worked loose the button of the skinny-legged slacks that hugged her curves. Did she know how goddamned delectable she looked? How the sight of her turned him into a creature ruled by base desires? He eased the pants down over her ass and took a moment to appreciate the sight of her shimmying them the rest of the way down before she kicked them off along with her shoes. She wore a silky black thong that perfectly matched her bra. Her ass was a work of fucking art. He must have stared a beat too long because Charlie glanced at him from over her shoulder.

Her brow furrowed with doubt. "I figured I should dress the part from head to toe." He sensed her unease in the tenor of her words. Didn't she know how perfect she was? "Is it too much?"

"Charlie," Mason said on a breath. "The sight of you right now is enough to take a man to church."

Her nervous laughter made his chest ache. "I assume that's a compliment."

"It's the best compliment." Her body could cause an atheist to have a spiritual awakening.

In this hotel room, away from their mutual responsibilities and missions, Mason could pretend that they were free from everything that fettered them. Why not buy into their fantasies for a few hours? Tell reality to go to hell and live in the moment. He could be a smuggler. A cheat. A liar and a hustler. He could be a criminal. She could be all of those things as well. They could live dangerously. Recklessly.

Because tomorrow, Mason knew that reality would once again come crashing down on the both of them.

Chapter Sixteen

Charlie's brain had switched to autopilot the second Mason put her back to the wall. She hated to admit that it had taken her pretending to be a criminal to experience the most exciting week of her life, and it was only getting better as the night—well, technically morning—progressed.

Working undercover was like living in a parallel universe. One where someone as extraordinary as Mason Decker whispered heated things in her ear. Kissed her with the most sinful intent she'd ever experienced. Left a trail of flames on every inch of her skin that he touched.

Her passions had always been career-oriented. She'd never wanted someone with such immediate and blinding intensity.

He wound his fist in the hair at her nape and eased her head to the right. His mouth was a brand as it made contact with her neck. A moan gathered in Charlie's throat. The possessiveness of his grip, the way his mouth claimed her, sent a rush of excitement through her bloodstream. Her pussy clenched as though in anticipation of what might happen next. The breath hitched in her chest as his teeth grazed the sensitive skin below her ear. Charlie reached back to wrap her hands around his thighs. Her nails dug in and Mason groaned.

"When I'm done with you, you won't give Kieran another passing thought."

Kieran who? As far as Charlie was concerned, Mason Decker was the only man on the planet.

He continued to lick, bite, and kiss her neck. He kept one hand wound in the length of her hair and the other reached around to fondle her breast. Charlie arched into his touch, her nerve endings fired all at once and she was flooded with pleasure. There was nothing shy or tentative about the way Mason put his hands on her. With intent. He touched her as though he knew what it would evoke in her.

How much more could she take before Mason reduced her to a begging, quivering bundle of sensation and want?

"Tell me you want me, Charlie."

The words left her lips on a breath. "I do."

"Only me."

How could Mason possibly think there would be anyone else after this? "Only you."

He angled his body over hers and Charlie rested her forearms on the dresser as he bent her over. His hand abandoned her breast and she swallowed down a whimper of disappointment. His palm wrapped around her torso. Her eyes drifted shut from the delicious heat. Slowly, his fingers followed the contours of her body, to her hip and then over her ass. Her heart hammered in her chest, her breath raced as Mason fiddled with the tiny strip of lace at her crease and ran his fingers beneath it.

"Do you like that, Charlie?"

"God, yes." She could barely work the words past her lips.

He ventured lower, between her thighs. Mason's fingers teased her opening, skirted the sensitive outer lips of her labia and her clit. She'd never been touched so perfectly before. Charlie spread her legs wider in invitation but Mason continued to pet her slowly. Featherlight touches that stoked her desire without bringing her any relief. He dipped the tip of one finger inside of her. Just deep enough to further test her resolve.

"How about that?" he asked close to her ear.

This time, Charlie did nothing to stifle her moan. "Deeper." She didn't care if she sounded wanton. Her pussy ached, her clit throbbed. Mason continued to tease her, and the only thing that would bring her any measure of relief was his cock buried deep inside of her.

"Not yet," he murmured. "I want your walls down, Charlie."

He wanted her inhibitions obliterated? No problem. She was practically there already. "I don't beg." Mason might have Charlie where he wanted her, but she wasn't about to let him know it yet.

"You will," he assured her. "Give me a second."

Flames of desire licked at her and Charlie's stomach did a dazzling backflip. His mouth met the back of her neck once again and she shuddered. Her back arched as she tried to deepen the thrust of his finger, but Mason pulled back. He nipped her shoulder and the quick sting sent a rush of wetness between her thighs.

"Don't move."

A smile curved Charlie's lips. "Not an inch."

She and Mason both were used to being in charge.

Charlie enjoyed the power play. Encouraged it. She'd been prepared to march into this room tonight and take control. Instead, she'd given it all to Mason. And oh, God, did it turn her on.

Mason continued with shallow strokes of his finger. His hand splayed out across her ass and Charlie bucked as his thumb ventured higher up the crease to circle the opening and the tight ring of nerves. No one had ever touched her there before. Hell, no one had dared. The sensation wasn't unpleasant. Rather, the slow, easy circles he made around the opening enhanced Charlie's pleasure to the point that slow sobs built in her throat. Her hips rocked into the contact and Mason nipped at her shoulder once again.

She stilled as a thrill chased through her. Already this was the most intense, exciting encounter of her life, and they'd only just begun.

Charlie gripped the dresser as she tried to steady her careening world. Mason released his grip on her hair in favor of returning his attention to her breast. He pulled the cup of her bra down and teased her nipple to a stiff, aching peak. She cried out as pleasure crested within her, so many sensations that melded together to cast a haze of mindless pleasure over Charlie's brain.

Her only coherent thought was: *more.*

More of his mouth on her. More of his skillful touch. More of his commanding control that gave her no choice but to offer herself up to him.

With each gentle stroke of his fingers, Charlie's grip on the dresser tightened. Her muscles contracted to the point that she shook. Her breath came in quick pants. Every nerve ending in her body fired. She drowned in pleasure. How much more of this could she take before she broke apart?

As much as Mason wanted her to. He was in charge.

"I need to come." It wasn't a question of wanting anymore. She needed release like she needed food, water, *air*.

"Is that what you want, Charlie?" Mason's voice slithered over her in a low growl. "For me to make you come?"

He wanted her to beg. And for the first time in her life, pleading for something seemed not only to be her best option, but absolutely vital to her survival. His finger slid up to circle her clit and Charlie cried out. "Yes. Please."

She didn't have to see Mason's face to know he wore a smug, satisfied smile.

He pulled away. Bereft of his touch, Charlie's chest hollowed out. She didn't know she could miss something with such instant and resounding impact. When his hands found her hips, she wanted to cry out with relief.

Mason gripped the waistband of her thong and dragged it down her thighs. He went to his knees and Charlie's body went taut with anticipation. He brushed his thumbs over her swollen lips and up the crease of her ass before burying his face between her thighs.

Charlie's world spun out of control when his mouth covered her sex. He tongued her opening and a low whimper escaped her. The wet, silky glide of his mouth was heaven and hell all at once. A delicious torture that she couldn't get enough of.

"Oh my God, Mason."

His fingertips dug into the flesh at her hips. He held her still as he lapped at her pussy, slow, purposeful licks followed by deep, hungry sucks that made her cry out. He took her labia between her teeth and pulled gently away before releasing her from his mouth. Charlie had never experienced anything so intense. So damned visceral. So *wild*. His tongue explored every inch of her. He circled her clit before delving back into her pussy.

This moment had no comparison. Mason had no comparison. Tonight was a game changer. Who would have thought she'd have to take a walk on the opposite side of the law in order to get everything she'd ever wanted and more.

The first taste of her was heaven.

Being with Charlie wasn't simply scratching an itch, as Mason had suspected it would be. Instead, touching her, tasting her, coaxing sweet mewling sounds from her, had struck him with a sense of intimacy that left him shaken.

Instead of getting her out of his system, Mason worried that Charlie had worked her way deeper. Into his bones, his blood, every cell. This was no longer about a simple infatuation. It was an obsession.

And he wanted more.

He wouldn't be satisfied with simply a taste. Mason's cock throbbed in time with his heart, so damned hard that it hurt. He wanted to bury himself deep inside of her. Relieve himself of the desperate want that pooled in his gut like molten metal. He wanted to fuck her hard and deep, make her scream his name before she came apart. And when they'd both found release, he wanted to start all over again and build them back to this place where nothing mattered but the two of them and what they felt.

By the time the sun rose, Mason wanted Charlie to be irrevocably his.

Her thighs trembled against his cheeks as he swirled his tongue over her tight, swollen clit. He could make her come like this. Feel every spasm against his tongue.

God, he wanted to. Wanted that power over her. And not because it made him feel more like a man to have it. No, it was because Charlie had freely given it to him. Had entrusted him with her pleasure. To take care of her. She'd sacrificed her own power and given herself over to the moment. To the passion that swept them both up in its violent storm. Mason wanted her to come again and again. He wanted her so damned sated that it would ruin her for other men.

Selfish? Absolutely. But Mason had never claimed not to be.

Nothing mattered more to him than her pleasure. Mason lapped and sucked at her pussy, grazed the sensitive flesh with his teeth. Charlie's cries grew more impassioned, her breaths heavy. She arched her back, pressed herself against his mouth. Her hips rolled with every thrust of his tongue.

"Don't stop, Mason. I'm almost there."

He wasn't about to stop.

Charlie's body went still and Mason increased the pressure of his tongue on her clit. She gasped, the sound accompanied by a low moan as the orgasm vibrated through her thighs. Her pussy contracted against Mason's mouth and he continued to lap at her, drawing out her pleasure for as long as possible. The sound of her desperate moans echoed through the hotel room. It bounced around in Mason's head, filling him with a sense of smug accomplishment that he could evoke that reaction in her.

Her cries grew silent and Charlie collapsed against the dresser. Mason kissed the backs of her thighs, the perfect globes of her ass. He stood and kissed his way up her spine, across to one shoulder and then the other. He kissed the back of her neck. Below her ear. Her temple. He could kiss her for hours.

"I'm Jell-O." Charlie's low laughter sent a shiver over Mason's skin. "I'm going to have to be hauled out of here on a luggage cart tomorrow."

"We're just getting started." Mason unfastened the clasp of her bra and guided the straps down her arms. "You have no idea what Jell-O feels like yet."

She let out a contented sigh. "Are you saying it gets better?"

"I told you"—Mason smoothed her hair away and put his mouth to her neck once again—"I'm going to make sure that you never think of another man after tonight."

"There are other men . . . ?" The low, sensual purr of Charlie's voice was enough to renew the surge of lust that coursed through him. "I had no idea."

He loved her dry wit. Mason was dead serious, though. When they left this room in the morning, there would be no doubt in Charlie's—or Kieran's—mind who the better man was.

Mason took Charlie's hand. As she stood and turned to face him his breath stalled. Her cheeks were flushed with color, making her eyes seem so much bluer. The strawberry-blond locks of her hair framed her face in a wild tangle. Even her lips seemed redder. Fuller. Begging to be kissed again.

Charlie's shoulders hunched as she brought her arms in front of her and her knees turned inward. Her gaze dropped low and to the right. Was she trying to hide her body? Good Lord, the thought of her hiding any part of herself was downright criminal.

"Let me see you." Mason took her hands in his and guided her arms away from her body. She kept her eyes pointed at the floor. "Charlie. Look at me."

Slowly, she brought her gaze to his. For the first time

since he'd met her, her expression was unsure. Charlie Cahill, who took down crime syndicates and smugglers. Who whipped an entire staff of seasoned agents into submission with nothing more than a withering stare. Charlie, who walked into a den of Russian mobsters and owned the room as though they worked for her, not the other way around. This woman, who exuded so much confidence, could barely meet his eyes when he took in the glory of her naked body.

"You're the most beautiful woman I've ever seen." Mason hoped his words conveyed the reverence he felt. "God, Charlie. You're fucking perfect."

She looked away. "I'm not."

Mason guided her face back to his. "You are." He kissed her slowly. "Your mouth is perfect." He let his fingertips wander over her collarbone before they dipped to her upturned breasts. He took their weight in his hands and brushed the pads of his thumbs over the points of her nipples. "Your breasts are fucking amazing." A corner of her mouth hitched into a seductive half smile. Jesus, she didn't have a clue how enticing she was. His hands wandered lower, over the flare of her hips to her ass. "This ass is a masterpiece," he said. "I want to have it bronzed."

"You do not."

"The hell I don't. I'd cast those fantastic cheeks and have it on my wall by tomorrow if you'd let me."

Charlie's answering laughter loosened the tightness in his chest. "That would be quite the conversation piece."

"Priceless."

A flush rose to her cheeks. How many men had told Charlie that she was beautiful? Sensual? Desirable? Mason would tell her every day for the rest of her life if she looked at him with the same heat that smoldered in her eyes right now.

She didn't say another word. Instead, Charlie leaned in and kissed him. Mason's lips parted as her tongue darted between his lips. He swallowed down her contented moan as she deepened the kiss. His arms went around her as her fingers dove into his hair. Her kisses were precise. Languorous. Slowly, they built into something more frenzied and urgent. The flames of their passion blazed white-hot once again and Charlie murmured against his mouth, "I want you."

It was Mason's turn to feel a pleasant rush from the compliment. "You can have me." She could have any damned thing she wanted from him. All she had to do was ask.

Charlie pulled away. Mason resisted the urge to pull her back to him, to revel in the petal softness of her skin on his. She led him by the hand toward the bed and Mason followed. He was helpless to do anything but what she wanted. The realization shook Mason to his foundation. So far gone to Charlie, he'd trade his own goddamned high moral standards for a few minutes with her. He'd already run headlong toward a life he'd turned his back on for her. What else would he do before it was all said and done?

She stopped at the foot of the bed. Mason swallowed a groan as she pulled her full bottom lip between her teeth. Indecision marred her delicate features for a moment before she reached down and slid his boxers over his hips and down his thighs. Her eyes widened as her gaze raked him from head to toe. The admiration that flared there caused Mason's cock to harden to stone. He kicked his boxers the rest of the way off and stood still for her appraisal.

She glanced up at him from beneath lowered lashes. So coy. And so goddamned sexy. "Talk about a masterpiece."

A rush of pure lust shot through him. Tonight with her wouldn't be enough, and he knew it. Mason wouldn't be satisfied until all of Charlie's nights belonged to him.

Every last one.

Chapter Seventeen

No one had ever made Charlie feel as though she burned from the inside out. And never had anyone helped her to feel so comfortable in her own skin. So confident in her sex appeal. Mason made her feel beautiful. Sensual. Wanted.

Bold.

With the same detailed attention he'd bestowed on her, Charlie kissed Mason's neck, sucking gently before grazing him with her teeth. She kissed her way to the hollow of his throat, where her tongue dipped briefly before she went lower, across his collarbone, over the muscled hills of his pecs, down the firm ridges of his abs. Her hands wandered to his back and her fingers traveled the groove of his spine cut into the muscles there. Charlie's gaze settled at the V at the juncture of his hips and thighs. She ran the flat of her tongue along one deep slash, and Mason's body went taut. A satisfied smile curled her lips as she repeated the action on the other side.

He groaned.

"You're going to drive me crazy if you keep that up."

"I owe you," she murmured against his skin. Another

lick. "Your tongue just did some pretty wonderful things to me."

Charlie's hands glided down the small of Mason's back to cup his ass. She dug in with her nails. Mason grunted as he gave an involuntary thrust of his hips. Her hands moved lower as she went to her knees, her nails scraped the backs of his thighs before coming around to the front. She eased him backward and he settled at the foot of the bed.

In the courtroom, Charlie's skills could never be called into question. In the bedroom . . . she wasn't as sure. She wanted to give Mason what he'd given her only moments before—earth-shattering pleasure that left him out of breath and shaking. She wanted him to remember tonight for the rest of his life. Because Charlie already knew she'd never forget it.

Her eyes met Mason's. She lost herself in the endless green depths. His nostrils flared and his jaw squared. He reached out and threaded his fingers through her hair. Charlie held her breath. Waited for his grip to tighten, to make her feel that sense of being possessed that caused a thrill to chase through her veins.

The freedom she felt at giving over her control was an aphrodisiac she hadn't expected. Mason was a temptation she hadn't anticipated. Nothing had gone according to plan since the day she'd stepped on that elevator and come face-to-face with his grim countenance. And still, she wouldn't have it any other way. His fist wound tighter in her hair and her heart beat madly in her chest. Gently, he urged her where he wanted her to go and Charlie was more than willing to follow his lead.

She took the hard, silken length of him in her hand before flicking out with her tongue at the swollen head of his erection. Mason sucked in a sharp breath and groaned on the exhale. The muscles in his thighs bunched and flexed as he caged her between them. Charlie took him deeper into her mouth, just to the crown, and sucked gently. He'd teased her. Enticed her. Brought her to the point of begging. Could she do the same to him? Could she shatter his inhibitions as he'd done to her?

There was only one way to find out.

Mason leaned back on the mattress and braced himself with his free arm. Charlie came up higher on her knees and took him deeper into her mouth, sucking hard before pulling back and letting her teeth scrape over the sensitive tip. She dared a quick glance up at him from beneath lowered lashes and heat pooled in her belly when she found his attention focused on her. She kept her eyes on his. Flicked out with her tongue once again. Mason's eyes widened and the muscles in his stomach twitched reflexively.

Winning her first case couldn't rival what she felt right now, knowing that she evoked that intense reaction in him.

She continued to build that passionate response with light passes of her tongue, gentle suction before taking him deeper and hollowing her cheeks as she increased the pressure of her mouth. Charlie was sure to keep her pace slow and easy. Lazy. As though there was nowhere else she'd rather be than lounging between his thighs.

There was something decidedly illicit about the way his hips pumped with each dip of her head. The way his fist released and contracted as it gripped her hair and held her right where he wanted her. Low grunts and groans that quickened the blood in her veins and made her thighs slick with arousal.

Charlie's fingers once again found the base of Mason's

cock. His free hand came to rest on top of hers and he urged her to take his girth in her fist and squeeze. "That's it," he said between panted breaths. "Don't stop." His hips bucked as she took him deeper into her mouth. "Just like that." His words were nothing more than a low growl. He kept his other fist in her hair and thrust even deeper into her mouth.

The glide of him between her lips bordered on euphoric. His crisp scent and salty taste only added to her enjoyment of his body. It became a sensory experience. The sight, sound, taste of him drove her mad with want. She took him as deeply as she could. Swirled her tongue against his shaft as she sucked. She worked her mouth up and down his length, increasing her pace until Mason's breath came in ragged pants that caused a swarm of butterflies to swirl in Charlie's stomach. His muscles grew taut, his thighs began to quake. Anticipation coiled within her. She'd brought him to the edge of his control and she couldn't wait for him to topple over.

Mason leaned forward. His hand abandoned her hair to cup the back of her neck as he held her still. Charlie tipped her head up to look at him. His brow was pinched as it came to rest against hers and his breath came in heavy pants that brushed her face. "I need to fuck you," he said in a desperate whisper. "Now."

Charlie wasn't about to argue. Her own desires had been rekindled and burned with the heat of an unchecked wildfire.

Mason pulled her up to her feet. His mouth descended on hers in a crushing kiss that left her breathless and wanting more. When he let go of her to cross the room, she wrapped her arms around her middle as though to hold in the heat of his body that he'd taken away. He retrieved his wallet from the bedside table, pulled out a shiny metallic packet and tucked it between his fingers. His gaze smoldered as he strode back to where Charlie stood, every step precisely placed. Mason Decker truly was a living, breathing work of art. She wanted to pinch herself. Just to make sure she wasn't dreaming.

"My dad always told me, never leave the house without two things: a condom and bail money."

Charlie laughed. "Sort of a sordid combination, don't you think?"

Mason's gaze darkened, but a wry smile curved his full lips. "He wasn't exactly good at the whole fatherly advice thing."

Charlie's heart ached for Mason. She could only imagine what his life had been like growing up. The things he'd seen. Taken part in. The choices he'd been forced to make. That he'd wound up the exact opposite of Kieran—of his own father—was a feat in itself. He hadn't succumbed to the glitz and glamour of the criminal lifestyle Jensen had tried to sell to him. Instead, Mason had formed his own opinions and morals. He'd taken the high ground when his upbringing suggested otherwise. For that, Charlie had nothing but a deep admiration and respect.

There was so much more to Mason than anyone saw. She'd gotten a glimpse of it, though. It warmed her heart to think that he deemed her worthy. And it forged an intimacy between them she wasn't sure she was prepared to feel.

Mason rounded the bed and came to a stop inches from her. He bent his head over hers and inhaled deeply. "God, you smell good."

She didn't think she'd ever get enough of the compliments that flowed so effortlessly and honestly from his lips. "You can thank my shampoo." Accepting those compliments didn't come quite as easily for her.

"No," Mason said with a laugh. "It's not your shampoo." He ran his nose down her temple and Charlie's head tipped back as though she had no other choice. He inhaled again at her throat before putting his mouth to her. "You smell like the ocean. Salty and clean." He kissed her again and she shivered. "You smell like sex." He took her hand and guided it to his stiff cock. "See what you do to me, Charlie? Feel how hard I am for you."

She took him into her hand and stroked from the tip to the thick base.

"Do you want me to fuck you, Charlie?"

Her stomach did a backflip before it drifted back into place. "Yes."

"Tell me you want me."

They'd played this game before, but Charlie was happy to indulge him. Especially because every word from her mouth was the truth. "I want you."

"Only me."

"Only you."

"Good."

He shouldn't have needed to hear those words from her yet again. It wasn't like Mason was some untested, unsure pup. Doubt scratched at the back of his mind. There was a piece of him that had always felt empty. Somehow, Charlie managed to fill that space tonight. It made Mason greedy for more. He couldn't kiss her enough, taste her enough, touch or take her scent into his lungs enough. He vowed she'd be ruined for any other man after he was through with her, but it was he who had been ruined.

He was goddamned lost. To her.

Mason pulled her close. Her eyes, clear and endless blue, stared back at him. Her lips, so inviting, parted on a breath. He brushed the pad of his thumb across the flawless blushed skin of her cheek and let his fingers wander to the wavy strands of strawberry blond that framed her face. She was everything he could have ever wanted. He refused to acknowledge that once they got back to San Francisco, the spell would be broken.

His mouth found hers in a slow and sultry kiss. Mason's need for her burned like a cinder in his gut, pulsed through his veins like molten lead, and ate away at his chest. If he didn't fuck her—didn't take her hard and deep right now—he'd go out of his damned mind. There would be time for softly spoken words and gentle caresses later. Now, he had to purge this damnable need from his system before he cracked.

Charlie answered his kisses with building fervor and intensity. Her mouth slanted across his, her tongue traced his bottom lip before sliding against his in a sweet, slippery tangle. His cock throbbed hot and hard, his muscles burned with unspent energy. The heat of her skin met his, her lush breasts pressed into his chest. The head of his cock brushed the crease of her thighs and Mason groaned into her mouth.

He turned and took her down to the mattress. Charlie let out a squeal of surprise and the brilliance of her smile rivaled the sun. He kissed her petal-soft lips, her cheek, her shoulder. His mouth found her breast and he sucked her nipple before dragging his teeth over the sensitive peak. Charlie gasped as she arched into the contact, her expression blissful as her eyelids drifted shut.

Mason came up on his knees, tore open the packet and rolled the condom on with a groan of relief. He couldn't wait to take her. To join their bodies once and for all. He trembled with need as he settled himself between her thighs and braced himself with one arm beside her as he guided his cock between her parted legs and probed at her opening.

Charlie's hips rolled up to meet him and he thrust home. Their mutual sounds of relief surrounded him. She needed this as badly as he did. He stilled inside of her, almost fearful to move, to break the spell that held them both suspended in the moment. She squeezed him tight, her inner walls clenching around his girth.

"Charlie, look at me."

Her eyes fluttered open and Mason brushed her hair away from her face. He held her gaze as he moved slowly over her, shallow thrusts of his hips that caused Charlie's lips to part as she drew in tight little breaths. She was so beautiful like this: flushed with passion and completely undone. His lips found all of the places he'd already explored. Charlie's legs wrapped around the backs of his thighs and her heels dug in as she urged him to go deeper. Swept up in a whirlwind of passion, Mason obliged, grinding his hips against hers as he buried himself to the hilt. She drew in a gasping breath that released on a low, sultry moan. With every press of his hips, her clit slid against his shaft, intensifying the sensation.

There wasn't a thrill in the world that could compare to fucking Charlie. Mason thought he'd known excitement, but his life up until now was a pale representation. Adrenaline coursed through his veins, his heart pounded in his chest. Their panting breaths and low moans accompanied the sounds of their bodies meeting and parting in the quiet room. They had been reduced to creatures of frenzied, raw want and need.

They shared the same goal and Mason was going to get them both there.

"Harder, Mason," Charlie panted. "It feels so good."

Good didn't cover it by a long shot. Mason didn't think there was a word in any language to properly convey what he felt right now. He wrapped his arms around her, anchored her body to his own as he fucked her hard and deep, purging himself of the emptiness that had consumed him until the day Charlie walked into his life.

Charlie pushed up and rolled them until Mason was on his back. Her thighs lined up with his and her heels pressed against him as she began to ride him. The sight of her straddling his cock, her breasts swaying with every roll of her hips, her flushed skin, her hair like a wild summer sunset, blinded him with lust. He settled his hands at her waist and pulled her down hard, thrusting upward to take her as deeply as he could. Charlie gasped, her head rolled back on her shoulders.

She reached down and guided his hands to her breasts. "You're going to make me come," she said between pants of breath. "Don't stop."

Never. He molded his palms to the perfect roundness of her and squeezed gently. Charlie moaned her approval and he upped the ante, rolling her tight nipples between his fingers. Her head snapped up and her eyes went wide. Charlie cried out as she came, deep wracking sobs of pleasure. Chills broke out over her skin and he let his hands roam over the raised flesh that covered her arms, torso, the backs of her thighs. Her pussy clenched him tight and a rush of warmth bathed his cock.

"That's it, Charlie," he crooned as she rode out her pleasure. "Come for me."

With every cry from her lips, every tight contraction

of her body, she brought him closer to his own release. Mason fucked her with abandon. His hips bucked. His fingers gripped her. He pulled her down hard over his cock. His sac tightened, pressure built at the base of his shaft and a rush of sensation exploded through him as he came. One wave crashed after another. A violent storm of pleasure blasted through him. Mason's back came up from the mattress and he buried his face in the crook of Charlie's neck. Ragged breaths escaped his lungs and he wrapped his arms tight around her as he slowly came down from his own euphoric high.

Fucking amazing.

For what felt like forever, they simply held each other. Charlie's fingers threaded through his hair and Mason shivered at the contact. Her breath brushed the outer shell of his ear and she whispered, "I can't wait to do that again."

Mason's rumbling laughter filled the silence. That made two of them. "I can do better," he promised. "You'll see."

She pulled away to look at him. Her sly smile was the most seductive thing he'd ever seen. "Better?" She cocked a skeptical brow. "Are you implying that you were holding out on me?"

"Not exactly." Mason felt his own lips tug into a silly grin that he couldn't suppress. "But I'm a firm believer that practice makes perfect."

Her smile dimmed a fraction. "You must have had a lot of practice, then."

The truth was, he hadn't. Mason's career had always been more important than his sex life. Aside from a few random girlfriends here and there, Charlie had been the first woman he'd been with in almost a year. "Not really," he replied. "I'm just obsessed with impressing you."

She smiled. "Oh yeah?"

"Yeah." He took a few errant strands of her hair between his thumb and forefinger and stroked the silken length. He was absolutely obsessed with her hair as well. The color, the texture, everything. "Are you? Impressed?"

"I think I can safely say that now I truly know what Jell-O feels like. Does that answer your question?"

He kissed her once. Slowly. "We have a few more hours before we have to get ready to fly out. Let's shoot for making you feel like something a little less solid this time."

Charlie's smoky laughter stirred his lusts once again. "Like I said, they'll have to wheel me out of here on a luggage cart."

"I take it that means you're up for the challenge?"

She leaned in and took his earlobe between her teeth before drawing it into her mouth and sucking. "Absolutely."

Chapter Eighteen

Mason stared up at the ceiling. His brain wouldn't settle down enough to allow him to sleep. The warmth of Charlie's hand splayed over his chest, her body tucked close to his, her head resting on his shoulder, comforted him. The even rise and fall of her breath as she rested was a welcome distraction from the thoughts that plagued him.

He'd chosen his path a long time ago, just like Kieran had. So why did he suddenly feel so guilty about the way everything was going down?

"Did you know my dad's a lawyer?" Her sleepy voice sliced through the silence.

Mason wrapped his arms tighter around her. "He is?"

"Yeah. Corporate law. He wanted me to join his firm after I passed the bar."

Apparently Mason wasn't the only one in a contemplative mood. "Why didn't you?"

Charlie let out a slow sigh. She traced a pattern over his left pec and he let out a sigh of his own at the pleasant sensation. "I sort of resented him for pushing me into law in the first place. I guess I figured if I was going to be this thing that he'd molded me to be, I was at least going to choose how I pursued it."

He and Charlie were more alike than he'd thought. "Was he disappointed?" If Charlie's dad was anything like Mason's, there was no question how he felt. "That you chose criminal law?"

"Devastated," she said with a quiet laugh. Their hushed voices penetrated the darkness, binding them together in something that Mason knew he would never be able to disentangle himself from. "You would have thought I'd decided to become a drug dealer or something. He said if I was going to practice criminal law, the least I could do was become a defense attorney. That I could make a name for myself taking on high-profile cases."

"No guts, no glory, huh?"

"No glory, no money," Charlie replied drily. "Civil servitude wasn't what my dad had wanted for his daughter. Probably because his own reputation would take a hit. I could single-handedly prosecute and put away every criminal in the country and it wouldn't be enough to impress him."

"When my dad found out I was entering the academy, he shit a brick." Mason still remembered that visit. It was the last time he'd seen him until a couple of weeks ago. His dad's expression of betrayal and disgust was burned in his memory. "He called me a traitor, accused me of siding with the people who'd put him away. He even asked if I'd tipped the cops off before they arrested him. He said I was conforming to a system designed to keep people like us down. That Kieran was his true son—the only person in his life still loyal. I didn't talk to him again after that. I wrote him a couple of letters. Tried to open up the line of communication. He ignored me, though. Didn't want to have anything to do with me until a couple of weeks ago."

It sucked that he'd been made to feel like a disappointment for not following in his dad's footsteps. And Charlie had felt the same way. Whatever happened to loving your kids unconditionally?

"Did you?" Charlie's voice was little more than a whisper. "Tip off the police?"

Mason let out a soft snort. "No. He got caught because he let his ego get the best of him. That's how they all get caught. But they never acknowledge it. It's always someone else's fault, you know? It's never their wrongdoing. It's society's stupid laws. Someone's always got it out for them. I can't tell you how many times I heard it growing up. 'I'm just tryin' to make a living. What's so wrong with that?'"

Charlie put her lips to Mason's shoulder. The gentle kiss caused his stomach muscles to clench and his cock to stir. "Following your own path was brave, Mason. I wish I could have done that."

"What would you have done?" He couldn't help but wonder what interested Charlie. He wanted to know everything about her. "If you weren't working for the DOJ right now, what would you be doing with your life?"

"I honestly don't know." The sadness of her tone sliced through him. "For as long as I can remember, my dad hammered law school into my brain. I didn't have time for fun growing up because I was always studying. I wouldn't get into a decent college or a good law school if I let my focus slip. I didn't date. I didn't play sports. I didn't even really have girlfriends. I hit the books all the time. I worked toward my dad's goal for me without ever once wondering what it was that I wanted for myself."

Mason might have lost his family in the process, but he was glad he'd had the balls to follow his heart. His dad's lifestyle had never sat well with him. When Jensen was teaching him and Kieran how to properly forge a master's artwork, or how to effectively hustle someone, Mason had secretly resented it. It bothered him to think that his dad and Kieran shared the same pride and ego. That their disdain for the law equaled Mason's respect for it.

"How do you feel about it now?" Did Charlie feel as trapped in her life as Mason sometimes felt in his? There were days when he needed an escape so badly that he considered changing his name and finding a jungle somewhere to disappear into.

He felt her shrug against him. "The same way I felt about it then, I guess. Like I have no choice but to keep going. Keep proving myself. Beat my dad at his own game."

Mason knew all about that. He'd been trying to prove a point to his dad for fifteen years. Hell, longer. "You'll never live up to his standards." He had plenty of experience in that department. "So why even try?"

Charlie drew in a slow breath. "Because if I'm not the best, then my entire life has been wasted. If I don't have any bragging rights at all, when I look back at all of the years I spent on *his* dream, I'll realize what I've lost, and it'll break me."

"Life is what *you* make it, Charlie. Not what other people make for us."

"Is that why you're doing this now?" she asked. "To prove that your father and Kieran have absolutely no influence on your life?"

Okay, so he was a bit of a hypocrite. Sure, Chief Deputy Carrera had come to Mason specifically because of his connection to Kieran. He'd been maneuvered. Leveraged. And maybe at the end of the day none of them were more upstanding or righteous than his dad, Kieran, or any of the people they associated with. Mason had been living in his dad's—and Kieran's—shadow for most of his life. The stigma of his family had kept him from moving up the ranks with the San Francisco PD. It had nixed his chances at being accepted into the U.S. Marshals. It had landed him a job with Customs and Border Patrol and he'd spent nearly a decade pretending to live the criminal life, setting up smugglers and thieves in order to bring people just like Kieran to justice. Rather than allowing him to escape his upbringing, everyone in Mason's life had used his past to benefit them. Just like now.

"Maybe I should take some of my own advice once in a while."

"Why did you take this job, Mason?" Charlie brought her head up as though she could read the truth in his expression through the dark. "I read your file. You got screwed."

At least someone besides him was willing to admit it. "For the same reason you work so hard to win every single case that comes across your desk," Mason said. "I want to prove my dad and Kieran wrong. I want them to know that they didn't win."

Charlie reached up and cupped his cheek. "Win what?"

Mason let out a bark of disdainful laughter. "I don't know."

"Everything is black and white for us," Charlie said softly. Her voice was like a caress, reaching out through the dark to tickle Mason's senses. "Right or wrong. There's no in-between. We can't be compromising because there's no room for compromise. Guys like Kieran, like your dad, and even Katarina, they live in the gray. They have the sort of freedom that we don't. They can be as compromising as they want because they make the rules as they go. That's why we fight back, Mason. Not necessarily because it's the right thing to do, but because it's not fair that they get all of the leeway and we get none."

"You're beginning to think like a criminal."

"Not beginning," Charlie said. "I've always felt this way. It's not fair that I have to follow the rules and they don't. That's why I fight so hard to put them away. Because I'm jealous of that freedom. I've never had it easy, so why should they? It's childish and petty, I know. I've never told anyone that. But it's the truth."

Her trust in him caused Mason's chest to swell with emotion. "It was my dad's lack of conscience that got to me." Kieran had always teased Mason for being a bleeding heart. "He didn't care who he hurt, who he swindled or stole from. He always found a way to justify what he did. *They have insurance*, or *The guy's got millions, what does it matter if I free him of a few hundred thousand?* or *It's not my fault if they're too stupid not to know they're getting a forgery.*" Mason filled his lungs with air and held his breath for a moment before letting it all rush out. "I don't think getting ahead is a good enough excuse. People struggle all the time. They grow up disadvantaged. And not all of them are out there running cons."

Charlie pushed herself up until her face was inches from him. "You're a good man, Mason. Probably the best I've ever known."

* * *

Charlie had known early on that there was so much more to Mason than the stern-faced, cranky, take-no-shit persona he let everyone see. They had more in common than she ever would have guessed, and yet she knew that at the end of the day, Mason was the better person. His standards were so high Charlie could only aspire to reach them.

"I want to be," Mason said. The deep timbre of his voice rumbled through her, and Charlie shivered. "But I'm just as selfish as Kieran and my dad are. I made a promise to Kieran that what I did would never come between us. I should have walked away from Carrera's offer. Instead, I'm using Kieran so I can get what I want."

"It's for the greater good," Charlie assured him.

Mason snorted. "Is it?"

"Yes." She believed that. It's why she was so damned passionate about this task force. "Honestly, I don't know why or how Kieran got involved with Faction Five, but they're bad news, Mason. It doesn't matter that they're white-collar criminals. That they're educated and sophisticated. They're hiding behind positions of power and abusing that power for monetary gain. And who's that going to hurt? Everyone. It's a tear in the very fabric of the law. It's the worst sort of entitlement and it shows people like Kieran that their disdain for the system is justified. It'll open the door for terrorists and political usurpers to join their ranks and enjoy the same sort of autonomy. This group has to be stopped before they amass any sort of legitimate power. So what if you benefit from it? Stopping them isn't selfish. It's *necessary*."

"This isn't like Kieran." It was the first time Charlie had ever heard Mason speak of him with honest affection. "He's always worked alone. Syndicates aren't his thing. Especially if it means giving them any power over him. He's a free spirit. He doesn't take anything seriously."

"Maybe he's tired of gaming the system on his own." Charlie didn't know much about Kieran, but she agreed with Mason. Answering to a syndicate didn't seem like something he'd enjoy. "Faction Five could offer him a layer of protection that he's never had before."

"Could be." Mason didn't sound convinced. "He doesn't do anything without first having a good reason. But this syndicate . . ." He blew out a breath. "It doesn't make any sense. It's not Kieran's style. I just don't understand how he got mixed up with them."

Charlie settled herself against Mason's chest. "Do you think he's under duress?"

"No one forces Kieran to do anything," Mason said. "It's part of his charm."

She laughed. "Are you going to be able to go through with this?" Charlie had been concerned from the start, but now that she knew Kieran, had seen him and Mason together, she wondered if he'd be able to continue to manipulate the man who was as close to him as a brother.

"Yes." There wasn't an ounce of doubt in Mason's response. "He knows what he is and he knows who I am. I think we both realized it would come down to this someday. We couldn't keep our lives separate forever. Whatever happens, I'm ready for it."

Charlie hadn't thought twice about using Mason to gain Kieran's trust and infiltrate Faction Five. Her only concern had been the win. Now, though, guilt pulled at her chest when she thought of what she and the U.S.

Marshals office had asked him to do. What they'd held over his head in order to get his cooperation. In the end, were they any better than Kieran? Mason seemed to be the only innocent person in all of this.

"If anyone deserves to get something good out of this, it's you."

"I'm not a saint, Charlie."

She smiled at the humor in his tone. Somehow, she doubted it. "Tell me one thing you've ever done that was bad."

"Okay. When I was thirteen, I painted a reproduction of one of Van Gogh's *Irises*. My dad sold it to a collector for a quarter million dollars."

Charlie nearly choked on her intake of breath. "You're kidding me?"

"Nope. I did a damn good job."

Jensen Decker was a well-known forger. Charlie had never suspected that his son had inherited his artistic talent. "Did you know he was going to sell the painting?"

"Of course. He told me the money was going into my *college fund*."

Charlie figured it hadn't been the first time his father had told him something like that. "What happened to the money?"

She felt Mason shrug against her. "Who knows? Dad had a knack for spending money faster than he could make it."

"Have you ever painted anything that was an original?"

Mason's fingers brushed her bare shoulder. The simple up-and-down motion coaxed goose bumps to the surface of Charlie's skin and caused a rush of warmth to flood her. His touch evoked an instant reaction in her, and her mind drifted to their earlier heated moments. She couldn't feel an ounce of shame that even after exhausting herself, she was more than ready to have him inside of her again.

"Sometimes I paint when I'm stressed out," he said. "I never hang anything, though. It's more just for me. I'm not looking for any attention for it."

So humble. Charlie went balls out for glory, and Mason lived his life as low-key as he could. If she had anything to be ashamed of, it was her own ambition.

"I'd like to see your paintings sometime."

"Oh yeah?" His tone became sly and Charlie couldn't help but smile. "Trying to find a way inside my bedroom, huh?"

"Is that where you keep the paintings?"

"In my closet."

"Then, yes." Charlie splayed her hand over the bulging muscle of one pec. "I'm definitely trying to find a way into your bedroom."

Mason bent his head over hers and kissed her. Gone was the frenzied, passionate urgency that had consumed them before. He savored her mouth. Kissed her slowly and thoroughly. His hands explored her body, unhurried. Charlie settled down onto the pillow and Mason slid down beside her. They kissed in the darkness. Mouths meeting, tongues brushing, breaths melding into one. They touched. Stroked and caressed each other until the flames of their passion rekindled. And still, Mason took his time with her. His fingers dipped between her thighs and slid between her slick folds.

He teased her. Enticed her. Whispered dirty, heated things close to her ear. He tasted her mouth, her throat. Kissed his way down her stomach and sealed his mouth over her sex once again. Charlie's back arched off the bed as he licked and sucked, brought her to heights of pleasure so intense, she didn't know how much more she could take before her world exploded and left her weak and shaken.

With every caress, every touch of his lips, Mason treated her as though she meant more to him than some random hookup. He treated her as though she was precious. Beautiful. Desirable. He stirred her emotions to the point that tears pricked at Charlie's eyes and her chest ached.

"Fuck me, Mason." She needed to feel him inside of her. Filling her. Stretching her. She needed that joining of their bodies. "Please."

He rolled away from her, toward the bedside table, and she heard the sound of the packet being torn open before he settled himself between her thighs. Charlie shook with anticipation, worse than any addict desperate for her next high. She reached up and wrapped her fingers around his stiff length before guiding him to her opening. He thrust home with a groan of relief and she hooked her ankles around the backs of his knees as he drove forward, pulled out, and fucked into her again, hard and deep. Charlie cried out, her nails digging into his shoulders as she came up off the mattress to meet the forward momentum of his hips. His breathing became heavy and ragged. His arms shook on either side of her. His muscles grew taut as he ground his hips into hers.

Time didn't exist when it was just the two of them like this. It stretched out infinitely between them, leaving nothing but sound, sensation, and pleasure so intense it brought tears to Charlie's eyes.

"You feel so good." Mason's heated words at her ear vibrated along Charlie's flesh. "You're so tight. So perfect. God, you're so slick and wet. I can't get enough of you, Charlie."

He couldn't get enough? Charlie was beginning to

wonder how she'd function on a daily basis without wanting to drag him where they could have a few stolen moments alone. "Fuck me harder." She needed to come, to feel that wild abandon with him again. "Don't stop until I come."

Mason obliged her and then some. He fucked her without mercy, driving hard and deep, thrusting with a desperation that she understood all too well. Whatever this was between them burned hot and bright. It consumed them in unquenchable flames. "Come with me, Charlie." Mason's words were a low growl in her ear. "I'm close. I want your pussy squeezing me when I come."

Dear God. When he spoke to her like that, how could she do anything other than what he asked of her? Pleasure built and crested with every powerful drive of his hips. At her center, Charlie felt her body gather in on itself as though compressing to the size of an atom. Her thighs began to tremble and her muscles grew taut. A gasp lodged itself in her throat and she held on to Mason as though he was the only thing anchoring her to the earth.

"Oh God!"

The orgasm exploded through her. Charlie cried out as Mason fucked her. Waves of sensation crested and broke like the ocean at high tide. With every drive of his hips, Mason prolonged her pleasure. His breath became uneven and ragged in her ear and Mason's body went taut. He let out a low groan as he came and his wild thrusts soon became disjointed and lazy before his body came to rest on top of hers.

Amazing.

They came down from the high together. Kisses. Caresses. Slow, measured breaths. His heart beat against hers, and Charlie closed her eyes as she relished the almost imperceptible thump. Seconds passed. Minutes.

She had no idea how long they lay like that, but when Mason finally rolled away, she felt his absence with a gut-wrenching ache.

Charlie floated somewhere between wakefulness and sleep. "Have you always been claustrophobic?" It was hard to imagine anything scaring Mason or making him uncomfortable. Ever since the flight to L.A. she'd been curious.

"My mom died when I was two." The low timbre of his voice lulled her closer toward sleep. "My dad was gone a lot. One time, when I was five, he left me with a neighbor and she shut me in the closet for eight hours. When he came home and found me, I was pretty freaked out. I'd never seen him so angry. He threatened the babysitter. Told her if he ever saw her face again, he'd put her in the ground. I didn't know what it meant at the time, but I guess I must have been pretty traumatized because it freaked my dad out. He took all the doors off the closets after that. It was literally the only time growing up that I felt like he wanted to take care of me. The older I got, the harder he got."

"Mason." Emotion clogged Charlie's throat. "I'm so sorry. That's awful."

He kissed the top of her head. "My dad was a bastard, but he never let me be scared of enclosed spaces when he was around. He tried to distract me and keep my mind off it. You did that for me." He paused. "You make me feel like I can breathe, Charlie."

Her heart pounded at the admission. "You make me feel like I can breathe too." It was true. Being with Mason somehow made everything okay. That sort of comfort was a rare commodity.

Mason pulled her close and Charlie tucked herself against his body as she let sleep take her. She was officially lost to him. There was no going back.

Chapter Nineteen

Last night had been the best one of Mason's life. Charlie had let him forget, if only for a few hours, what he was really doing in L.A.

He'd passed Kieran's test, and in doing so, set in motion something that he couldn't ever undo. Charlie thought he was a good man? A good man was loyal. A good man didn't turn his back on his family. A good man didn't use his own brother for intel and turn him into a government asset.

Mason wasn't a good man. He was barely a decent human being. Whatever Charlie saw in him was an illusion. He was Jensen Decker's kid, for shit's sake. That was a stigma he wouldn't ever escape.

"I'll meet you in the lobby in twenty minutes?"

Mason looked up at Charlie. She waited by the door, sleepy, disheveled, and so goddamned beautiful she took his breath away. He crossed the room to where she stood and reached past her to open the door. His arm brushed her breasts and he recalled how their lush fullness felt, bare against his skin. Mason's cock perked up and he willed the bastard still. They needed to get their asses to the airport and back to San Francisco. Playtime was over.

He didn't want it to be over, though. As far as Mason was concerned, whatever this was between him and Charlie was just getting started.

Charlie gazed up at him. Did she have any idea how sexy she was when she played coy? Being close to her for the rest of the day and not touching was going to *kill* him. He leaned in close and kissed her once. It would have to be enough to sustain him for now. When she pulled away, a slow smile spread across her rosy lips. "Don't be late," she murmured as she ducked under his arm and hurried down the hallway.

Mason leaned out into the hallway to watch her go. He straightened and looked to his left to find Kieran standing just outside the door to his own room at the end of the hallway. Ashamed of his own smug satisfaction at having gotten one up on Kieran, he met his stoic gaze for only a moment before ducking back into his room and letting the door shut behind him.

From the day his dad had taken Kieran in, Mason had fought to prove he was just as good as Kieran. As smart. As successful. As charismatic and charming. As goddamned hard. And Mason had always come in second. *Always.*

Until last night. Mason had taken something that Kieran wanted. And despite the fact that his interest in Charlie hadn't been spurred because of Kieran's interest in her, it still made him feel as though he'd finally gotten the point across that he was Kieran's equal. He only hoped that Charlie wouldn't get caught in the middle of this power play that still existed between them even after so many years.

Twenty minutes didn't give Mason much time to get showered and ready to go. He'd slept all of about two hours and he wanted to stand under the scalding hot spray of the shower and let the water relax his taut muscles. What he really wanted was to be standing under the jets with Charlie, lathering her body and letting his hands slide over every slippery inch of her.

Mason groaned and braced his arm against the shower wall. He didn't think he'd be able to get her out of his head if he tried. With a flick of his wrist, he turned the knob to the right. He sucked in a sharp breath as the cold water hit him and he forced himself to stand under the spray until the icy missiles dulled his racing thoughts. Playtime was over. Back to business. He'd managed to pass Kieran's test, but that didn't mean he'd gained his unwavering trust. It didn't mean Mason would confide in him about his involvement with Faction Five.

Since he'd taken this assignment, Mason's focus had been on what he'd get out of it if he was successful. The U.S. Marshals Service had been his endgame since the day he'd joined the police academy. Now, though, he wasn't thinking only of himself. He wanted Charlie to have the win. To be able to prove to her father and anyone else who'd ever doubted her that she was a force to be reckoned with. He'd do whatever was in his power to get that for her. He'd hand Faction Five to her on a silver fucking platter.

Mason finished his frigid shower and dressed. He slung his duffel over his shoulder and headed for the lobby. His gut tightened at the prospect of facing Kieran. He hadn't taken Charlie from Kieran. It wasn't a betrayal. It felt like one, though. It didn't matter how much time had passed. Or that they hadn't talked in years until recently. Kieran was still Mason's family. Was it guilt over what had happened between him and Charlie that got under Mason's skin? No, it was the shame that nagged at him since day one: He was manipulating Kieran. Deceiving him. The task force claimed to want Faction Five more than Kieran. That the information he could provide them was worth more than his arrest. Mason knew they were blowing smoke to placate him. They'd arrest Kieran as soon as the opportunity presented itself. What made Mason feel like an asshole was that he pretended the possibility of Kieran's arrest wasn't inevitable, to justify his own selfishness.

Charlie and Kieran were already in the lobby when Mason got there. They sat together on a couch, deep in conversation. It seemed the task force hadn't needed Mason at all. Charlie had managed to easily dazzle Kieran. She could have single-handedly infiltrated Faction Five. She was capable of anything.

"Hey." She flashed him a blinding smile that made Mason's chest ache.

He wanted to return the gesture but he couldn't manage more than a slight grimace. "Hey."

Her expression fell. Mason wanted to kick himself. His eyes slid to Kieran, who pinned him with an accusing glare. From here on out, things were bound to get shittier and a hell of a lot more tense. It wouldn't do him any good to come across as regretful or even guilty. Charlie wasn't a prize to be won. And he wasn't going to let Kieran treat her like one. They were all adults. Time to put childish rivalries behind them.

Kieran cocked a sardonic brow. A sly, half smile curved his lips. He was up to something. Who the hell knew what. Kieran was always working an angle. What was important was for Mason to be sure he kept one step ahead of him.

"How was your night?" Kieran's confident expression didn't waver. "You look a little tired."

If he was trying to bait him, it wasn't going to work. "Hotel beds," Mason responded. "They kill my back."

Kieran checked his phone as though totally unconcerned with how Mason spent last night or any other night. He pushed himself up from the couch and held his hand out to Charlie. "Our car's here. Ready?"

She gave him a pleasant smile and let him help her up. "Ready."

Mason tried not to appear too crestfallen when she walked out ahead of him, beside Kieran, to where the car waited. They weren't a couple by any stretch of the imagination. Pretending that they were wouldn't do anything but make Mason look like a sap. Not exactly great for his street cred.

Kieran settled in next to Charlie in the backseat, leaving Mason to flank him by the window. His mood took another spiraling dive. "What's our cut?" He'd planned on waiting until they were back in San Francisco to talk business, but he felt the sudden urge to ruffle Kieran's feathers.

"What do you mean?" The innocence in Kieran's tone made Mason want to slap him.

"You know damn well what I mean. You made ten million off Katarina last night and didn't have to lift a finger for it."

"Someone had to kill that warlord to get the diamonds," Kieran replied.

"Someone did," Mason agreed. "But it wasn't you."

Kieran's answering chuckle grated on Mason's nerves. There was no end to his arrogance. "Doesn't mean I didn't have to work to get my hands on them."

Whatever. It probably hadn't taken more than a quick phone call. Hell, Mason wouldn't be surprised if someone from Faction Five had offed the warlord. It wasn't as though Mason wanted any of the money.

Hell, if he'd wanted to make millions, he would have followed in his dad's footsteps to begin with. But Mason had committed to the part he was playing. He'd told Kieran he was in it for the money. There was no point in not acting as though that wasn't the most pressing thing on his mind right now.

"You knew you had a snowball's chance in hell of getting Katarina to pay your price. She's wise to your bullshit. That's why you brought Charlie and me along. Without us, you wouldn't have that considerable paycheck. We agreed to your test, but neither of us agreed to work for free."

"I didn't agree to pay you, either."

Always a loophole. This was why Mason had shunned the life he'd been brought up in. There was *no* honor among thieves, no matter what anyone said to the contrary.

"This is bullshit and you know it, Kieran."

Mason couldn't explain why his temper crested so quickly. So far, everything had gone according to plan. Hell, after last night with Charlie, he could safely say everything had gone better than according to plan. So why was he so annoyed? Why did every word out of Kieran's mouth make him want to punch him in the face?

"If you're in it for a few bucks, Mason, I can cut you a check and we can call it a day." Kieran turned to Charlie. "Whaddya say, Charlie? Want to follow Mason's lead and bug out, or are you prepared to make an investment for an even bigger payday?"

Mason leaned back in his seat and caught sight of Charlie. To think that he'd once doubted her ability to keep her cool in an undercover situation. After only a week of tutelage, she was a seasoned pro.

"I want the big payday," she said without missing a

beat. "But that doesn't mean that I'm okay with being kept in the dark."

"You could learn a thing or two from her, Mason." Kieran cast a sidelong look Mason's way. "She knows how to play the game."

It took a sheer act of will to keep her eyes off Mason. To not behave as though her entire world hadn't been changed in the course of a few amazing hours. Charlie couldn't help but smile. When she'd left his hotel room, she believed that nothing could quash her upbeat mood. Mason's current sour countenance was doing a pretty good job, however.

"Charlie doesn't know you like I do."

Mason's dark tone sent a shiver up Charlie's spine. Why the sudden animosity? Mason was supposed to be playing nice with Kieran, not antagonizing him.

"If I didn't know better, I'd think you were trying to insult me, Mason."

Kieran was answered with silence and Charlie stepped in to keep their quickly sinking ship afloat. "We want the payday," she said. "Both of us. I'm willing to concede that we didn't do much of the legwork. But we should at least be compensated for our time."

Kieran grinned. Charlie had known him long enough to realize when he was trying to use his charm to manipulate the situation to his advantage. "A free trip to L.A., a nice meal, and a luxury hotel aren't enough compensation?"

Charlie kept her expression stern. "No."

Kieran's smile grew but it didn't reach his eyes. For the first time since they'd met, Charlie felt as though she might be pressing her luck. It was easy to forget that Kieran Eagan lived his life on the opposite side of the law. And like Mason said, he wouldn't hesitate to protect his own interests first.

"All right. So tell me, what do you think your services are worth?"

Charlie had no idea. It's not like she'd studied any illegal-diamond-broker rate sheets. Her dad always told her that it was important to consider her time as more than valuable. People paid for her expertise and it was okay to put a value on that knowledge. Of course, he'd later scoffed when she explained the government pay scale to him. *They're devaluing you, your education, and your expertise.* There was a pretty good chance that Kieran and her father shared a similar philosophy.

"I want a hundred thousand," she said. "And Mason should get double for not only negotiating the deal, but for having to deal with Katarina afterward."

"From the way Katarina made it sound this morning on the phone, Mason hardly suffered for those two extra hours."

A spark of jealousy flared in Charlie's esophagus and she swallowed it down. Kieran was trying to get a rise out of one of them, and she for one wasn't going to take the bait. "Doesn't matter." Charlie looked away. "He spent that time with her whether it was pleasant or not."

Kieran turned his attention to his right. "I didn't realize you needed Charlie to negotiate your paychecks for you, Mason."

Charlie leaned back to look at Mason. His mouth formed a grim line and his bright green eyes narrowed with annoyance. "We're partners," he said simply. "I trust *her*."

The rib didn't go unnoticed. "Considering CBP is still cutting you a paycheck, you can understand why trust might continue to be an issue for us."

Mason faced Kieran. "Isn't that why you brought us down here? To reestablish some trust?"

Kieran hit Mason with the silent treatment again. It was totally his favorite intimidation tactic.

"We don't need you, Kieran." It was a bold move, but Charlie wanted to prod at Kieran's pride. "Mason and I can find our own niche in this business. It'll take us longer to turn a real profit, that's all. Which is why Mason reached out to you in the first place. We wanted to fast-track, not take the scenic route."

"You're certainly not shy about admitting that you're using me." Kieran's tone was a little too sour for someone who gave the impression he didn't care.

"How did you get a leg up?" Charlie dug her heels in. "Did you make your own way or use Jensen's connections to give you an immediate boost?"

"It's a family business," Kieran offered by way of an explanation. He'd never freely admit that he owed his success to Jensen.

Charlie gave him a pointed look. "It still is."

Was it wrong to play off Kieran's sense of family in order to get what she wanted? If it came down to it, Charlie didn't doubt that Kieran would throw Mason under the bus if he had to. At the end of the day, Kieran's loyalty was to himself. So was Charlie's. She'd do whatever it took to bring Faction Five down. If that meant manipulating Kieran's only weakness—Mason—to get it, then so be it.

Kieran didn't chuckle this time. He didn't flash a charming grin or try to dazzle Charlie with his words. He contemplated her for a long moment. Discomfort at being so closely scrutinized made her squirm in her seat. A nervous tremor skittered up her spine and Charlie willed her breaths to remain calm and even, despite the fact she felt like hyperventilating.

He didn't look away from Charlie when he said, "Is that what we are, Mason? Family?"

Charlie burned with curiosity as she forced herself not to make eye contact with Mason. She wanted to see the expression on his face, if only to try to gauge his current mood.

"We are," Mason said after a tense moment. "You know that. Even if you don't trust me enough to bring me in on whatever you've got going on. Like Charlie said, we'll do all right on our own."

"You think?"

Kieran's words dripped with sarcasm. Even though Mason had given her bits and pieces of insight into his childhood, Charlie couldn't even begin to imagine the history that lay between him and Kieran. Their lack of mutual parentage didn't make them any less brothers. And brothers fought. She simply had to do what she could to smooth this momentary bump in the road between them.

"Yeah." Mason's response lacked even an ounce of humor. "Doesn't matter who's signing my paychecks. The people who matter know what I'm capable of. My job doesn't change who I am. Who *my* father is."

Kieran flinched as though he'd been stung.

The car pulled up to the unloading area at the airport. Kieran shifted in his seat and let out a frustrated breath. "One hundred thousand for Charlie. One and a half for you. That's my final offer. Take it or leave it."

"We'll take it." The car came to a stop and Mason didn't waste any time climbing out and rounding the car to wait for the driver to open the trunk.

They needed to skirt the one sore spot in Mason and Kieran's relationship if this was going to work. If Charlie had to play the peacemaker and placate the both of them in order to keep everyone happy, so be it.

Kieran moved to get out, but Charlie grabbed him by the arm.

"Listen, Kieran. I'm not gonna lie. We need the reputation you've built. Mason's just being stubborn and trying to push your buttons. You're both Jensen's kids as far as anyone in the business is concerned. It was my idea to reach out to you, not Mason's. I wanted to work with you. Mason can be helpful. He's helped me to skirt the feds for months. I just need you to know, I'm in. No matter what."

Kieran's gaze narrowed and his lips thinned. "And if I don't want to work with Mason?"

She was afraid it would come to that. But there was no way she was letting go of her only chance at infiltrating Faction Five. "Then I'll respect your decision."

Kieran regarded her for a brief moment. "Good."

If Mason knew she'd just made a deal with Kieran, he wouldn't be happy about it. Charlie hoped that Kieran's sour mood would pass and Mason would never have to find out.

She didn't want to be on the receiving end of Mason's anger. Especially if he thought she'd betrayed him.

Chapter Twenty

"So basically, the trip to L.A. was a bust."

"Not necessarily. We walked away with a couple hundred thousand dollars and some street cred."

Mason rolled his eyes as he relaxed back into his chair. A couple of weeks ago, Charlie wouldn't have been quite so cavalier. If he'd given her a snarky comeback like that, she would've read him the riot act. Not anymore, it seemed. Charlie Cahill was the queen of 'tude.

Chief Deputy Carrera looked about as thrilled with Charlie's flippant response as Mason was. Because Kieran still hadn't fully let his guard down, they'd agreed that a full debriefing with the entire task force wasn't a good idea. Mason had picked Charlie up from the Fairmont and they'd driven around for a good hour before he was sure they weren't being tailed, and met Carrera at the rendezvous site, a little hole in the wall coffee shop at the opposite end of the city.

"What do you think, Mason? Is this a waste of time, or do you think Kieran is ready to trust you? If not, we can't keep Charlie in this situation for much longer. It's dangerous, not to mention a huge liability."

That was an understatement. Mason gave Carrera a nod of acknowledgment. "Kieran likes to be the one holding all of the cards. But I don't think he's going to string us along." Mostly because Mason knew that Kieran's interest in Charlie wasn't strictly professional. He wouldn't let her simply walk away.

"It's been almost a week," Carrera pointed out. "I was hoping to have Charlie clear of this by now. So far it's not looking good. We went into this knowing it could be months or longer before Kieran gave you anything solid. That sort of timetable isn't going to work for Charlie."

It was true that stings like this could take months, even years, to conclude. Kieran was in charge. Period. Mason wanted what Carrera wanted: for Charlie to be free and clear from this part of the operation as quickly as possible. "Like I said, he's trying to get a point across. And yeah, I think he's ready to trust me."

"Trust *us*," Charlie interjected. "And how about asking Charlie what she thinks about all of this?" Mason cringed at her accusing tone. He didn't like being talked about like he wasn't there, so why would she? "I think the both of you are delusional if you think Kieran's going to easily accept any limited future involvement on my part. I knew when I got involved that this wouldn't be over in a few days. I'll do what I have to do." She leveled her gaze at Mason. "For however long it takes."

Damn, she was stubborn. But Mason admired her determination. True, it was stupid to think that Kieran would hand over the keys to the castle so soon—or accept Charlie fading off into obscurity. Mason could hope though, couldn't he?

"What if Kieran cuts you loose?" Carrera definitely wasn't convinced. "He's got ten million in seed money that could very well be going to Faction Five, thanks to your little field trip. He might not need you anymore."

If Carrera thought Kieran would turn that money over so easily—or that a criminal syndicate as big as Faction Five would be satisfied with a measly ten million—he was crazy. "That money was for Kieran." Mason was almost positive. "He used Charlie and me to prove to Katarina that he was worth her respect. That's not seed money. It's a trophy."

"Could be." Carrera was skeptical, but the chief deputy didn't know Kieran like Mason did. None of them did.

"I agree with Mason," Charlie chimed in. Mason appreciated the solidarity, but honestly, he didn't want her out in the field any more than Carrera did. "At least in that L.A. was personal and not professional. He's not going to leave us high and dry. I'm not willing to throw in the towel yet."

That was the problem. Charlie's tenacity wouldn't allow her to quit. It could be months. Hell, a year, before Kieran deemed them worthy of knowing his secrets, and Faction Five could be up and running in full swing by then. There was no possible way Charlie could live out of a hotel for the next year, abandon her job, and follow him and Kieran on whatever wild-goose chase his brother dreamed up, no matter what she thought to the contrary. There had to be another way. A faster way to get Charlie and the task force what they wanted.

"How do you know Kieran is involved with Faction Five?" Up until now, everyone had been pretty tight-lipped on the intel they had. "If you don't even know who's running the outfit, how can you know that Kieran's got the inside track?"

"About six months ago, we arrested a hacker who'd

been on the run for several months. He tried to make a deal by offering up a little information." Carrera fiddled with his paper coffee cup before he met Mason's gaze. "He said there was talk about an up-and-coming crime syndicate that was about to make some big waves in the underground. Gave us the name Faction Five."

Carrera's information wasn't anything new. They'd already gone over this when Mason had been brought on to the task force. "Wait a second." Mason looked from Carrera to Charlie. "If these guys are so secretive that you can't even identify their members, how did some third-rate hacker know about them?"

"He'd come across interactions between Faction Five and a couple of potential recruits on the Internet," Charlie said.

"Kieran was one of these potential recruits?"

Charlie rolled her lip between her teeth. "Not exactly."

Jesus Christ. All of this time spent getting close to Kieran, and Mason was starting to believe the most informed people on the task force weren't even sure what they were dealing with! His head pounded. The residual stress that hadn't worn off after L.A. pooled in his gut and sent a renewed surge of agitation through him.

"*Not exactly* isn't going to cut it, Charlie." He couldn't help his curt tone. "I need to know everything that you know from here on out."

Charlie's gaze met Carrera's. "I told you in the initial briefing that Faction Five reportedly comprises members from various government and law enforcement entities. We're working on the assumption that the *five* in Faction Five represents the number of founding members. The problem is that the second they sensed we might be on to the group's existence, they disappeared. We don't have any leads on who might be running the show. Their membership is obviously loyal. So loyal we can't pinpoint any of the members or leadership structure."

They might as well be chasing ghosts. "That still doesn't tell me how you know that Kieran is involved with them."

"A few months ago, the CIA started monitoring a Twitter user who went by the handle BlackDragon. The tweets seemed nonsensical, but they got some code crackers on it and realized that BlackDragon was sending out invitations to certain individuals. Offering up a business opportunity to high-level players who could afford to buy their way in. Whoever set up the account knew what they were doing, though, and we weren't able to track the user to an IP address."

Technology made it easy for people operating outside the confines of the law to communicate. Twitter, Snapchat, Facebook . . . any and all social networks could be used to send and receive esoteric messages. Sure as hell beat using the classifieds. Mason had worked several cases for CBP that involved social media. Coyotes especially used social media to their advantage. The smuggling of people across the U.S. borders was just as lucrative as smuggling precious gems.

"We monitored the account for six months," Carrera continued. "And BlackDragon finally got a bite."

"Kieran?" Mason found it hard to swallow. Kieran was old-school. No way would he use social media as a tool. Besides, he was well established in the trade. He'd handled every aspect of his business for years. He didn't need a leg up to make a fortune. His business was already well established.

"No, not Kieran." Carrera spun his coffee cup between his palms. "Andrew Gentry."

Gentry's reputation almost rivaled Mason's dad's. He'd been a heavy hitter in his day, but rumors had circulated for years that he'd given up the life. It seemed the more Carrera tried to explain, the more tangled the story became. None of it made sense.

"Gentry?" Mason scoffed. "He's my dad's age. I'd be surprised if he even knows how to turn on a computer, let alone use social media."

"It wasn't quite that simple," Charlie added. "It was more of an *I know a guy, who knows a guy, who knows a guy* situation."

Yep. A total tangled mess. "So you put surveillance on Gentry?"

"Yeah," Charlie said. "He never met with anyone in person. Whoever Gentry communicated with, they exchanged messages hidden in books at local libraries. We weren't able to intercept any of the messages."

Now that was more Gentry's speed. Sometimes the tried-and-true ways were the best. The Internet was forever. Gentry obviously knew that.

"After a while, Gentry quit going to the libraries," Charlie said.

"But Kieran started showing up?"

She gave him a sad smile. "Yep. It was a bit of a surprise, since the rumors were that Kieran was living somewhere in Europe. Once a week for a month and a half, he made a stop at a library. Then, he completely stopped. The trail went cold."

Mason didn't have to guess what had happened next. "And Carrera reached out to me."

Charlie didn't respond. She didn't have to. Mason had been their last resort, and he'd played right into their hands.

"What if all of this is for nothing?" Mason asked.

They didn't have much to go on. In the back of his mind he wanted them all to be wrong. He didn't want Kieran to be involved in any of this. "There's no proof that Kieran is trying to buy his way into Faction Five. You could be wrong."

"We could be," Charlie agreed. "But I'm betting we're not."

"So we keep going." Did Mason have any other choice at this point? "We wait for Kieran to contact us again and see where the trail leads."

"That's the general consensus." Carrera took a sip from his cup. "But the sooner we get Charlie out of this, the better."

"No way. I already told you, I'm in for however long it takes."

Here we go. Mason knew that talking her into taking a backseat role would be a wasted effort. That didn't mean he wasn't going to try.

If Charlie had known she was about to be ganged up on, she would have considered phoning in to this meeting. "I've proven I can handle it," she replied. "There's no reason not to use me. Besides, if I'm suddenly not in the picture anymore, it'll throw up a red flag."

Charlie didn't want to admit to Mason that she'd given Kieran the impression she'd used Mason to get her an introduction. His mood was bad enough already; there was no reason to further ignite his ire. Cranky Mason was a hell of a lot harder to deal with. In fact, *raging pain in the ass* pretty much covered it.

He'd kept his distance from her since L.A. Not even so much as a phone call. Charlie's own agitation over his silence put her in a less than congenial mood herself. She hated to think that what had happened between them was just a one-night stand. But with the way Mason had iced her out the past week, coupled with his stoic treatment of her now, Charlie felt like he was sending her a pretty clear message.

She didn't think it would hurt so badly, but the pain of his rebuff sliced through her rib cage.

"Why will it throw up a red flag?" Mason pinned her with an accusing stare. "I'll tell him that what happened in L.A. spooked you and you've reconsidered our business relationship. Easy enough."

Fine. If he wanted a fight, she'd give him one. "I don't think he'd buy that explanation."

Mason's gaze narrowed. Charlie was pretty sure if it were possible, daggers would be shooting out of his eyes right about now. "Why?"

The one word hung in the air. Carrera leaned forward as though pretty damned eager to hear this one.

Charlie squared her shoulders and knocked her chin up a notch. "I might have told him that it was me who'd wanted to do business with him in the first place and that I'd used you to make the introduction."

A quiet moment passed while Charlie envisioned the steam building up pressure in Mason's head.

"You did what?"

Somehow, the level calm of his voice was so much scarier than an angry shout. Charlie cringed. "You two were arguing. We were losing him and—"

"We weren't losing him." Mason's jaw clenched. "We've always argued, Charlie. It's part of who we are." He raked his fingers through the length of his dark hair and let out a frustrated gust of breath. "You know, this would all be going a hell of a lot smoother if everyone would quit assuming that they know Kieran better than I do."

"Nobody's assuming that."

Mason turned his attention to Carrera and cocked a doubtful brow. "You're trying to manage him. You're trying to manage us both, and that's where you're fucking this up."

"So far, there hasn't been a single aspect of this operation that's been managed," Carrera said with disgust. "We're so off the rails we're not even close to the tracks anymore." He gave Mason a look. "I wouldn't know how to manage you if I tried."

Charlie sensed the coming storm of Mason's temper. Too bad Carrera seemed oblivious.

"And yet, you offered me a job in exchange for my help. Who made you do it?" Mason's tone escalated and drew the attention of a few people in the coffee shop. His eyes met Charlie's. "Ah. Figures."

It figured that Mason would make the leap to assume that she'd been the one to bring him on to the task force. It hurt to think he assumed she'd railroad him like that after everything that happened between them in L.A. Or was it simply her ambition and own need to take control of the situation that had him riled and disdainful? Not for the first time, Charlie wished she could get into Mason's head and see what he was thinking.

Mason's gaze smoldered as he looked from Carrera to Charlie. "I told you when I came on that this had to be done *my way*. And so far, all anyone's done is hover, butt in, and try to take over a situation and manage someone they know *nothing* about." It didn't take a genius to know that Mason was addressing her directly. "You need to let me handle this from here on out. Period. If you don't, you're going to lose the only connection you might have to Faction Five. Is that what you want?"

He might as well have ended that sentence with *Charlie?* Mason wasn't the only one dealing with frustration. Ever since they'd gotten back from L.A., Mason had behaved as though nothing had happened between them. Hurt sliced through her as he looked at her with nothing more than casual interest. Charlie wanted to kick herself for thinking that an intense intimacy had been forged between them in that hotel room.

Pathetic.

"You know what I want," Charlie snapped. Mason's eyes widened a fraction of an inch and Carrera sat back in his chair and cleared his throat. She was tired of making amends for the way she'd botched Mason's plans with Kieran. She'd made a mistake and she'd apologized for it. "But even you have to admit that Kieran isn't totally sold on the idea of working with us. You can't cut me out now. It needs to be business as usual."

"Business as usual?" Mason scoffed. "Wanna fill me in on what exactly that is? Because there is nothing about this situation that's even close to business as usual."

Now he was just being difficult. His attitude ignited Charlie's anger. *Stubborn ass.* "I'm not going to let you bait me into an argument, Mason."

"Oh, there's no baiting," Mason assured her. "And I'll argue my point until I'm blue in the face."

Of course he would. "Because you're stubborn to a fault."

Mason's eyes went wide. "I'm stubborn?" Charlie bristled at his incredulous tone. "Seriously, Charlie, you're crazy if you think—"

The muted sound of Mason's cell ringing cut him off. He fished his phone out of his pocket. "It's Kieran."

Charlie's stomach knotted with anticipation. Carrera leaned forward in his chair, attention focused on Mason, who slid his finger across the screen. His gaze met Charlie's for the barest of moments before he answered. "What's up?"

Mason kept his expression blank as he listened, which only helped to crank Charlie's anxiety up into the stratosphere.

"Yeah." Mason paused. "Okay." Another long pause that lasted at least a year. "Whatever."

Charlie felt like she might crawl out of her skin at any second. The suspense was killing her. Mason's grouchy, disinterested tone didn't help either. His approach to dealing with Kieran was thinly veiled hostility. Charlie couldn't fault him, she guessed. Had she been in court, it would have been her approach in dealing with the defense.

"I can do that," Mason said after a moment. "I'll need a few days to get everything set up, but it shouldn't be a problem."

The longer they talked, the antsier Charlie got. She wished Mason would wrap up the call already. The suspense was killing her!

"Why do you need her for this?" Mason's gaze slid to his left, and Charlie's jaw clenched. He was trying to cut her out! Dirty, rotten traitor.

The chances of her being able to prosecute this case were slim-to-none, thanks to her involvement in the undercover aspect of the operation. If Mason managed to get his way and benched her, she'd be practically useless. She wouldn't be proving any points to anyone if that happened.

Mason's expression darkened and tension pulled at his shoulders, tightening his T-shirt over the muscled expanse of his back. "It might take her a few days to line someone up, but I'm sure she can do it."

Another silence passed. "I'll be in touch," Mason said as he wrapped up the conversation. "Later."

He ended the call and shoved the phone back in his pocket. Charlie stared at Mason, her eyes practically bugging out of her head. "*Well?*"

Rather than address her directly, Mason turned to Carrera. "Kieran needs to move a large shipment of gems into the country. Four days from now. He wants me to get them past customs and to keep the feds off his back."

"And Charlie?" Carrera asked.

Mason let out a long-suffering sigh. "He wants Charlie to line up the buyers."

"Why?" Carrera seemed as skeptical as Mason. Did neither of them think she was competent enough to pull this off?

"My guess is he doesn't want the sale connected to him." Mason's brow furrowed and his jaw squared with the words. Something bothered him. "He pulled the same thing in L.A. Sort of. He could have negotiated the sale to Katarina, no problem. But he wanted to put a cushion between them."

"He could be trying to figure out a way to cover his tracks," Carrera suggested. "Making sure he could work with Faction Five without anyone being able to make the connection."

"Maybe," Mason said. "Or his motives could be entirely personal."

Carrera's brow furrowed. "How so?"

"He's got a thing for Charlie," Mason said darkly. "He could be looking for an excuse to see her again."

"Shit."

Carrera's displeasure didn't fill Charlie with confidence.

"Mason's exaggerating." She turned the stink-eye on Mason. She wasn't exactly excited about Carrera reporting that little tidbit to the rest of the task force when he briefed them. "It's not like that."

"The hell it isn't." Mason met her look for look. "Which is why we should get her out now."

"I'm not going anywhere," Charlie said. They could try to get her out, but she'd be damned if they succeeded. "I can handle myself. Period."

Carrera and Mason exchanged a look. The chief deputy's resigned sigh made Charlie want to pump her fist in the air. "We'll play it by ear. If having her around keeps Eagan happy and distracted, it'll only help us in the long run."

"Jesus." Mason's disgusted tone pricked at Charlie's chest. "This is a fucking joke." He turned to Charlie as he stood. "Hope you're happy. You're getting exactly what you want."

Without another word, he strode from the coffee shop and let the door swing shut behind him.

What in the hell was wrong with him? If he thought he could treat her with disdain and simply walk away, Mason had another think coming. He wanted to go toe-to-toe with her? So be it.

Chapter Twenty-One

Mason slammed the front door and strode into his living room. He paced from wall to wall, back and forth, back and forth, as he tried to burn off the anger that pooled and burned in his muscles. No one seemed interested in exercising the least bit of caution, especially Charlie. *Goddamn it.* Mason's fist connected with the wall and he let out a grunt of pain. The drywall cracked, marred with a streak of crimson. Not even his bleeding knuckles could distract him from the agitation that twisted his gut.

Fucking Kieran. Fucking Carrera. Fucking task force. Fucking ambition.

From the start, Charlie had disregarded the danger of her situation. Blind to anything other than the glory, the *win*, she'd run headlong into something she knew nothing about. Had zero experience with. All Mason wanted to do was get her *out*. Keep her as far away from Kieran's world as possible. And not only had Charlie insisted she stay right where she was, she'd managed to convince Carrera that Kieran's interest in her would benefit them in the long run. Was there anyone on this task force who had their damn head on straight?

A knock came at Mason's door. He glared in the direction of the offending sound, knowing full well who stood on the other side. Stubborn didn't even begin to describe Charlie. Her hardheadedness was absolutely exasperating. He'd spent days trying to get her out of his head. To pretend as though he wasn't dying inside every time he talked to her, saw her, got within touching distance of her. So many days practicing detachment, and she'd shown Mason how much their night together meant by offering herself up to Kieran on a silver platter.

Mason knew he had no right to be jealous. Charlie wasn't his. He wanted her to be, though. That got to him more than anything. He didn't care about the job, the glory, none of it. Not anymore. The only thing that mattered was *her*.

Another round of obnoxious knocks started up. It seemed his relationship with Charlie stemmed from their antagonism. She couldn't help but wind him up. Mason stalked to the door and threw it wide, to find her standing on the front steps, arms folded across her chest, her expression livid.

"You're seriously just going to walk away from me like that?"

She must have run to her car and followed hot on his heels after he'd left the coffee shop. He fought a smile as he pictured her, enraged, outraged, and prepared to throw down for whatever wrong she perceived had been committed against her.

That indignant fire was one of the things Mason loved about her. Unfortunately, it was also one of the things that drove him up a freaking wall.

"Yeah," Mason said as a matter of fact. "I'm a grown-up. I can do what I want." Charlie stomped past him, into the living room, and Mason closed the door behind her.

"You're a pain in the ass, is what you are."

"I'm a pain in the ass?" *Laughable.* "I'm not the one who's out of her depth and refuses to admit it."

"Out of my depth?" Charlie's voice escalated with disbelief. "This is my task force. I know exactly what I'm doing."

"And you won't let me forget it, will you?" Mason asked. "That you're the boss. That *every* decision is yours to make. I guess I shouldn't be surprised that you're throwing your weight around again. It was made pretty clear to me today that you're not even above extortion to get what you want."

"I can't believe you'd jump to that conclusion." Charlie leaned forward, hands on her hips. "It was Carrera who suggested it would be in the task force's best interest to offer you a position with the Marshals Service in exchange for your help."

Mason sneered. "So I'm supposed to believe that you hadn't done your homework and didn't know a job with the Marshals Service was the one thing I wanted?"

Charlie met his gaze head-on. "Yes! You were in that boardroom with me, Mason. I didn't have a clue who you were or what your connection to Kieran was. Carlos insisted we bring you on. I didn't want you." She looked away as though embarrassed to make the admission. "You're stubborn, opinionated, have a problem with authority, and you quit your job with CBP. I saw no value in adding you to the task force. I told you, Mason, there isn't anything I won't do to bring Faction Five down. I thought you'd accepted that about me."

Her words hit with the impact of a blow to his gut. "What else are you willing to do for the win, Charlie?"

Mason wished he could take back the words the second they left his mouth. He waited for the inevitable crack of her palm across his cheek but it never came. Instead, she leveled her icy blue gaze at him. Her silence was far worse than any other punishment she could dish out. Hurt accentuated her delicate features as she turned and headed for the door.

The eerie, pre-storm quiet of Charlie's hurt and anger settled on Mason's shoulders and pressed him toward the floor. It compressed his lungs. Squeezed the air from his chest. He forced his legs forward and reached the door as Charlie pulled it open. His fingers closed over hers on the knob and he eased it shut.

"What happened to your hand?" she asked without turning to face him.

Mason stared down at his bloodied knuckles. "My temper got the better of me." He kept his fingers twined with hers. "I think I let it get the better of me more than once today." It wasn't much of an apology, but it was a start.

"What do you want from me, Mason?" Charlie disentangled her hand from his and let it drop from the doorknob. She turned to face him. Anger still smoldered in her eyes, though with considerably less heat.

Where to begin? Mason couldn't think of anything he *didn't* want from her. His want of her was all-consuming. Nothing mattered anymore. Not Kieran, not the job, not even Faction Five—whoever the hell they were.

He stepped up to her and wound his fingers in the silky length of her hair. His mouth found the outer shell of her ear. "I want everything, Charlie."

She drew in a slow breath and angled her head toward his. "So do I, Mason. And that's the problem."

His hopes deflated like a week-old balloon. "Always the job . . ."

"You want everything. Why can't I have everything I want, too?"

Mason pulled away. He smoothed his palm over her hair that a moment ago he'd held gathered in his fist. He'd vowed to keep their relationship strictly professional after L.A. Why was it so damned hard to keep his distance from her? Charlie was intentionally antagonistic. Ambitious to a fault. Hardheaded with a king-size chip on her shoulder. Tough and brave. Beautiful and passionate. She was the perfect storm. Everything he admired and desired wrapped up in one hell of a package.

How could he be anything but obsessed?

"I want *you*, Charlie." The anger that hadn't fully dissipated made an unwelcome reappearance. "Damn it, I don't give a single shit about anything else. Why do you think I want you as far away from Kieran as possible?"

Her anger reignited. "This is about Kieran? Jesus, Mason. When is this rivalry between you two going to end?"

Mason raked his hands through his hair before brushing it forward with a forceful flick. He blew out a frustrated breath. He might as well be banging his head against the wall, as much good as it did him. "This isn't about Kieran. This is about you, Charlie! If what you say about Faction Five is accurate, they're beyond dangerous. They'll go to any lengths to keep their identities a secret. Do you realize the position you've put yourself in? You could be killed!"

"I—" She averted her gaze. "The task force needs—"

If not for the gravity of the situation—not to mention his total exasperation with her—Mason would have taken a moment to enjoy how cute she was when she got flustered.

"I don't care what the task force needs." Mason

stepped up until he stood chest to chest with Charlie. He guided her face up to meet his. "*I* need you to be safe. *I* need to know that you're okay. At the end of the day, *I* need to know that I didn't put you at risk." He swallowed against the emotion that gathered in his throat. "I can't have you out in the field while I'm worrying that I can't protect you. It messes with my head. My focus is shot."

"I never said I needed you to protect me. I know what I'm involved in."

Mason lived in a constant state of vacillating between wanting to kiss Charlie and needing to shake some damn sense into her. "I know I don't need to protect you. I *want* to!" Mason wrapped his arm around Charlie's waist and hauled her against him. "Damn it, Charlie, I think I'm—"

Charlie put her lips to Mason's before he could finish his sentence. She didn't know why, but she was terrified of the next words that might come out of his mouth. It was too soon for the intense emotions she felt, and knowing that Mason might feel them too shook Charlie to her core. They'd been playing make-believe for too long. Eventually, Mason would come to his senses. When that happened, Charlie had to be sure that her heart was guarded so her entire world didn't shatter from the pain of losing someone she'd never truly had.

Mason slanted his mouth across hers and deepened the kiss. His tongue traced her bottom lip before he took it between his teeth. Hands groped for bare skin as they tore at each other's clothes. Their breaths became wild pants as their passion built to the point of combustion.

Charlie drew in a sharp gasp as Mason thrust his hand past her waistband and into her underwear. His fingers found her clit and slid against the sensitive flesh, already swollen and dripping wet.

His lips moved against her mouth as he rasped, "I need to fuck you, Charlie. Right now."

"Yes." She couldn't think of anything but having Mason inside of her, his large hands on her body, his mouth branding her everywhere it touched.

Mason took her hand and led her up the narrow stairs of his town house to the bedroom. He didn't waste any time in reaching for her shirt and pulling it up and over her head. His mouth met her throat as he released the clasp of her bra and a second later it landed behind him on the floor next to her top. Mason tackled her to the bed, yanked off her shoes, her pants, her underwear. She lay on the bed, bare to his gaze, and he stared at her for a long moment.

"Goddamn, Charlie," he said on a rush of breath.

Warmth infused her as he quickly undressed. He reached for the dresser and grabbed a condom from the top drawer. Charlie's breath raced, her heart pounded. This had been the longest week of her entire life, being away from Mason.

The gates of their restraint had been opened and all of that pent-up need flooded her. Mason rolled on the condom with a purposeful stroke and Charlie couldn't help but admire the sight of him as he stood before her. His body had no equal.

Mason grabbed Charlie by the ankles and pulled her down the mattress toward him before he rolled her over to her stomach. His hands fastened onto her hips as he hitched her ass up and drove home. Charlie let out an indulgent moan as he filled her and began to thrust. She rocked her hips back to meet his forward momentum, intensifying the sensation from the increased force.

Her fists wound into the heavy coverlet on Mason's bed and she gripped it as though it was the only thing grounding her. Each wild thrust of his hips felt better than the last, each new shock of pleasure that shot through her caused Charlie to cry out for more.

Mason's body came down over hers. He kept one hand on her hip and the other circled her stomach before it slid between her thighs. Charlie sucked in a breath as his fingers found her clit. He slid the pad of one finger over the sensitized knot of nerves as he continued to pound into her. His breath was hot in her ear as he rasped, "Come for me, Charlie."

"Mason. Oh, God, yes." Her thighs trembled with each flick of his fingertip and Charlie spread her legs wider to give him better access. The intensity of his finger circling her clit while he pounded into her nearly short-circuited her brain. Charlie squeezed her eyes shut. The sound of Mason's body slapping against hers, his breath as it brushed her neck, his touch, the way he filled her so completely, and the delicious friction as he fucked her was more than she could take. A violent tremor shook her as her world burst into myriad particles of stardust. Charlie cried out, wracking sobs of pleasure that echoed off the walls around her. Chills broke out over her skin, her heart hammered in her chest. Wave after wave of pleasure stole over her as Mason's caresses became softer.

"You squeeze me so tight when you come," Mason said close to her ear. His words came from between panted breaths, distorted by the force with which he pounded into her. "I can't get enough of it."

His hand wandered up her torso to cup her breast. Mason held her body against his as he fucked her harder, faster. She reached around and gripped his thigh as she urged him deeper still. Charlie knew exactly how he felt. When it came to Mason there was no such thing as enough. Her want of him was a bottomless chasm, endless and unfillable.

It brought her to heights of desperation she didn't know she could feel.

Charlie lost track of time, space—hell, even her own body. She was weightless, formless, floating on a cloud of bliss. Mason's low moans became desperate grunts as his body slapped against hers. His breath in her ear transformed into rasping growls and every muscle on his body went rigid to encase Charlie in stone. A shout burst from his lips as he came. The thrust of his hips became wild and disjointed. He drove hard and deep as he held her body against his and when he had nothing left to give, he collapsed beside her on the bed.

"You drive me crazy, Charlie." She strained to hear his whispered words. "I can't even be in the same room with you without wanting to tear your clothes off. Even when I'm not with you, I'm thinking about you. I need you to understand what that's doing to me. It's pulling my focus. I can't afford to let my guard down with Kieran. You're a beautiful distraction. When I'm with you, nothing else matters. Do you understand that? If you want Faction Five, you have to give me the space and clarity of mind to do my job."

The emotion in his words gutted her. She rolled onto her side, away from him so she wouldn't be forced to look him in the eye and see the honesty in his expression as well. She'd been seduced by the excitement of working the case, being right in the middle of the action. She'd enjoyed playing a part and leaving the reality of her life behind for a little while. And though she hated to admit it to herself, she'd even enjoyed the attention that Kieran bestowed on her.

Charlie had always been the smart girl. Level-headed. Organized and focused. She'd never been the desirable woman. Beautiful. Wanted.

She'd been selfish and hadn't once considered how all of this affected Mason.

His weight left the mattress. Charlie glanced over her shoulder and watched as he walked into the bathroom and pulled the pocket door closed. The faucet came on and she listened to the sounds of Mason cleaning up. A chill settled on her cooling skin and she pulled the coverlet around her.

How in the hell had they gotten to this crazy place? When Charlie had stepped into that elevator and taken in Mason's cranky countenance almost a month ago, she never would have guessed this was where they'd end up. He'd totally thrown her a curveball.

Charlie's life was all about control. Her parents had steered the course of her life from childhood; and after she'd passed the bar, she'd given herself over to her job, letting it define her, shape her, dominate her time and her thoughts. Being with Mason allowed her to let go of that control inch by inch. He made her feel wild and unfettered. She couldn't plan her next move because he made it impossible to gauge what it should be. That lack of control didn't frighten her, though. Instead, it empowered her. She could trust Mason and she could trust herself with him.

She simply had to be brave enough to give him the reins and let him run. The question was, could she actually do it?

Chapter Twenty-Two

Charlie's nerves were shot. Ever since their wild afternoon at Mason's town house, she hadn't been able to shake the guilt over her selfishness. It had taken him opening up to her when they were both still raw and shaken from their passion, for her to see what all of this was doing to him. She had to hear the stress and worry in his voice to realize that she needed to take a step back and let him do his job.

Thanks to her own silly ego, they were stuck doing at least a couple more jobs with Kieran, and hopefully once they were completed, she could take a backseat and give Mason the space he needed to see this assignment through.

It hadn't been a problem to give Kieran what he wanted. Thanks to Mason and CBP, Kieran had managed to get the first of several considerably large shipments of gems into the country without anyone even batting a lash. He'd breezed through customs, and with Mason's help had transported the stones to a safe-deposit box until they could fence them.

"Looks like you're up, Charlie. Dazzle me with the wealthy buyers you've set up."

Kieran had let his guard down a little since L.A. He appeared more relaxed and at ease. His smile reached his dark eyes as he sipped from the wineglass. Charlie swore she'd never met a man more into gourmet dining—or wine—than Kieran Eagan. He should've shunned his criminal lifestyle and become a restaurateur a long time ago.

Again, everything had been orchestrated to impress Kieran. Undercover FBI and U.S. marshals would pose as buyers and supply Kieran with the money that he needed for his business endeavor. Once the arrests were made, the government would seize the money and everything would be tied up in a neat, easy-to-prosecute bow. At least, that was Charlie's hope. She wanted everything from here on out to run without a hitch. Mason deserved it.

"I've got buyers lined up in San Francisco, Seattle, and San Diego," Charlie replied. "I also have buyers wait-listed in L.A. and Portland."

Kieran raised his glass in a silent toast. "Impressive. Who are they?"

"Two are jewelers," Charlie said. "San Francisco and Seattle. They'll purchase the bulk of the product. Do you have the Kimberley certificates?"

Kieran nodded. "A stack of them. The forgeries are good. No one would know the difference either way."

It was true. The current system for policing the export of blood diamonds was certainly flawed. It was an easy thing to forge a Kimberley certificate and pass the stones off as coming from a conflict-free zone.

"Who are the other buyers?"

"Private collectors." Charlie took a sip from her glass. "I've promised the largest stones to them."

Kieran chuckled. "Of course. Do you have a projection of what we stand to make from the combined sales?"

Charlie shrugged. "Somewhere around twenty million."

"Very nice."

Kieran had made sure to separate Charlie from Mason for this particular meeting. Anxious energy skittered through Charlie's veins, but she kept her nerves under wraps. Deputy marshals were posted a block down the street, surveilling the restaurant from their car. Knowing someone was close made Charlie feel better, but she had to remind herself that she couldn't let her guard down.

"Why aren't you fencing the diamonds yourself?" Charlie's goal for today's meeting was to try to get Kieran to reveal some part of his involvement with Faction Five. "You've got plenty of connections and fences you trust. Why use me at all?"

Kieran's voice dropped a couple of decibels to a sensual rumble. "Don't you want me to use you, Charlie?"

She'd expected him to come on to her. He'd made no secret about his interest when they'd been in L.A. That didn't make Charlie any more comfortable to be alone with him.

She let her lips relax into a coy smile. "I wouldn't have come otherwise. But you understand my curiosity."

"You said you used Mason as a way to connect with me," Kieran said. "Why? You already have connections to buyers."

"True," Charlie said. "But I didn't have the diamonds."

"I'm not as well connected as you think." Kieran

drained his glass and poured another. "I need buyers with deep pockets."

"For what?" Adrenaline trickled into Charlie's bloodstream. Would he finally confide in her?

His expression turned sour. "I need to raise a shit-load of capital in a short amount of time."

"Thinking of fleeing the country?" Charlie forced a smile, but she really hoped this wouldn't end up being an international manhunt.

"Not yet." His expression turned wily. Back to the mischievous Kieran. "But everyone has to pay the price of doing business, Charlie. Even someone like me."

"How much?" Charlie came to play hardball. She doubted Kieran would expect anything less.

"Too damn much."

Vague. Not to mention frustrating. He'd netted a little under ten million from Katarina. If Charlie managed to bring in another twenty, he'd be on his way to earning a hell of a lot of money. What was Faction Five's buy-in price? They could stand to make billions depending on the kind of members they allowed to join their ranks. An international crime ring with all the autonomy in the world. The implications of what they could accomplish with that sort of power and backing made Charlie's head spin.

"I don't understand." Any chance of finding Faction Five dwindled with every tangled word from Kieran's mouth. "You promised us an epic payday. What it sounds like to me is that you're using us to do the leg-work and buy you out of debt."

Kieran sat back in his chair and blew out a breath.

"If that's the case," Charlie continued, "I don't see any reason for us to work together."

She stood and Kieran grabbed her by the wrist. "It's . . . complicated."

She leveled her gaze. "I can't work with you if I don't know what's going on."

"Are you sleeping with Mason?"

The question knocked the air out of her lungs. "I don't see how that has anything to do with anything." He was deflecting, changing the subject in order to steer the focus onto her. "And besides, it's not any of your business."

He leaned in close. "What if I want it to be my business?"

Mason would throttle her if she used Kieran's infatuation to gain the upper hand. But Charlie didn't see any other way. Maybe in this instance it would be better to ask forgiveness than permission.

Charlie leaned down until her face was mere inches from Kieran's. "Give me what I want, and maybe I'll give you something you want."

His gaze smoldered. "All right." A slow smile spread across his lips. "We're set for tomorrow's sale, right? Seven o'clock. I'll pick Mason up and then we'll swing by your hotel."

Charlie answered with an indulgent smile of her own. "It's a date."

He let go of her wrist. "I'm going to let you in, Charlie. Just be patient for a little longer."

Charlie had no choice but to be patient at this point. "Thanks for dinner." She turned and walked away, her heart lodged somewhere in her throat.

If she managed to string Kieran along, hold his interest for a little bit longer, maybe she'd finally get some answers. But oh man, was Mason going to be pissed when he found out how she was going to get them.

* * *

"Jesus Christ, Charlie. What part of *don't encourage him* did you not understand?" Mason couldn't be mad at her—she'd used what she had to work with at the time. Still . . . she was obviously trying to worry him into an early grave. He raked his fingers through the length of his hair. "Did he at least act as though he was taking the bait?"

"I think so." Charlie sat on the couch in her suite, surprisingly relaxed for someone who'd been dropped into the deep end of the pool. "He said he'd pick us up tomorrow at seven."

Mason's nerves were shot. Aside from tomorrow's sale, Kieran had done a damned good job of keeping Mason and Charlie separated. No way was Charlie going to be alone with Kieran again without a wire or some kind of backup. It wouldn't be an issue to get Carrera to post some marshals to keep an eye on Charlie after tomorrow, since Mason would once again be busy helping to bring another shipment of gems into the country.

"None of what he said makes sense," he said. Generally, Kieran could be counted on to be up-front. He never pulled punches. And so far he'd been more forthcoming with Charlie than Mason.

"Tell me about it." Charlie chewed her bottom lip. The simple act was enough to distract Mason, and he gave himself a mental shake. "That's what worries me. What if we have this all wrong? What if we've spent countless resources chasing our tails? If after all this time we find out that Kieran has nothing to do with Faction Five and we've just helped him to pay off a very large debt?"

Kieran was smart. Smarter than their dad ever was. Smarter even than Mason. It would be one hell of a con to trick the government into picking up the tab on his mountain of debt. It would go down in history as one of the greatest heists of all time. For Charlie's sake, he hoped that wasn't the case.

"There has to be more to it than an elaborate con." But what? Mason had been racking his brain for hours and still had no idea what to think. "We need to know more about Faction Five to start to put the pieces together. Like, where are they based? Do they own any assets? There's always a paper trail. We just have to find it."

Charlie snorted. "Believe me, we've tried. They aren't based out of anywhere. We can't find any holdings, no trails, or even a crumb that would lead us to someone whose membership we could confirm. They're like the illuminati."

"A myth?" Mason laughed.

"No," Charlie said solemnly. "So secret that no one believes they exist."

Conspiracy theories aside, Mason agreed with Charlie on one thing: They needed some answers and they needed them now.

"Don't you have any hackers on the payroll? Social media experts who can help to decipher what you already know?"

"Of course," Charlie said. "But as soon as the owners of the social media accounts realized what we were up to, they went old-school."

Right. The libraries. "And in all that time watching the libraries, you never found a common denominator? One person who had shown up at all of the locations?"

"Nope," Charlie said. "We had eyes on every person in and out. No one did anything out of the ordinary."

"Damn it, this is frustrating." Mason's teeth ground.

"We should bypass all of this cloak-and-dagger bullshit and let me beat the information out of Kieran."

"You'd like that, wouldn't you?" Charlie said with a laugh.

Mason let out a slow sigh. "You have no idea."

The little bit of levity helped to lighten the mood, but it didn't change the fact that they'd made absolutely no progress in a little over two weeks. Charlie's brow furrowed as she stared at some far-off point, lost in thought. Mason could almost hear the gears cranking. Her beauty took his breath away. It made him wish she'd let him say the words he'd wanted to say at his town house a few days ago: *I think I'm falling in love with you.*

Perhaps it was better left unsaid for now. At least, until their lives went back to some semblance of normal. Mason didn't want Charlie to be able to use the undercover investigation as an excuse for his feelings. And she would. Ever pragmatic, she'd try to explain his love away rather than see what was right in front of her face.

"Wait a sec." A thought struck and Mason grasped on to the idea as it solidified in his mind. "You watched the people who came and went from the library and never found out who was leaving messages for Kieran, or how."

"Right." Charlie gave Mason a curious look. "We had people on the outside and the inside. We kept our distance from Kieran because he's too smart not to know when he's being followed."

"What did he do while he was there?"

"He'd wander the aisles, pick a book, read for a while, put the book away, and leave. We checked the book each and every time afterward. There was no pattern. The books were random. No notes tucked inside, no words in the margins. Not even a pencil mark."

He could have taken a note with him, but Mason was starting to think Faction Five would never leave a paper trail of any kind. "And he didn't talk to anyone?"

"No." Charlie shook her head. "From what I remember from the reports, he'd exchange a few polite words with the librarians, but that was it."

Mason's eyes widened a bit as he waited for the light-bulb to go on in Charlie's head. Realization dawned but she remained skeptical. "You think the library employees were his contacts? It seems far-fetched that each librarian at every branch he visited was somehow involved with Faction Five, don't you think?"

Sure. But at this point, anything was possible. "Maybe not directly involved," Mason said. "Maybe one day, some guy slips a library employee a hundred bucks and says, give a message to this other guy when he shows up today. There's no paper trail, plus it keeps the marshals and FBI from putting their finger on a specific mark."

"If that's how it went down, it's sort of genius."

And definitely old-school. "It's simple too. No muss, no fuss."

"It can't be that simple." Charlie pulled her bottom lip between her teeth in concentration. Mason's gaze was drawn to the action and he lost his own train of thought as he wished he was pulling that lip between his teeth right now. "It would implicate the library employees for starters, and it would expose Faction Five."

"I don't think it was quite so blatant." Mason chuckled. "I doubt they were giving detailed instructions or their plans for world domination."

One corner of Charlie's mouth hitched in a smile. The unassuming—and sexy—expression caught Mason off guard. He felt his jaw go slack and quickly snapped it shut.

"If everything was in code, then Kieran would have to know about it beforehand," Charlie said. "What sort of code could they have used that both Faction Five and Kieran would have previous knowledge of?"

"Depends." Mason cupped the back of his neck and massaged some of the tension away. "Smugglers have their own special language. So do thieves and con artists. It would've been easy for Kieran to communicate with anyone who knew how to speak to him. If any of Faction Five's members are law enforcement, they'd be privy to some of that language."

"Why didn't we put you on the task force from day one?" Charlie shook her head. "We'd be way ahead of where we are right now. My God, Mason. Your knowledge surpasses everyone else's by *miles*."

He gave a sheepish shrug and tried not to let the bitterness get to him. "I'm sure no one thought they could trust me. Sort of comes with the territory when you're Jensen Decker's kid."

"You've been totally screwed over." Charlie's expression turned sad, her eyes wide, limpid pools of blue. "I'm so sorry."

"Don't be." He cleared the unwanted emotion from his throat. "It's not like it's nothing I've ever dealt with before. Besides, I'm not bringing that much new information to the table. Just shedding the light from a different angle."

"Still, this is huge!" Charlie couldn't contain her excitement, and pride surged through Mason that he had been the one to make her feel that way. "We'll have to be careful, especially with Kieran becoming more trusting of us, but we can investigate the library employees and see what we find."

"It's a start," Mason agreed.

"Who knows, with this angle, plus my date with Kieran tomorrow, we could finally make some actual headway."

So far, this undercover operation was anything but typical, and it bothered him. It should have run by the book, especially with the agencies and people involved. It was almost like they'd been given as little intel as possible. Been intentionally confused and left in the dark. He hadn't been able to shake his doubt from day one, and it rankled. And it didn't help that Kieran continued to be equally confusing and cryptic.

Mason couldn't bring himself to express his worry. Not when Charlie's eyes lit with bright enthusiasm and hope. He wanted this for her. Wanted her to have the validation she'd been searching for. A niggling thought at the back of his mind kept scratching, though. He'd wanted to believe that Kieran was acting under duress. That there was no way he'd get involved with a syndicate that could bring so much heat on him. If Kieran was in deep with Faction Five, it put Charlie in even more danger if she was discovered. Mason couldn't bear it if anything happened to her. He needed to be one step ahead of Kieran, and right now he was clearly falling behind.

His only option at this point was to go to the one person who knew Kieran better than Mason did. Looked like he'd be paying dear old dad another visit. And soon.

Chapter Twenty-Three

"I'm pretty sure we don't need a babysitter, Kieran."

"My diamonds. My rules."

If Mason had it his way, they would've taken Kieran out of tonight's equation. Charlie would have turned the stones over to the undercover marshals, they would have transferred the money to Kieran's account, and there'd be no need for the pretense. Lazy, maybe. But what he really wanted was to take Charlie back to his place for a repeat of the other day. Kieran had done his damnedest to keep them apart for the past few days, and when they were together, he was always around. Hovering.

"Fine." Mason did nothing to hide his annoyance. "Then at least make yourself useful."

He shoved the small case full of stones into Kieran's hands. Charlie gave him a warning look as she climbed out of the car. Mason grumbled under his breath. This wasn't a three-person job by any means. Of course, if anyone was in danger of being cut out, it was Mason. His responsibility was to get the gems through customs. He should have been thankful Kieran decided to bring him along, when he could have simply come here with Charlie.

The last thing Mason wanted was for the two of them to have any more alone time than necessary.

The Marshals Service had commandeered Hendrickson's Jewelers for their front. Running a con on a con man wasn't an easy thing. Especially when dealing with one as infamous as Kieran. Mason swore under his breath. With each passing second his mood further crumbled into an unsalvageable mess.

Charlie stepped up to him, all smiles and feminine charm. "Ready?"

Her blue eyes sparked with fire, and Mason fought the urge to pull her against him and put his mouth to hers. He glanced over his shoulder to find Kieran watching them with more than mild interest.

"Ready." Mason wanted to get this shit over with and call it a night. The sooner, the better.

The undercover marshal played his part well. Charlie wheeled and dealed and worked her supposed magic on him. He made counteroffers, rejected some of the imperfect diamonds. Kieran supplied the forged Kimberley certificates. By the time everything was said and done, the marshal had transferred eighteen million dollars into Kieran's offshore account. Kieran verified the transfer from his tablet, pleased as hell to have netted another huge payday. One more job out of the way. Hopefully one step closer to Faction Five. Time to get rid of Kieran for the night so Mason could spend a little one-on-one time with Charlie.

"Let's celebrate!" Kieran was in high spirits, of fucking course. He'd just made a mint.

Mason's own cranky snort in response had more to

do with his displeasure at having to share Charlie with anyone for another second than Kieran's excitement over another successful sale.

"You're such a foodie," Charlie teased. That she'd gotten to know Kieran well enough to realize that, only served to further agitate Mason's temper. He had no problem admitting to himself that he was jealous. What bothered him was that he'd never felt it with such a burning intensity before.

It wasn't because of Kieran. He'd competed with him for girls' attention before. No, Mason was jealous because Charlie meant something to him.

"And proud of it." Kieran climbed into the driver's seat of the rental, leaving Mason once again to sit in the back. Alone. The enamel ground on his teeth as he clenched his jaw shut. At this rate, it would be hours before he got Charlie alone. "And in that vein, we need to hit Gary Danko. They've got a juniper-crusted bison steak that's amazing. Another huge payday deserves a five-star meal."

"We can't eat there." Charlie gave a rueful shake of her head. "It'll cost a fortune."

"Yeah," Mason grumbled. "Let's just hit a drive-through and grab a burger." Whatever got rid of Kieran faster.

Kieran's mocking laughter let Mason know that a drive-through wasn't an option. "You need to get used to luxury, Charlie." He leaned over the center console toward her, and Mason fought the urge to jerk him up-right. "You're going to be a very rich woman, thanks to me."

Mason rolled his eyes. He wasn't sure how much more of Kieran's flirtatious banter he could take. Kieran straightened and checked the rearview mirror.

Both of the side mirrors. Mason caught his reflection and his suddenly serious countenance.

"What is it?" Kieran could rock the playful and carefree vibe, but he never let his guard down. He had eyes like a hawk. And he took his personal security very seriously. He didn't respond, and the fine hairs on Mason's arm stood on end. "Kieran?"

He glanced Charlie's way, further intensifying Mason's anxiety. "We're being followed."

Charlie turned to look at Mason from over her shoulder, her usually soft face lined with concern. It could have been the marshals tailing them, but he didn't think so. *Shit.*

"You sure?"

"Three cars back, older dark blue BMW," Kieran replied.

In the gray twilight, the color was tough to make out, but Mason noticed the car. Way too conspicuous for someone with any training. What the hell?

"Mason?" Charlie's voice quavered.

"It's all good." Kieran didn't hesitate to offer up assurance. "Comes with the territory."

Or rather, assurance in the way that criminals assured one another. Mason reached out to lay a hand on her shoulder and gave a tight squeeze. "We've got about twenty thousand in diamonds on us still." Any hustler with half a brain who saw them go into the jewelry store after hours would have known what they were up to.

"Oh my God, we're about to be robbed, aren't we?"

Kieran laughed at Charlie's horrified tone. Not helpful. Not even a little bit. "If worse comes to worst, we're out twenty K to some punk-ass gangbangers. That's all."

Mason rolled his eyes. Kieran, always so damned cavalier.

"Can you lose them?" Given the choice, Mason would rather end the night conflict-free.

Kieran's eyes met his through the mirror and he flashed a confident grin. "Won't know until I try."

Oh Jesus. "Hang on, Charlie."

Kieran swerved into the next lane and hooked a hard right. Charlie gripped the oh-shit handle with one hand and braced her other on the dash. The tires squealed and the back end fishtailed before Kieran righted the car. Mason kept a lookout for any sign of the BMW.

"To your right, Kieran!"

The BMW cut through a side alley and emerged beside them. Kieran hit the brakes before Mason could get a good look at the car's passengers, and swerved to the left. Horns blared as he cut across traffic. Charlie let out a squeal as an oncoming car nearly clipped their bumper.

"Jesus Christ, Kieran!" Mason's heart lodged in his throat. If they'd been T-boned, Charlie would have been toast. "Be careful!"

"Do you want careful, or do you want to shake these guys?" Kieran stayed insufferably calm despite their circumstances. "Because you can't have both."

"Not dead or dismembered would be good," Charlie said.

Kieran chuckled. "I'm not making any guarantees."

"You're not funny."

Mason seconded that. Kieran might live for the thrill, but Charlie didn't. Mason didn't want her near danger of any kind. He checked under Kieran's seat and found the two Glocks they'd tucked there for safekeeping. They'd learned their lesson after L.A., and Mason decided not to go anywhere with Kieran unarmed. He'd rather be prepared to make a stand than go down before he had a chance to defend himself.

Kieran hung a left into a narrow alley and doubled back the way they'd come. "My guess is, they'll try to cut us off again. They won't think we'll double back."

Wrong. Kieran came to an abrupt halt as the BMW blocked their way out of the narrow alleyway. He threw the car into reverse and another car pulled in at the other end, boxing them in.

"Son of a bitch." Kieran let out a snort of disgust. "Guess we're in it now."

"Yeah." Mason handed one of the Glocks over the seat to Kieran. "I guess we are."

Kieran didn't waste any time getting out of the car. All they needed was for his smart mouth to get them into trouble. Mason leaned over the seat and said close to Charlie's ear, "Stay put. It'll be okay."

She gave him a tight nod of acknowledgment, her eyes wide with fear.

What an absolute fucking nightmare. He'd hand over the diamonds, no questions asked. Anything to defuse what could be a deadly standoff.

Charlie thought she might swallow her tongue. She was sick and tired of people telling her everything was going to be all right when it clearly wasn't. The whole just-another-day-at-the-office mentality was getting old. Fast.

Mason got out of the car and put his back to Kieran's. If this was the sort of thing that regularly happened undercover, Charlie wanted none of it.

"Lose the piece, motherfucker!" an angry voice called out.

Kieran's mocking laughter didn't do anything for Charlie's fraying nerves. Was there anything that scared him? "Yeah, that's not gonna happen." His stance remained relaxed, his expression calm.

"Whatever you think we have, you're welcome to it!" Mason said. Kieran gave him a look from over his shoulder that said, *Really?* "We don't want any trouble."

"Speak for yourself," Kieran said in a conversational tone. "I have zero patience for gangbangers. No imagination and totally not willing to work for a living. I think we should put them in their place."

Charlie's eyes rolled so hard she thought they might fall right out of her head. Dialing 9-1-1 seemed like a much better solution to their problem.

"You might not want trouble, but you got it!"

Charlie took note of their assailants. Rough, tough, clearly violent, and without conscience. Kieran might be right that they lacked imagination, but it was clear they meant business. They had something these men wanted. Nothing was going to stand in the way of that.

"Here!" Charlie scrambled out of the car and held the black case with the remainder of the diamonds aloft. "This is what you want, right? Take it and leave."

Kieran looked at her as though she'd lost her damned mind. He might not be willing to let go of twenty grand, but Charlie would much rather let the diamonds go than die.

"Don't you think that's the sort of decision we should be making as a group?" His brow arched curiously. "I mean, the stones are mine after all."

Really? "No, I don't. You said it yourself, worst case, we're out twenty K. I'm not dying over a few thousand dollars in flawed diamonds, Kieran."

Kieran laughed off her comment. "No one's going to die today, Charlie. At least, none of us."

Again, not the response she was looking for.

"I have a better idea!" Kieran shouted. "Why don't you come over here and suck my cock!"

Oh dear Lord. Charlie's gaze flitted to Mason, who didn't look the least bit surprised by Kieran's cocky show. "Get in the car, Charlie." The urgency of his instruction got her moving in a hurry. "Now." Apparently, Mason had been in similar situations with Kieran. She ducked back into the front seat at the exact moment Kieran opened fire.

Oh God! She was going to die in a dirty back alley. *Not* the way she wanted to go out.

Gunfire erupted around them like angry thunder. Bullets struck the window and Charlie ducked well below the dash. Adrenaline dumped into her bloodstream and her teeth chattered from the violent tremors that shook her body. Both Kieran and Mason dove back into the car. The engine roared to life. Kieran rolled down his window and stuck his arm out, squeezing off several wild shots before he put the car into reverse and punched the accelerator. The tires squealed in angry protest and Charlie covered her ears as more shots rang out, this time from the backseat.

If they made it out of this alive, it would be a freaking miracle.

"Hang on!"

Charlie was really beginning to hate those words. Not a second after Kieran said them, she was thrown forward with a violent jerk. Her head smacked into the dashboard and the coppery tang of blood invaded her mouth as her teeth bit into her cheek. The screech and smash of metal meeting metal as they crashed into one of the cars caused Charlie's heart to lurch up into her throat. Dark spots swam in her vision and her breathing became rapid and shallow. Passing out would definitely be a better alternative than dying from a heart attack at this point. At least if she was unconscious, her heart might stop trying to beat out of her rib cage.

They met resistance and Kieran punched his foot down on the accelerator. Angry shouts accompanied the thunderous gunshots and Charlie couldn't tell what was friendly fire and what wasn't. Kieran put the car into gear, drove forward, threw it back into reverse and crashed into the vehicle blocking them one last time. Their car swung out into the street and once again Charlie felt as though she was being whipped from one end of the vehicle to the other.

"Hold on, Charlie!"

Mason's voice was a beacon, reaching through the confusion in her mind. She held on to the sound, to the unflinching reassurance in his deep, rumbling tone. He wouldn't let anything happen to her. She knew it as well as she knew herself. They'd get out of this alive because Mason would make sure they did.

Kieran slammed the shifter into drive and the tires squealed against the pavement as he took off down the street. Charlie didn't dare look up, and chose to remain blind to their surroundings as the car lurched and wove through traffic. Kieran's countenance remained calm, his jaw set with concentration. He probably got into dicey situations like this regularly. Charlie, not so much.

"Are they following us?" Kieran might be calm, but Charlie couldn't curb the frantic worry in her own words. "Where are they?"

The rush of wind through the windows accompanied the occasional honk of a horn as Kieran continued to speed down the narrow streets. He didn't let up on the gas, didn't stop at a single light. It was a wonder they hadn't drawn police attention or been smashed into oblivion, which was a true testament to his driving skills.

Twilight gave way to full dark and Charlie remained crouched beneath the dash. She couldn't bring herself to look up. To take a deep breath. To relax a single muscle. Hell, she didn't think she'd ever be able to relax again after tonight. They'd almost been killed. And whereas she wanted to blame Kieran's rash behavior for the shootout, she had a distinct feeling that if he hadn't acted, the outcome would have been the same.

Jesus.

The air drained from Charlie's lungs and she fought for a breath. Mason leaned over the seat toward her, the lines of concern etched into his face, accentuated by the encroaching darkness and the light from the dash.

He reached down and grabbed her by the hand, hauling her over the center console and into the backseat. "Hey!" Kieran complained as she kicked his arm. "Careful. I didn't avoid getting shot tonight to get my arm broken." Charlie couldn't muster a response. She still couldn't believe he was so cool and collected. It would take her a month to calm down from this!

Mason gathered Charlie in his arms and held her close. Emotion rose in her chest, threatening once again to choke her as she fought for a few decent breaths.

"Shhhh." His warm breath in her ear was a welcome comfort. "It's okay, Charlie. You're okay. Just breathe. I've got you."

She relaxed against him. When Mason held her, she felt as though nothing could touch her. "I-is anyone hurt?" Her teeth chattered on the words and she willed herself to sound strong.

"I'm fine," Mason assured her. "Kieran?"

"Please." He let out an arrogant snort. "As if any of those children had the skill to hit any of us."

Cocky even in the face of death. But Charlie couldn't deny that she was glad they were all relatively unscathed.

"What about you?" Mason's fingers lightly caressed her temple and Charlie sucked in a sharp breath. "You've got a nasty bump. Are you hurt anywhere else?"

She looked up to find his jaw clenched, lips thinned. His brilliant green eyes blazed with an angry fire, as though he was ready to turn around and beat those gangbangers to a bloody pulp.

"I hit my head on the dash," she said. "I'm okay though."

Kieran looked over his shoulder. "You sure?"

"I'm sure."

A quiet moment passed. Kieran turned down Lombard toward Charlie's hotel. "Well, this rental is seriously fucked," he remarked as though they were talking about a recent fender bender. "That's going to cut a chunk out of our profits."

Mason chose not to respond and Charlie followed his lead.

"Any idea who they were?" Mason broke the silence.

"None," Kieran said. "You?"

"No." Charlie looked up at Mason's dark tone. Something had him riled, but she didn't know what. "But you can bet your ass I'm going to find out."

"Good." Kieran looked up into the rearview mirror. "Those little shits are going to regret trying to rob us."

The rest of the drive passed quietly. When Kieran pulled up in the hotel's breezeway, she put her mouth close to Mason's ear. She hated that she couldn't stop trembling. "Will you stay with me tonight?"

His eyes met hers. "Yeah. Of course."

Charlie let out a relieved breath. She was still way too shaken up to be alone. Something didn't add up. The attempted robbery had been too well timed. Mason knew it. She saw the suspicion in his eyes. She couldn't shake the thought that someone wanted them dead.

"Want me to wait for you?" Kieran asked Mason as he got out of the car and let Charlie out as well.

"Nah. I'm good. I'll call you in the morning, though."

Kieran looked from Charlie to Mason and back again. His mouth turned down like a kid who'd just had his cookie taken away. He let out a resigned sigh. "All right. I'll pick you up tomorrow afternoon, Charlie, for our meeting."

Oh crap. She'd forgotten all about it. The thought of going anywhere with Kieran and *without* Mason sent a renewed rush of anxiety into her bloodstream. One last meeting, she promised herself, and then she'd fade into the background and let Mason take over. "I'll be ready," she said. "Good night, Kieran."

"Take it easy." He put the car into gear. "Later, Mason."

They stood in the breezeway and watched the battered Mercedes drive off.

"Thanks for staying." Charlie's voice sounded small in her ears.

"I'm not going anywhere." Mason held her tight.

Thank God. Charlie didn't think she could handle being alone tonight. It scared her that over the course of a month she'd become so dependent on the comfort of Mason's presence. And she didn't see that changing anytime soon.

Chapter Twenty-Four

"Where are we going?"

Kieran slid into the driver's seat and buckled his seat belt. "You'll see."

Charlie didn't like not knowing where they were headed. Especially after yesterday's near miss. She was still pretty shaken up and without Mason beside her, she felt entirely too exposed.

Both Mason and Carrera had insisted that she wear a wire, but Charlie hadn't been comfortable with it. Not when Kieran was still a little twitchy as well. Instead, Carrera had made her agree to a tail. Carrera put two of his best men on it, and they'd guaranteed her that Kieran wouldn't be the wiser. Mason hadn't been quite so lax, though. He didn't trust a couple of marshals following in their car to keep an eye on her. Not with the way Kieran had gone grand-theft-auto through the streets of San Francisco last night. He'd activated the find-friends app on Charlie's phone. That way he could personally keep an eye on her. She had to admit, knowing he could monitor where she was made her feel a hell of a lot more comfortable.

Tonight wasn't the night to be wound up and nervous. Kieran needed to see her at ease. Relaxed. Business as usual.

"Just an FYI, I'm not a huge fan of surprises."

Kieran's eyes lit with an impish spark. "Really? I am."

"Okay, then why don't you tell me where we're going, and later I'll jump out from around a corner and scare you. It'll be a win-win."

He chuckled. "Are you worried?"

Charlie leveled her gaze. "Should I be?"

"No. I won't let anything happen to you."

Somehow, Charlie didn't find Kieran's words all that reassuring. She had a sneaking suspicion that once again he'd intentionally separated her from Mason. Best-case scenario, his reasons were purely selfish, which Charlie could easily deal with. Worst? He was on to them. In which case, she sure as hell hoped those marshals tailing them were good at their job.

The sun hadn't quite set yet, and reflected off the water in the bay like a pirate's lost treasure beneath them. Kieran turned the radio up and Charlie wished he'd turn the damn thing off. Rather than pass the time in silence, she decided to use it to her advantage. She could do a little reconnaissance of her own.

"Did you know Mason was looking for you before he contacted Jensen?"

Kieran's lips quirked in a half smile. "What makes you think that?"

"Mason said the reason you've eluded an arrest for so long is because you're one step ahead of the feds all the time. And that you know what they're going to do before they do it, which is why no one can ever pin anything on you."

"I had no idea he spoke so highly of me," he said with a laugh.

"Is it true?"

Kieran's expression grew serious. He kept his eyes on the road, but Charlie noticed the squaring of his jaw. "I have friends here and there who throw information my way every once in a while."

"I could use a few more friends like that." Boy, wasn't that the truth? Charlie needed intel on Faction Five. It would be nice if some concerned acquaintances threw her a bone here or there. "I figured you've eluded capture for so long by simply staying out of the country."

Kieran shrugged. "I had a reason to come back."

"Does that reason have anything to do with our errand tonight?"

"More or less."

Gah! She was so tired of his cryptic responses. Spit it out already! "It's lucky for me you decided to come back. Me and Mason."

"You really trust him?"

"I do." Kieran might have lingering doubts about Mason, but Charlie was going to quash them. "He was about to quit CBP, you know." He'd already quit by the time the task force snapped him up, but Kieran didn't need to know that.

Kieran's gaze slid to the side. "Why's that?"

"They wouldn't promote him. Used him for undercover work and to give them insight on smuggling rings and whatnot. But they made it pretty clear that because of his familial ties, he wouldn't ever see advancement."

Kieran snorted. "I warned him. Before he made the stupid decision to enter the police academy, I told him they'd treat him like a pariah. But Mason had to prove himself to the world. I guess he thought he'd do it by going in the polar opposite direction of his family. Now he's got wasted years under his belt when he could have been making some real money. What did it net him—breaking from the pack—taking the honorable route? Not a damn thing, that's what."

It was obvious that Mason's departure from the family business was a sore spot. One that hadn't quite healed for Kieran. Charlie hoped that when it was time to arrest Kieran, she could protect Mason somehow from having to take any responsibility for it. Of course he'd said he had no qualms about bringing Kieran down, but Charlie knew that he still considered Kieran family. If she could spare him that emotional fallout, she would.

"I like Jensen," Charlie remarked offhand. "Of course, he's got a reputation for being likable."

Kieran's jaw squared once again. Charlie wondered at the sudden change as his lips thinned and his gaze narrowed on the highway. His hands gripped the steering wheel until his knuckles turned white. He let out a slow and measured breath, as though trying to temper his anger, before his body relaxed by small degrees. "Jensen is a legend." His response lacked the warmth with which he spoke of Mason. "He took me off the street, gave me a home, a brother. Taught me everything he knows."

Those were all statements of fact, but Kieran failed to mention anything about having any true affection for the man who'd become a father to him.

"It must have been nice for you and Mason both." Charlie wanted Kieran nice and relaxed. As far from agitated as possible. "I bet his childhood was pretty lonely until you showed up."

"Yeah," Kieran said. "Jensen is all smiles and charm

when he needs to be, but don't let that fool you. He's ruthless as a fucking wolf."

A reminder Charlie needed. She'd become complacent over the past couple of weeks. Charmed by Kieran and Katarina and even Mason. Their larger-than-life personalities easily seduced her. Still . . . there was honest affection between Kieran and Mason. True brotherhood.

"You looked out for him. Didn't you?"

Kieran shifted in his seat. "We looked out for each other."

Jensen Decker, the quintessential gentleman thief, obviously had a darker side to his personality that few knew anything about. "You're still looking out for each other," Charlie pointed out.

"After a bit of a hiatus." Kieran's tone soured. "But that's all in the past now. Right?"

A chill danced the length of Charlie's spine. "I hope so. Especially if you can hook us up with whatever cash cow you've got the inside track on."

"You really don't like being in the dark, do you?"

At least there were some parts of Charlie's personality that she didn't have to fake. "I freaking hate it."

Kieran snorted. "Control freak."

"Yep, and proud of it."

"Mason's problem has always been his undying faith in the system," Kieran said. "Makes no fucking sense, either. We were taught the system was broken. That so-called honest men were more corrupt than any criminal. For some damned reason, Mason didn't believe Jensen. Maybe if the old man hadn't been such a lousy son of a bitch to him as we got older, Mason would've been more inclined to trust him."

With every word out of Kieran's mouth, Charlie realized there were a good couple decades of emotional baggage that both he and Mason carried around. When she first met Mason, her impression had been that he carried an unnecessarily large chip around on his shoulder. Now she realized that chip was totally justified. After all, he'd been jerked around by everyone: his dad, his brother, the very system he'd had so much faith in. Was there anyone or anything in this world that hadn't let Mason Decker down at some point?

Even Charlie had let him down. She'd put her own ambition before him. Before anyone. At the end of the day, was she any better than Kieran or Jensen?

"You never believed in the system, did you?"

Kieran snorted. "No. Jensen was right about one thing. The system's corrupt. I've met more ruthless criminals on the right side of the law than I ever have on the wrong side of it."

Charlie bristled. She'd always been so confident in her path. So righteous in her need to prosecute those who broke the law. So sure that her side was the right side. The *only* side. Over the course of the past month, she'd come to realize life wasn't simply black and white. There was so much more to right and wrong than the decision to be one or the other.

By the time all of this was said and done, Charlie prayed she could continue to see the difference between the two and make the right choices.

Mason's leg bounced as he sat in the visitors' room at San Quentin. Kieran's third shipment of diamonds was safely stashed in the safe-deposit box, and now it was time to shake the bushes. A niggling thought scratched at the back of his mind, something he hadn't been able to let go of since they'd gotten back from

L.A. He'd learned in the course of his life that when something came easily it was usually because someone wanted it that way.

Mason had been given far too many liberties since being brought onto the task force. Charlie too. He'd been undercover enough with CBP to know how it worked. There was no way the U.S. Marshals Service would be so lax in the way they handled undercover operations. Even with Mason's smart mouth and un-willingness to follow orders, he'd had to play it by the book. All it had taken with Carrera was a few grumbled protests and they'd let the reins loose.

None of it made sense.

Including the ease with which they'd transferred his dad to San Quentin.

Jensen strode into the room with the confidence of a king. Unease slithered up Mason's spine and tight-ened the muscles across his shoulders. His gaze landed on Mason. Mild shock accentuated the lines of his face for the barest moment, but Jensen quickly recovered and replaced the expression with passive disinterest. He took a seat across from Mason, completely at ease despite the cuffs that bound his wrists and ankles. That look of confidence rattled Mason because it only helped to confirm his suspicions.

"You seem surprised to see me."

"Two visits in one month." Jensen shrugged. "This must be a special occasion."

"I want you to tell me everything you know about Faction Five."

Mason wasn't here for small talk. He wanted answers and he wasn't going to stand being kept in the dark for another goddamned second.

Jensen responded with a cocky grin. "What's that?"

Mason's jaw clenched. He'd beat the information

out of his dad if he had to. Charlie was headed God knows where to meet God knows who with Kieran. The only thing Mason knew for sure was that she was in trouble. He needed to find out just how much trouble.

"Don't play your fucking games with me." His jaw clenched and unclenched with agitation. "I'm not some newb you can snow with your smiles and personality. Don't forget, *Dad*, I know exactly who you are and what you're capable of. Your bullshit doesn't work with me. So I'm going to ask you one more time before I beat the ever-loving fuck out of you. What do you know about Faction Five?"

Jensen's smile melted from his face. His bright gaze darkened and a sneer curled his lip. Finally, Mason got a glimpse of the man he knew as his father. The ruthless, selfish bastard who had only ever looked out for himself.

"Enough to know you're in way over your head, boy."

Mason fixed his dad with a stern stare. "What did they offer you? What do you get now that Kieran's working to raise the money to buy your way in?"

A corner of Jensen's mouth hitched. He settled back in his chair and regarded Mason for a quiet moment as though trying to decide how much to reveal. "Freedom." He drummed his fingers absently on the table. "And after that"—his smile grew—"whatever the hell I want."

Complete autonomy. Faction Five offered its elite membership carte blanche. The opportunity to conduct business with the freedom of knowing there would never be any chance of arrest or prosecution. What was a multimillion-dollar buy-in compared to the hundreds of millions he stood to make, given the opportunity to operate without law enforcement breathing down his neck? And the worst part? Jensen hadn't had to lift a fucking finger to do it. He'd let Kieran and him—his own goddamned sons—do all of the heavy lifting for him.

"You son of a bitch," Mason spat. "You knew all along what I was doing, didn't you?"

"Let's face it," Jensen said. "You were never very good at the long con, son."

Son. The word made Mason's teeth itch. "And Charlie?"

Jensen chuckled. "You mean, Assistant U.S. Attorney Charlotte Cahill?"

Mason's heart pounded against his rib cage. His lungs compressed, squeezing every last bit of air from his chest. "You knew all along who she was, didn't you?"

"It was important to keep up appearances," Jensen remarked. "For Kieran's benefit. After today, though, I won't have to play games anymore."

Anger pooled in Mason's gut. Kieran had been as much a victim as Mason and Charlie. Jensen had played them all. But he hadn't orchestrated it on his own.

The realization made Mason nauseous as he said, "Carrera set it all up."

Jensen smirked.

Adrenaline raced through Mason's veins as his worst fears were confirmed. The chief deputy was one of the five. He'd promised to personally keep an eye on Charlie, which meant she was as good as dead.

Charlie had been on the right track. Sort of. A couple more weeks and she might have had it all figured out. The task force had been set up for failure from the very beginning. Jensen had planned it so that his kids would be saddled with the task of raising his buy-in, thereby proving his worth to Faction Five. He'd conned them all. Tricked them into doing his dirty work for him while he sat back and watched from the comfort and protection of his jail cell. And when it was all over, anyone not on board would get a bullet to the head. Namely, Charlie and Mason.

"Why keep Kieran in the dark at all?" It took a sheer act of will not to launch himself across the table and wrap his hands around Jensen's throat. "Why not tell him everything?"

"Kieran could have raised the funds on his own," Jensen admitted. "But it would have taken him a couple of years to get it done. This way was faster, not to mention easier."

Mason snorted. Dipping his hands into the government's coffers probably filled his dad with a smug sense of satisfaction.

"Besides," Jensen said, "he never would have knowingly turned on you. He wouldn't have let me use you."

"Someone has to take the fall for the money the feds transferred to Kieran for the fenced diamonds." The realization was a punch to Mason's chest. They'd played Kieran's game, paid him *millions* for the diamonds he'd smuggled into the country, under the assumption that when the case was wrapped up, the government would reclaim the funds. "Seems like the powers that be would've kept you from doing anything that would shine the light of suspicion on them."

"What do they care where I get it from as long as they get their money?" Jensen remarked. "Someone will take the fall for it. It won't be them. Or me."

Mason's gut clenched. "Charlie."

"That was the plan." Jensen let out a chuff of breath. "She sorta fucked that up when she marched in here after you the other day, didn't she? Kept you on your toes, though."

"It's all right," Mason said. "I can roll with the punches."

The original plan must have been to kill Mason off and let Charlie be responsible for the lost money and botched investigation into Faction Five. Once again, Mason had thrown a monkey wrench into his dad's plan. "What now?" he asked. "Let me take the fall for the money the government is going to lose? What about Charlie? What happens to her now?"

"It's outta my hands." Of course his dad would find a way to have zero accountability.

"Who planned the robbery with the gangbangers last night?" Mason studied his dad's expression, but the bastard didn't even flinch. "You or Carrera?"

"You give me a hell of a lot of credit." Jensen narrowed his gaze at Mason. "If you think I can orchestrate something like that from in here."

He might not be connected now, but once he paid his multimillion-dollar tithe to Faction Five, Jensen would be damned near omnipotent. As one of their elite membership, with the power to pretty much do whatever the hell he damned well pleased, he'd be set for life.

"What happens to Kieran when all of this is said and done? Are you bringing him along for the ride, or will you leave him high and dry as well?"

Jensen had the decency to show the slightest bit of remorse in his answering scowl. "Kieran knows how the game works. He'll understand."

The hell he would. Mason knew Kieran better than anyone. Even his dad. Family meant more to him than anything. Kieran wouldn't take a betrayal lightly.

"You think you know him." Mason returned his father's hard stare. "But you don't."

"And you do?" Jensen laughed long and loud.

"You're damned right I do."

"We'll see about that."

Mason wanted to use his fist to wipe the smug expression from his dad's face. "What's that supposed to mean?"

"Wonder what Kieran will think when he finds out who Charlie really is. She's a hot piece of ass, no doubt about it, but that won't mean much when he finds out she's been working with his own brother to fuck him over this entire time."

Shit.

Mason launched himself across the table and grabbed his dad by the collar of his ugly orange jumpsuit. "If anything happens to her, so help me God, I'll wring the life out of you with my bare hands!"

Urgency vibrated through Mason's limbs as he held fast to Jensen's collar. He needed to get to Charlie. Now. Hell, it might already be too late.

Chapter Twenty-Five

The house Kieran pulled up to didn't scream international crime syndicate headquarters. Instead, it was simplistic and boring, so *suburban*, that Charlie wondered if they were even in the right place. He put the car into park and killed the engine. Sat for a silent moment before he turned to face her.

"What you are, Charlie, is a small piece of what is going to be a massive empire." Kieran's gaze bore through her, his dark eyes intent and serious. "A crime syndicate unlike anything there's ever been before. No rules. No fear of arrest or prosecution. Whatever we can dream up, we can do."

Giddy anticipation raced through Charlie's veins. Finally, some definitive answers! She kept her excitement under wraps and canted her head to the side as she regarded Kieran. "No accountability whatsoever?"

He beamed. You'd think Kieran had dreamed up Faction Five all on his own. "None."

She kept her expression skeptical. "How do you think you're going to manage that?"

"It's already been managed."

"Is that what we're amassing money for?" She let her lips curve into a sweet smile. "The ability to work without restriction?"

"Exactly."

"No one's completely immune from the law," Charlie said, dubious.

"Mason managed to keep you from being thrown in jail," Kieran pointed out.

"True." Charlie eyed the house in front of them. Nervous energy churned in her stomach and burned in her chest. She rubbed at her sternum as though to banish the sensation. Being separated from Mason didn't sit right with her. Why would Kieran bring her to meet with any of Faction Five's leaders and leave him behind? "But Mason is one tiny piece of a much larger puzzle. I got lucky."

"We're taking luck out of the equation."

"How so?"

Kieran reached out and traced the pad of his finger along the back of Charlie's hand. His gaze heated and she swallowed down the nerves that refused to calm. "The game's about to change, Charlie. And I'm bringing you along for the ride."

She cleared her throat. "What about Mason?"

Kieran's gaze darkened. "Come on. There's someone I want you to meet."

He got out of the car and Charlie took a quick moment for a few deep, cleansing breaths that did little to slow her pounding heart. Her hands shook and she gripped them tight, willing them to still before Kieran noticed the fear she couldn't seem to temper.

Charlie reached for the door handle and reminded herself that she wasn't alone. Carrera and a couple of deputy marshals were somewhere close. The GPS on her phone was active. It wasn't like no one knew where she was. Everything would be okay. She'd be okay. *Just breathe, Charlie. Don't lose it.*

Kieran pulled her door open at the exact moment she pushed. He held out a hand and Charlie took it, hoping like hell he wouldn't notice her sweaty palms. "This doesn't look like the sort of place an international crime ring would set up shop." She kept her tone light and airy, forced any hint of a tremor to the pit of her stomach.

"Looks can be deceiving." Kieran flashed her a wicked grin.

"I guess that's true." Charlie forced herself to laugh. They made their way down the narrow walkway toward the house. With every step placed, her anxiety built. "Don't you think Mason should be here for this? I mean, we are partners and this seems like a pretty important meeting."

"We can fill him in later." Kieran's reassurance didn't do anything for Charlie's nerves.

"Sure." What else could she say?

"Relax." Easy enough for Kieran. Charlie wouldn't be able to relax until she was out of this mess and every member of Faction Five was behind bars. "We're about to be given the keys to the castle."

The keys to the castle? Or yet another set of hoops to jump through? Either way, Charlie supposed she was about to find out.

Kieran stepped up to the door and rang the bell. Fear compressed the air from Charlie's lungs as she waited to be greeted by whoever stood on the other side. She'd been less worried walking into Katarina's high-end strip club, surrounded by Russian mobsters, than she was this innocent-looking house. The door swung wide and Charlie felt as though she'd been

knocked in the stomach with a baseball bat as she came
face-to-face with Carlos Carrera.

She clenched her jaw to keep it from hanging wide
open. A slap in the face would have been less shocking—
and would have hurt a hell of a lot less—than what she
was seeing right now. Carrera? Part of Faction Five?
One of her own damned task force members had been
in league with the bad guys all along. She couldn't believe it. Didn't want to. There had to be another explanation. Like, he'd shown up early and made the call to
arrest everyone at the house. Surely that was it. It
couldn't be what it looked like. Charlie refused to believe the truth that was right in front of her face. Otherwise, she'd crack.

"Sorry about this, Counselor." Carrera pulled his
gun from the holster. "Kieran. Why don't you two come
in?" He held the gun casually at his side but the threat
was inherent in his voice.

"Counselor?" Kieran sounded as confused as Charlie felt. At least they were both in the dark.

With mechanical steps, Charlie moved forward. The
door closed silently behind them, but it might as well
have been the stone of her tomb sliding into place. Because she had no doubt she wasn't walking out of here.
She'd been intentionally separated from Mason,
duped by her own damned people and one of the men
she'd put her absolute trust in. Charlie had never felt
so betrayed in her entire life, and she knew that she
had no one to blame but herself.

She'd gotten herself into this mess and it seemed
there was no way of getting out.

"Put that gun away, Carlos. Jesus Christ." Kieran
looked like he was hanging on to his temper by the
barest of threads. Apparently he didn't like having a
gun pointed at him any more than Charlie did. He raked

his fingers through his dark hair and the expression reminded Charlie so much of Mason. "Would someone care to tell me what the *fuck* is going on here?"

"Jensen wanted to make sure his funds were secure before you knew."

Kieran looked from Charlie to Carrera. "Knew what?"

That lousy son of a bitch! Anger seethed beneath the surface of Charlie's skin, writhing and boiling. The theory that Kieran had been planning to con the government out of its money had been right . . . only Kieran didn't seem to be in on it. Had Jensen played them all? *Jesus.* Nausea rolled through Charlie and angry tears stung at her eyes. She'd been made a fool of. And the worst part of it all was that in this case Kieran was right: The worst criminals were the ones who claimed to be on the right side of the law.

"Charlie isn't who you think she is," Carrera said. The bastard didn't even have the decency to pretend to feel guilty as his gaze slid to Charlie. "She's an assistant U.S. attorney. In charge of the task force investigating Faction Five."

Kieran's eyes went wide, confirming Charlie's suspicions. He'd been kept completely in the dark. But why?

"Mason . . ."

"Mason knows," Carrera said. Kieran looked as though he'd just been punched in the gut. Charlie could relate. It totally sucked to have the rug pulled out from under you. "He's been working the case with Charlie. It's what Jensen wanted."

"Mother . . . fucker." Kieran took a step back. For the first time since she'd met him, Charlie got a glimpse of the hard-hearted, ruthless criminal. A deep crease cut into his brow and his nostrils flared with anger. A burst of nervous energy dumped into Charlie's bloodstream.

If Carrera didn't kill her, she was pretty sure that Kieran would get the job done.

"Kieran, it's not what you think." Charlie wasn't sure what she thought she'd accomplish by trying to defuse his anger. Any attempt to bullshit him at this point was only going to push him deeper into a rage. "Okay, so maybe it is what you think, but you have to understand that you weren't the target. We were trying to get to Faction Five, and you were our only lead. Mason cares about you. He never wanted—"

Whip-quick, Kieran pulled a gun from a holster beneath his jacket. The sound of him pulling back the slide effectively silenced Charlie. He leveled the barrel on her face and her heart pumped hard and fast with renewed fear. Carrera had set her up. There was no car with U.S. marshals keeping tabs on her, and even though Mason could keep an eye on her whereabouts through the app on her phone, why would he? As far as he knew, this was business as usual and Carrera had made it seem as though Charlie would be protected. She was miles from the city, miles from her only protection. There would be no rescue, no cavalry to march in and save the day. She'd betrayed Kieran Eagan, and according to Mason, he didn't take betrayal lightly.

She was screwed.

Carrera. That son of a bitch.

Mason sped through traffic, the engine of his Camaro growling angrily as he punched the accelerator and switched lanes. It had all been a lie. The offer to get him into the program at Glynco, his temporary deputy status, all of it. He'd effectively turned Mason into the one thing he despised, and he'd been so damned eager to believe the lies that he'd swallowed down every spoon-fed bite. He and Charlie both.

There was no one he could trust. Jensen had refused to reveal the identities of Faction Five's other members. From his dad's comments about gaining his freedom, Mason gathered that at least one of them was a federal judge. The other was Carrera. The task force already surmised that one member was a senator, and Mason figured the other could be a programmer or coder. It was pretty safe to assume the remaining member was another federal law enforcement officer. FBI or CIA maybe. It didn't matter if Mason didn't know the members' identities; they'd do anything to protect their secrets. They'd failed to kill them last night, but you could bet they wouldn't fail a second time.

Kieran was the only unknown variable. That didn't do much to bolster Mason's confidence. His brother would just as soon kill Charlie himself as protect her when he found out who she really was. Kieran didn't like to be played, and Charlie had used every wile at her disposal to keep him placated.

No one fooled Kieran Eagan and lived to tell about it.

Thank God he'd activated the app on Charlie's phone. Without it, he would have been dead in the water. Jensen sure as hell hadn't been forthcoming as to where Carrera had instructed Kieran to take her.

His dad had always only ever looked out for number one. It didn't surprise Mason a bit, though he couldn't banish the hurt he felt. That his own father would turn on him, conspire to have him killed, was a wound Mason didn't think he'd recover from. He'd deal with his own hurt later, though. Once Charlie was safe and Faction Five was put down for good.

Racing against the clock, Mason took off from San

Quentin. The app would lead him to Charlie's phone, but would it take him to her as well? If Carrera was smart, he would have told Kieran to pitch her phone into the bay or ditch it on the freeway. In which case, he was screwed. Carrera might be a slimy piece of shit, but he wasn't a seasoned criminal. Mason had to hope that he'd overlook a few details in his haste to get Charlie out of the picture. Then again, Carrera's haste might seal Charlie's fate. His heart pounded in his chest. Damn it, he couldn't get to her fast enough.

Thirty minutes later, Mason pulled into a subdivision that was so damned cookie-cutter, it might as well have been his own neighborhood growing up. Jensen found it entertaining to hide out among the middle class. He'd always said that their overinflated opinions of themselves didn't allow for them to suspect their neighbors of any wrongdoing. He hoped that Carrera had taken a page out of Jensen's book and chosen this place for Kieran to bring Charlie. If not, Mason was back at square one.

He parked his car a block from the address he'd pulled from the find-friends app and said a silent prayer that he'd find Charlie safe and sound. Mason ditched his car and took off at a jog, past the similar façades of the houses crammed next to one another, the perfectly manicured lawns, the luxury SUVs and practical sedans parked in the driveways. It was a life that Mason had been forced to pretend he had as a kid. While other kids' parents left for their offices and respectable jobs, Jensen was flying out to fence a quarter million in diamonds or con some poor sap out of his life's savings. He'd resented the lies, the deception, his entire life. And now, he was an unemployed Customs agent with a U.S. marshal's badge that was probably as counterfeit as the Kimberley certificates they'd been passing off to their buyers all week. Mason had become a vigilante, thanks to Carrera and his dad.

He'd make sure they paid for it, too.

Mason rounded the corner and slowed. Kieran's rental car sat parked in a driveway three houses down. Adrenaline dumped into Mason's bloodstream. He locked down his nerves and centered his focus as he approached the house and went around to the backyard. Charlie was in that house, and if she was in anything less than pristine condition, Mason would unleash the fury of hell on whoever hurt her.

Even if that man was his own brother.

Mason hopped the fence and dropped into the backyard, gun drawn. He strained to hear voices from inside the house but was answered with an eerie silence that made his heart stutter in his chest. The blinds were drawn, offering him cover, but at the same time preventing him from seeing inside.

"Would someone care to tell me what the *fuck* is going on here?"

The sound of Kieran's voice pierced the quiet. They couldn't have been here too long. Odds were good that Charlie might still be alive. Her voice followed on the heels of Kieran's demand, too frantic and muffled for Mason to make out what she said. A relieved breath decompressed his lungs. She was still alive. Thank God. For how long, though, depended on how quickly Mason could get his ass in gear and come up with a plan to get her out of there.

The sounds of voices quieted once again. Mason could account for Carrera, Charlie, and Kieran. Whether or not Carrera had brought backup, the odds were still stacked against Mason. He wanted to trust that Kieran wouldn't turn against him, but if Carrera had filled him in, chances were good that Kieran was pissed. He wouldn't forgive a betrayal of this magnitude and Mason wouldn't blame him.

He'd done his best over the years to stay as far away from Kieran's business as possible, and Kieran had returned the courtesy. Now though, thanks to Carreras's greed and his own dad's selfishness, he found himself in a position he'd never wanted to be in. What was done was done, though. No turning back now. Charlie needed him, and he'd be damned if he let her down.

Mason stepped up to the patio. Through a small gap in the vertical blinds he saw Charlie positioned between Carrera and Kieran. His heart sank to his stomach as he noted Kieran's outstretched arm and the gun he aimed at Charlie's head. Damn it, Kieran wasn't a violent man, but there were two things that would make him one: when someone threatened his life, or when someone betrayed him.

With his line of sight limited by the blinds, Mason couldn't be sure if there was anyone else in the house. It didn't matter. He needed to get Charlie out of there. Even if all he could do was distract Kieran and Carrera and whoever the hell else was inside long enough for her to run. He'd face a barrage of bullets if that's what it took. He was in love with Charlie. There wasn't a damn thing he wouldn't do to keep her safe.

Too bad he probably wouldn't live long enough to tell her.

Mason watched as Charlie was ushered farther into the living room and out of his line of sight. A flash of movement from inside the house caught Mason's eye. A body moved toward the dining room from the kitchen area and crossed to the patio door. Quick breaths puffed in Mason's chest as he spun away from the sliding glass door and pressed his back against the rough stucco exterior of the house. The patio door slid open with a whisper of sound and Mason waited to pounce.

At the first sign of a body emerging, Mason reached out. He grabbed the guy by the arm and swung him around with a forceful jerk. The gun dropped from his grip and Mason took him into a tight choke hold. He increased the pressure of his grip as the guy shoved and flailed, knocking Mason up against the side of the house. Any sound could alert Carrera to trouble, and Mason quickly shoved away, taking the fight around to the side of the house where there would be less chance of discovery.

The son of a bitch was strong and refused to go down easily. Mason let out a low grunt as he squeezed the bastard's throat in the crook of his arm, willing him to lose consciousness. He clawed at Mason's arm, batted wildly toward his face. His wheezing breaths quieted and he went limp in Mason's grasp.

One down. God only knew how many to go.

Mason retrieved the discarded gun and tucked it into his waistband. He sidled through the open patio door, his footsteps light. With his Glock held at the ready, Mason kept tight to the walls as he crept past the dining room and into the kitchen. The sound of Kieran's voice carried from the living room and Mason paused.

"I want to talk to Jensen first."

"You can talk to him after Judge Erickson signs off on his release. Until then, you're going to have to take my word for it."

Charlie scoffed at Carrera's words. Mason rolled his eyes. Could she try to *not* be so damned exasperating when her life was in danger?

"Judge Erickson is set to retire in six months," Charlie

remarked. "A whole hell of a lot of good that's going to do your secret club."

"What's she talking about?"

Uh-oh. Kieran's short-clipped words didn't bode well. What Carrera didn't realize was that Kieran played only one side: his own. He wouldn't risk his own safety and freedom by being involved in anything that wasn't absolutely foolproof.

Maybe for once, Charlie's tenacity would come in handy. Creating a little tension between Carrera and Kieran might just be the distraction Mason needed. Either that or her smart mouth would sign her death warrant. Mason hoped that for once luck would be on his side.

Chapter Twenty-Six

Charlie's brain raced to form a plan of attack. It seemed that division was her best bet at staying alive. If she could sway Kieran to doubt Carrera—and the security of Faction Five—even a tiny bit, she might be able to buy herself the opportunity to make an escape.

"The fuck sort of operation are you running, Carlos?" Kieran demanded. "Does Jensen know about this?"

"Charlie doesn't know what she's talking about." Carrera kept his gun trained on her, his expression emotionless. "The judge isn't going anywhere. Not when he stands to make hundreds of millions."

"What about Mason?" Kieran's dark eyes narrowed on Carrera.

"What about him?"

Kieran stared Carrera down. Charlie had never seen him look so dead serious and threatening. The silence grew thick with tension. Charlie looked from one man to the other.

Carrera let out a long-suffering sigh. "Someone's got to take the fall. As far as anyone knows, Mason went rogue. By the time we're done with him, there won't be a jury in the county that won't believe he stole the government's money and killed Charlie to cover his tracks. It'll work out to our advantage."

Charlie couldn't contain the words or the rage that scalded a path up her throat. "You son of a bitch!"

"Jensen knows about this?" Kieran's tone hinted at disbelief. Charlie couldn't help but feel sorry for him. His sense of family was so strong he couldn't conceive that Jensen would turn on his own son.

Carrera laughed. "Hell, it was his idea."

Something in Kieran's demeanor snapped. He swung his gun around and pointed it at Carrera. Charlie fought the urge to celebrate prematurely, but for the first time since she'd walked through the door, she felt a slight glimmer of hope.

"Bullshit." Kieran forced the word from between clenched teeth. "I don't believe you."

"Take it easy, Kieran." A slight tremor shook Carrera's voice. "I told you, he didn't want you upset, and that's why he didn't tell you."

"Tell me what?" he spat. "That he was using both of us to raise his buy-in for your fucking organization? What happens to me now that Jensen's freedom has been purchased? You gonna take care of me too, *Marshal*?"

Carrera's lip curled at the sneer in Kieran's voice. "Don't forget who you're talking to and what I'm capable of."

Kieran smiled. Cold, devoid of emotion. Serious and deadly. Charlie eased to the edge of the couch and dug her feet into the carpet. If bullets started to fly, she wanted as far from the action as possible.

"I think all of that perceived power is going to your head, Carlos."

"Perceived, my ass." He looked Kieran up and down, the disdain clear. "Fuck up Jensen's chance at freedom, and I'll be the least of your worries."

Kieran let out a sarcastic chuff of breath. "Jensen doesn't own me."

Carrera's brow arched curiously. Charlie fought the urge to shake her head at his arrogant stupidity.

"Fuck you," Kieran said. "Fuck Jensen, and *fuck* Faction Five."

The sound of a scuffle broke out from the kitchen, and all hell broke loose. Kieran turned and Carrera used his diverted attention to his advantage. He brought his gun up and fired. Charlie hit the deck. The shot went wide, missing Kieran, and he squeezed off a couple of retaliating shots, clipping Carrera's arm in the process.

"Get out of here, Charlie!"

Kieran's words stunned Charlie to the point that she could barely move. Was he actually going to help her? She scrambled to find her footing, but a hand wrapped around her ankle and jerked her backward. She kicked with her free leg and Carrera let out a grunt of pain as her heel connected with his face and he lost his hold on her. Her fingers dug into the thick pile of the carpet as she fought to stand. Kieran reached down, grabbed her wrist, and hauled her to her feet.

Never in a million years would Charlie have thought any of this would play out this way. But she was damned glad it had.

"Come on!"

They turned toward the front door, only to find their way blocked by another armed man. Charlie had counted three men besides Carrera when they'd come in, and two of them were currently unaccounted for.

Whoever he was, this guy wasn't messing around. He brought his gun up, aimed . . .

The shot rang out. Kieran hauled her against his body and turned, shielding her from the impact, and Charlie squeezed her eyes shut. She waited for the pain of a bullet tearing her insides to shreds but it never came. The sound of a body hitting the floor prompted her eyes to open and she found their assailant bleeding out on the floor.

"Charlie!"

"Oh my God, Mason!" Relief washed over her as he rounded the corner from the kitchen to get to her. And just as quickly turned to panic as he was tackled to the floor by Carrera.

"Charlie, get the hell out of here!"

Kieran's words barely registered as he gave her a shove toward the door. Fear froze her in place as she watched the butt of Carrera's gun come down on Mason's head. His grunt of pain gutted her, and the starch seemed to melt from her spine. If he died trying to protect her, she'd never forgive herself. Nothing in this world meant more to her.

The emotion clogged her chest and stole her breath. She loved Mason Decker. *Holy shit.* Probably not the best time for that epiphany, considering they weren't even close to being out of the woods yet.

Charlie gave herself a mental shake. This wasn't the time for self-reflection and searching her emotions. She compartmentalized that shit on the double and focused instead on getting the hell out of there like Kieran told her to. No one knew where they were and no backup would be coming. All she needed was the opportunity to alert law enforcement and get them here.

Carrera had fucked with her task force. Charlie was going to fuck with him.

She took off for the front door at a sprint. The muted sound of the silencer made the shot almost hard to hear, but Charlie sure as hell felt the wind of the passing bullet breeze past her ear. The threat stopped her in an instant and she turned to find Carrera on his feet, his gun leveled on her. Mason was stunned but not unconscious, on the floor cradling his head in his palms. Kieran remained calm through it all, his own gun trained on Carrera. His chest barely moved with his breath. Not a bead of sweat marred his brow. This was his world after all; Carrera was just visiting. The crooked marshal would be wise to remember that, but Charlie doubted he'd be smart enough to give credit where it was due.

"Mason? You good?" Kieran's voice didn't so much as quaver.

"Yeah."

Charlie allowed herself a breath of relief at Mason's grunted response. From the kitchen, one of Carrera's men emerged, looking a little worse for wear. Obviously the one Mason had fought with in the kitchen. Blood trickled from his lip and a split above his left eye. He limped to Carrera's side and hauled Mason to his feet by the scruff of his shirt and laid his fist into Mason's gut.

"Ooof."

The sound knotted every muscle in Charlie's body and she swore she felt the blow in her own stomach. The man's fist swung around one more time and Charlie flinched as Mason slumped over.

"Lay into him again," Kieran said to Carrera's guy, "and it'll be the last thing you ever do."

"You're not in charge here, Kieran," Carrera said.

Charlie wanted to punch him in the face, bash him over the head with something blunt and heavy. She could barely contain the anger that churned and boiled with every smug word out of his mouth. "Jensen said you'd play ball."

"Well, Jensen was fucking *wrong*," Kieran ground out. "I'm not anyone's bitch. Not his, and sure as fuck not yours."

"Why protect Mason when he's willing to sell you out? He would have arrested you. In a heartbeat." Carrera's incredulous tone only further prodded Charlie's temper. The man was a decorated U.S. marshal, for Christ's sake! What could have prompted him to turn his back on the vows he'd made to uphold the law?

Oh, right, millions of dollars and unchecked power.

"I offered him a fast track to a U.S. marshal's badge in exchange for your arrest, and he took the offer without even blinking."

Kieran's elbow dipped and his gun lowered a couple of inches. Charlie's stomach lurched up into her throat. "Is that true, Mason?"

Mason met Kieran's unflinching gaze. "More or less. You know how it goes, Kieran."

Charlie's jaw went slack. That wasn't true. The task force wanted Kieran for intel. His arrest had been the least of their worries. What was Mason up to?

Kieran's eyes narrowed and one corner of his mouth twitched. What Mason had promised to do was use Kieran's knowledge to help bring down Faction Five. Carrera wanted Kieran to believe differently. But how Kieran chose to interpret the truth of Mason's confession was a different story altogether.

Growing up with a con artist and a liar, you learned

pretty damned quick how to protect yourself. Kieran and Mason never lied to each other. At least not outright. His dad had constantly played them against each other when they were kids, just like Carrera had tried to do. Over the years, they'd learned to communicate in a way that would circumvent Jensen's bullshit. Kieran was more Mason's brother than Jensen had ever been his father. Mason trusted that Kieran would do the right thing.

He was a con artist and a thief, true. But he wasn't a heartless bastard. Not by a long shot.

"I think it's time we renegotiated terms," Kieran said.

"I don't have to negotiate shit." Carrera's disdainful sneer wouldn't do much for Kieran's mood, that was for sure. "Take her into the kitchen and sit her ass down," he said to the bastard who'd just used Mason's gut as a punching bag. "Mason too. And keep an eye on them without getting your ass kicked this time. I don't want any more trouble before we wrap this up."

Wrap this up, meaning put a bullet in their heads. Nothing had gone according to Carrera's plans so far, proving that he wasn't the criminal mastermind he thought he was. When his partners got wind of how badly he'd fucked this up, there'd be hell to pay. If Mason got his way, they'd all have plenty of time to hash it out behind bars.

Charlie's gaze met his and Mason fought to suppress the rage that boiled in his veins. At least she was in one piece and unhurt, but that she'd had to go through any of this at all made him want to beat the shit out of someone for retribution. The asshole to his right would do just fine. Mason would get his chance soon enough; he simply had to play it cool and wait for the right moment.

Kieran was going to get him that moment. He had no doubt.

Mason had barely made eye contact with Charlie. His worry for her damn near ate him alive and he couldn't risk losing his focus for even a second. But in the post-scuffle calm, he took in her wide, frightened eyes, pale complexion, and drawn mouth. His need to comfort her almost overrode his desire to beat Carrera and his cronies to a bloody pulp.

"It's going to be okay, Charlie." Her eyes met his, glistening with tears. "I promise."

She gave a shallow nod of her head as Carrera's goon grabbed her by the arm and led her into the kitchen. With one of his guys slumped against the wall, bleeding, and the other still unconscious in the backyard, their odds were even. They could tip at any moment though, so Mason needed to make the most of every second.

Likewise, Kieran needed to get to the point. They didn't have time to fuck around.

"Jensen didn't raise your multimillion-dollar buy-in," Kieran said. "*I did.*"

Carrera's partner poked the barrel of his Glock into Mason's back. A growl rose in his throat but he headed toward the kitchen and left Kieran to do what he did best. They continued to argue, Kieran talking circles around Carrera, and the crooked U.S. marshal doing his best to placate Kieran, before Carrera was forced to make a deal with him as well as Jensen.

In the kitchen, Mason reached out and caught Charlie's hand in his. A tremor vibrated from her fingers into his and his jaw clenched. He stepped up close behind her until her back met his chest. The warmth of her body was heaven. It banished every ache and pain that plagued him.

"How could I be so stupid?" He barely heard her whispered words. "He played us both."

"He did." Mason let her fingers slip through his grasp. "But he's not going to get away with it."

From the living room, a gun fired. No silencer, meaning Kieran had shot first. Mason brought his elbow back with enough force to crack the other man's skull. A pop of cartilage accompanied his shout of pain. Mason spun and brought his left fist around and connected with his gut. The guy went to his knees, doubled over, his face cradled in one palm.

Pop! Pop! Pop!

Kieran's aim must not have been stellar. The sound of bullets hitting drywall added to the cacophony. "Charlie, get under the table!" Mason shouted. He watched from the corner of his eye to make sure she did what he'd asked while he wrestled the Glock out of Carrera's accomplice's hand.

"Behind you!"

Charlie's warning shout drew Mason's attention. He whipped around in time to see the guy he'd put the choke hold on storm through the sliding glass door. He fired off two shots to Mason's one. The breath lodged somewhere near his sternum as he braced for the impact, but instead, the other guy slumped to the floor.

Too much demanded Mason's attention. By facing one assailant, he left the other unguarded. The crack of wood and a shout of pain had him spinning once again to find Charlie standing over the unconscious body of the guy he'd put the sleeper hold on, a dining room chair clutched in her fists.

The sudden rush of adrenaline left Mason shaky and unsteady on his feet. Charlie went to his side and it was clear from her own trembling form that she wasn't doing much better. "Kieran?" he called out. It had grown much too quiet in the living room for Mason's peace of mind.

"Yeah."

Mason let out a relieved sigh. "You good?"

"Yeah."

His response was a little too tight. Mason kept Charlie tucked behind him as he ventured back into the living room. Kieran had his gun to Carrera's head, his finger placed precariously on the trigger. He shook like a freaking leaf, his temper simmering under the surface of his barely contained rage.

"Let law enforcement deal with him." Mason kept his tone as calm as possible. He didn't feel any more under control than Kieran looked.

Kieran snorted. "He *is* law enforcement."

"No." Though Carrera sure as hell made a point for Kieran's opinion of cops. Mason wanted to coldcock the son of a bitch on principle. "He's not. He's a lying piece of shit, is what he is. You need to let the system deal with him. You're a lot of things, Kieran, but a murderer isn't one of them."

"He fucked us," Kieran said from between clenched teeth. "Jensen *fucked us.*"

Mason felt sorry for Kieran that he was only now realizing what Mason had known most of his life. "Yep. They fucked us," he agreed. "And the best way to fuck them back is to let them rot in their cells."

"You're a hypocrite, Decker. You know that?" Mason turned his attention to Carrera's sneering countenance. "You're so ready to put me in jail, but you're just going to let him walk? As if he wouldn't have put a bullet in your head if it would have benefited him somehow."

Mason had told Carrera from day one: No one knew Kieran like he did. Kieran had chosen his path a long time ago, and whereas Mason didn't agree with it, he also knew that Kieran tried to be a good man in his own way. He pulled a thick black zip tie from his back pocket and secured it tight around Carrera's wrists. "Carlos Carrera, you're under arrest for conspiracy and attempted murder. You have the right to remain silent . . ."

Carrera laughed as Mason read his Miranda rights. "You stupid son of a bitch," he spat. "You don't have the authority to arrest me."

The sound of sirens grew louder in the distance. A shoot-out like they'd just had didn't go unnoticed in a peaceful suburban neighborhood like this. Mason's gaze met Kieran's for a silent moment and he held it.

"I might not," Mason agreed. "But they do."

Kieran stepped up to Mason as the sound of sirens grew deafening. He pulled back his right arm and gathered his hand into a fist. Mason smiled at his brother a split second before his punch connected with Mason's chin. Stars swam in his vision and Charlie's surprised gasp filled his ears before he hit the floor.

Damn, Kieran really didn't pull any punches.

Chapter Twenty-Seven

"We're lucky Carrera refused to take the fall for Faction Five alone."

Charlie tapped her pencil on the yellow legal pad as she considered interim Chief Deputy Benson's words. Her concentration had been crap for the past month as she waited for the remaining members of the group to be arrested by the U.S. Marshals Service.

"We are," she agreed. "Not that it's made our job much easier."

So far they'd arrested Judge Joseph Erickson, and Captain Bruce Augusta from San Francisco PD along with Carrera. Senator Bob Penn was still unaccounted for—along with a huge chunk of Faction Five's seed money—and the marshals were closing in on the group's fifth member, Steve Jenks, a coder for the CIA who'd been spotted in San Diego and heading toward the Mexico border yesterday.

"It could have been a lot worse."

Charlie gave him a rueful smile. "Probably."

"We'll get Penn," Benson assured her. "Jenks too. It'll take a little time, but no one can hide forever."

"What about Kieran?" Charlie tried to keep the concern from her voice.

"I'll admit, he's going to be a little tougher to track down. So far, there aren't any leads, but we'll get a hit eventually."

After knocking Mason out, Kieran had taken off. The manhunt had been intense the first week, but Charlie knew he'd left the country almost immediately. He'd been a tool for Jensen to buy his way into Faction Five, and nothing more. He wasn't a relevant aspect of her case against Carrera and the others. When it came down to it, Kieran was another of their victims.

Charlie's focus wandered to her office window and the crystal-clear blue sky beyond. The moment when Mason had all but let Kieran coldcock him replayed in her mind. She knew there was no other way it could've gone down. They were brothers. Their bond was pretty damned unbreakable.

Charlie had always thought that life was so black and white. There were only two sides and you either chose the right one or you suffered the consequences. But maybe not all criminals were bad guys. After all, she'd certainly learned that not all good guys were honorable. Doing the right thing didn't always mesh with what fell within the boundaries of the law. For better or worse, Mason had done the right thing in letting Kieran go.

"How's Mason doing?"

The one thing Charlie made sure the task force made good on was Carrera's promise to Mason. She'd demanded that his application to the Marshals Service go through, and he'd been accepted to the training program at Glynco. He was the *only* reason Faction Five had been taken down. He deserved this. Charlie felt his absence every day, though. She didn't know it was possible to miss someone with such a deep, resounding ache. It distracted her, possessed her every thought.

She hadn't told him how she felt about him before he left.

Six weeks might as well be forever. What if their time apart made him realize that he didn't want her? What if all they'd had was the case and the task force, and everything he felt for her was a result of being thrown into that situation together? Worry gnawed at Charlie's stomach. Her feelings for him hadn't changed at all. If anything, they'd only intensified in his absence.

"Charlie?"

Benson's voice pulled her from her thoughts. "Sorry," she said with a nervous laugh. "It's been a long day. What did you say?"

"I asked if you wanted to go over the arrest records before Jensen Decker's hearing next week?"

"I think I'm good." Jensen's attorney was trying to broker a deal by offering up the names of possible Faction Five co-conspirators. It wasn't going to do him any good, though. Charlie was determined to make sure he never saw anything but the inside of a jail cell for the next couple of decades. "I'll give you a call if I need anything though."

Benson headed for the door. "Perfect. Have a good weekend."

She checked the time at the bottom of her computer screen. "You too." She'd promised to meet her dad for dinner tonight. Getting back to her life, her normal routine, should have felt good. Instead, Charlie found herself yearning for something more. At any rate, she could use a drink.

* * *

"You look tired."

Charlie's dad gave her a peck on the cheek as he settled down beside her at the bar. Charlie glanced at Lacey from the corner of her eye before casting her gaze upward. Lacey subdued her own amusement as she turned her attention to her customers at the other end of the bar. Charlie wished she had a similar escape route.

"I'm all right." She pushed the scotch she'd ordered for her dad over to him and he took a long sip. "I've had a few late nights this week, but my workload's been pretty light."

"You should've taken some time off." Her dad had insisted that she take a leave of absence after he'd found out what had been going on. Charlie appreciated his concern, but work was the only thing keeping her mind off Mason lately. If she didn't have work, she'd drive herself crazy thinking about him.

"I'm okay, Dad. Really."

"Do the marshals still have a security detail on you?"

"No. I put an end to that after the second week." Charlie appreciated that the USMS had taken her safety so seriously, but she wasn't about to waste resources on herself. "No one's going to come after me."

Her dad's brow furrowed. "You don't know that, Charlie. You pissed off some very important people."

True. But she knew the risks when she'd taken this job. If she allowed herself to be intimidated by people like that, men who deserved to be in jail would never be prosecuted. "I'll be okay, Dad."

He took another long sip from his glass. "That Eagan fellow still isn't accounted for. From what I've heard, he's bad news."

A rueful smile curved Charlie's lips. Kieran had everyone snowed. He wasn't half as ruthless or dangerous as he led people to believe. "He won't come after me."

"And you know that how . . . ?"

Kieran hadn't disappeared empty-handed. He had thirty million in cash that Charlie herself had helped to put into his hands. If she had one regret, it was that. She knew he didn't feel an ounce of remorse for taking it, either. It wasn't tough to picture him on some obscure beach somewhere, living a luxurious life. Probably retired. Hopefully retired.

"I just know, Dad."

They sat in relative silence for a while, each of them decompressing from their day. Charlie's mind inevitably wandered to Mason. What was he doing? Was he breezing through basic training? Was he happy?

"I'm proud of you, kiddo." Her dad's voice broke the silence and Charlie stared at her dad. He'd never uttered those words to her. Ever.

Emotion clogged Charlie's throat. "You are?"

"I couldn't be prouder."

Tears pricked at Charlie's eyes. "Thanks."

He reached over and hugged her. Charlie let her eyes drift shut as she relaxed against her dad's shoulder. She felt as though they'd reached a turning point. One where expectations didn't exist anymore. Funny, it had taken becoming a black-market diamond broker to get them to this point.

As per their routine, they took their drinks to a table and had dinner. They talked about work, their cases, the usual stuff. Afterward, Charlie said good-bye to Lacey and hugged her dad one last time before heading around the corner back to her office. She'd decided to grab the arrest records for the case after all. Anything to keep her mind off of Mason and how much she missed him.

Charlie stepped into the elevator and hit the button

for the sixth floor. The doors began to slide shut. "Hold the elevator!" She let out a sigh and reached for the button to open the doors at the same time a large hand slid into the opening to push the doors wide. Charlie looked up. Her heart beat a mad rhythm as her gaze met Mason Decker's. *Dear God.* Was it possible that he'd grown even more striking in the weeks he'd been gone?

"You had me worried there for a second." The deep rumble of his voice vibrated through her, coaxing chills to the surface of Charlie's skin. "I thought you were trying to shut me out."

Charlie looked up at him and a slow smile curved her lips. "I would *never* shut you out."

A hundred words sat at the tip of Mason's tongue. Words he'd practiced over again in the long month he'd been apart from Charlie. Instead of saying his carefully rehearsed speech, he took her in his arms and put his mouth to hers.

Sometimes actions spoke louder than words.

Mason hadn't known he could miss someone with such a crippling intensity. The past six weeks away from Charlie had nearly destroyed him. Not a day had gone by that he didn't think about her. Worry about her. Long to hear her voice, feel the softness of her skin. Kissing Charlie was a homecoming unlike anything Mason had ever experienced. It solidified his feelings for her in an instant. Every doubt that plagued him vanished.

His tongue flicked out at the seam of her lips and Charlie opened for him to deepen the kiss. The sweetness of her mouth intoxicated him, her sweet scent swirled around him. Mason wrapped his arms around her. He held her body tight against his as his mouth slanted over hers.

He was in love with Charlotte Cahill. He'd never loved anyone more.

The elevator door slid open to the sixth floor and silently closed once again. He barely took notice when the car lurched and started its descent, and he didn't stop kissing Charlie when the doors opened once again on the third floor and three passengers stepped in. The minutes melted away as they kissed, and when the elevator reached the ground floor and they were finally alone again, Mason pulled away to look at her. *Beautiful.*

"I love you, Charlie." The words tumbled from his mouth in a rush. "I should have told you before I left."

Because of Carrera's involvement, Mason's relationship to Kieran, and the fact that Kieran had managed to flee with thirty million of the government's money, there had been an internal investigation into the task force. He'd been ordered not to have any contact with Charlie, and once Mason was cleared of any wrongdoing, the interim chief deputy had sent him on to Glynco. There'd been no time to say the things he wanted to say to her, and he'd worried that when he came back, everything would be different. But one look from her told Mason everything he needed to know. She loved him too.

"I think those are the best words anyone has ever said to me." Charlie's beautiful blue eyes shone with emotion.

"I mean it, Charlie." He needed her to know, without a doubt, how he felt about her.

"I know you do." Her voice was barely a whisper. "I love you too."

"God, I missed this face." Mason cupped her cheeks and put his lips to hers.

"Just my face?" she teased.

He kept his lips over hers and said, "As soon as I get you alone, I'm going to show you—in detail—how much I missed every sexy inch of you."

The sound of a throat clearing drew their attention. An elderly woman stood with her hand bracing the elevator doors wide as she waited for Mason and Charlie to get out of the car. He flashed her a wide smile and showed her his badge. "U.S. marshal, ma'am. Official investigation. I'm afraid I'm going to have to ask you to wait for another car."

Charlie tucked her body against his and laughed as the woman released her grip. Mason reached over and hit the button to close the doors once again, shutting them out from the world.

"I can't believe you just did that," she said, laughing.

He kissed her again. "I promise it's the only time I'll abuse my power."

"Please," Charlie scoffed. "You're the last person on the planet who's in jeopardy of abusing their power."

"I'm not as squeaky clean as you think," he said. "I don't know if you know this or not, but I come from a pretty infamous family."

"I've heard the rumors." She nuzzled Mason's neck and his cock stirred behind his fly, more than ready to take this reunion somewhere a hell of a lot more private. "But I trust you."

"What do you need from your office?" Mason's voice rasped as he put his lips to Charlie's throat.

"It can wait until Monday," Charlie said.

"Good. Because we're going back to my place, where I can get you good and naked."

"That sounds like an excellent plan." Her hand ventured beneath his shirt and he shivered from the contact. "Besides, I thought small spaces made you uncomfortable."

He could suffer through it. For her. Anything for her. "One more trip up," he said as his mouth found hers once again. "I'm not ready to let go of you quite yet." The kiss deepened, intensified, until they were both breathless and panting.

Her hand slithered past his waistband to cup his erection through his jeans. "Maybe in the meantime, I'll make a trip down?"

Holy shit. "Are you trying to rattle me, Charlie?"

"Depends," she murmured. "Is it working?"

"Hell yeah."

She smiled as she stroked him through his jeans. "Good."

"Have I mentioned how much I missed you?"

Charlie snuggled in closer to Mason. Her head came down on his shoulder and her palm rested over his heart. They'd made love for hours. Questing hands, slow kisses, and tentative caresses became frenzied touches, hungry mouths, and low moans that filled the silence. The weeks apart from Charlie melted away by slow degrees, and the desperation that had eaten away at him was replaced with a contented glow that warmed his muscles and exhausted him. He was far from sated, though.

"You might have mentioned it once or twice," Charlie said sleepily. "Have I told you how much I missed you?"

Mason smiled. "You might have mentioned it."

Her mouth found his shoulder. She came up on her elbow and kissed across his collarbone over his pecs, as she rolled her body on top of his. Charlie straddled his waist. She bent over him and the fragrant waves of her hair teased his shoulder. Mason let his hands wander the supple curves of Charlie's body. A tremor shook her when he cupped the weight of her full breasts in his palms, and she let out a quiet whimper as his thumbs brushed the tight points of her nipples.

A month and a half apart had felt like years. But during those weeks of physical and mental exhaustion, Mason had found his priorities. He'd thought about the importance of family and shared history, and he'd come to realize that there was room in his life to let in a little bit of that gray area he'd shunned for so long. Life was too damned short to be uncompromising. Uncompromising men were admirable, sure. But they were unhappy as hell.

Mason planned to spend every day of the rest of his life blissed out and happy. With Charlie.

The wet heat of Charlie's pussy slid along Mason's shaft, redirecting his thoughts. She reached over to the bedside table and grabbed a condom from the drawer. "I hope you don't have anywhere to be this weekend," she said in a husky murmur. "Because I don't plan on leaving this bed until Monday morning."

"Monday?" Mason came up on his elbows. His mouth touched down right above Charlie's sternum and blazed a path over the swell of her breast. "I thought maybe you could take the week off."

Charlie's low laughter ignited Mason's lust. He kissed the tip of her breast before he drew her nipple into his mouth and sucked. Her hips bucked and the action caused her clit to slide against his shaft. God damn, she drove him crazy. Mindless. He'd never want anyone as much as he wanted Charlie. She was it for him.

"A week, huh?" He sat up fully and wrapped his arms around her, caressing down her spine. "Everyone at the office has been trying to get me to take it easy. Maybe I could stand to have a few extra days away . . ."

The salt tang of her skin and her floral scent took over Mason's senses. He committed the way she smelled, tasted, to memory, unwilling to let this moment fade. Mason knew that every time with Charlie would be like this, because every second spent with her was precious.

"A week off and then back to the grind," she said with a sigh. "I think we can handle it, don't you?"

Mason chuckled. "Definitely." He pulled back to look at her and brushed the hair away from her face. "I was thinking . . . that maybe we'd take a vacation. After everything settles down. Maybe toward the end of the year."

A curious smile graced Charlie's lips. "Could be fun. What did you have in mind?"

"How does Morocco sound?"

Charlie studied him for a silent moment. "Morocco?" Her eyes sparked with realization and she laughed. "They don't extradite to the U.S."

"Huh," Mason said. "I didn't know that."

Charlie's bright, knowing smile filled Mason with so much emotion, he thought his chest might burst. They'd both come so far since that day in the elevator, and Mason wouldn't have it any other way. Maybe together, they could have it all. The careers, the happiness, and maybe even the sense of family.

"Sounds like it could be an adventure." Charlie beamed, her expression so full of love.

"I'm up for an adventure." He held her tight and kissed her. "How 'bout you?"

She smiled. "Definitely."

Loved LOCKED AND LOADED?

Be sure to check out the rest of
Mandy Baxter's
U.S. Marshals series

ONE NIGHT MORE

ONE KISS MORE

ONE TOUCH MORE

AT ANY COST

Available now from
Zebra Books!

Connect with Us

Visit us online at
KensingtonBooks.com
to read more from your favorite authors, see books
by series, view reading group guides, and more.

for sneak peeks, chances to win books and prize packs,
and to share your thoughts with other readers.

facebook.com/kensingtonpublishing
twitter.com/kensingtonbooks

Tell us what you think!

To share your thoughts, submit a review,
or sign up for our eNewsletters, please visit:
KensingtonBooks.com/TellUs.